THE GREENBECKER GAMBIT

Ben Graff

The Greenbecker Gambit

Published by The Conrad Press in the United Kingdom 2020

Tel: +44(0)1227 472 874
www.theconradpress.com
info@theconradpress.com

ISBN 978-1-913567-02-6

Typesetting and Cover Design by: Charlotte Mouncey, www.bookstyle.co.uk

The Conrad Press logo was designed by Maria Priestley.

Printed and bound in Great Britain by Clays Ltd, Elcograf S.p.A.

THE GREENBECKER GAMBIT

BEN GRAFF

For my father, Colin Graff. The day you took the lid off your chess set, a whole new world came tumbling out. You taught me so much more than how to move the pieces. For my mother, Mary Graff. You were right to worry about where it might lead. The years move on so quickly, but I keep you both with me. x

'A desperate disease requires a dangerous remedy.'

Guy Fawkes

'Chess and me, it's hard to take them apart. It's like my alter ego.'

Bobby Fischer

'Any future is unknown - but sometimes it acquires a particular fogginess, as if some other force had come to the aid of destiny's natural reticence and distributed this resilient fog, from which thought rebounds.'

Vladimir Nabokov - *The Luzhin Defence*

'It's like everyone tells a story about themselves inside their own head. Always. All the time. That story makes you what you are. We build ourselves out of that story.'

Patrick Rothfuss - *The Name of the Wind*

'Go, go, go, said the bird: human kind
Cannot bear very much reality.'

T.S. Eliot – *Four Quartets: Burnt Norton*

AUTHOR'S NOTE

The Greenbecker Gambit is a work of fiction. As far as possible, all aspects of the story that relate to real events, at and away from the chess board, are factually accurate. Tennessee Greenbecker's thoughts on many of these happenings are entirely his own. Tennessee's interactions with both fictional and actual chess players only exist within the confines of this novel.

1. Sheer pyrotechnics

Waiting for the body to burn is making me impatient.

Good money has changed hands and I had expected a much better show. Other parts of London are doubtless already ablaze, while here the hapless officials in their high viz yellow jackets are struggling to make the bonfire smoulder. I am astounded by their amateurism.

In the distance pinpricks of red on the latticed arms of cranes shape the skyline like a modern-day forest. When morning comes, they will continue slowly reimagining the capital, building over the London that belongs to me, one new brick at a time. Burning and rebuilding. That is all there is. Everything starts and ends with fire.

A faraway rocket goes off. Traces of green and gold colour the sky before fading into nothing. Yet the display I have chosen has so far failed to offer even that. Even the Guy is a rather pathetic excretion of unevenly sculpted papier-mâché dressed in a too-good-coat. Perhaps there is a secret plan to save him for next year. I suppose that would be grounds to claim a refund.

Honestly, first Guy Fawkes lets everyone down by failing in

the simplest of tasks and now his replica will not burn. Still, I will not judge him too harshly. My sympathies are always with the man who is prepared to give something a go, rather than the critics who sneer from the side-lines.

I let out a shout of annoyance, but people turn to look at me and I pretend it was just a cough. This crowd is mainly families togged up in ski jackets and thermals, doubtless too warm for the night. Stuffing their faces with expensive burgers and hot dogs laden with red and yellow sauce, the smell of onions and processed meat stronger than the wisp of smoke from the bonfire.

Earlier, a steward glared at me when I reached into my ruck-sack for one of my cans, so instead I have stuck to a few mugs of prohibitively priced mulled cider, just to be sociable. It is also not long since a child waved a sparkler in my face, prac-tically singeing my beard, but her mother's shouts of 'come away now,' contained no hint of an apology. She perhaps had no idea as to who I am.

It is not always obvious to people when they are in the presence of greatness. I am wise enough not to expect too much. Not everyone can fully comprehend Tennessee Greenbecker, the foremost chess player never to be world champion. A better claim to that mantle than Korchnoi, Keres or Bronstein. Now all dead, as is my good friend Bobby Fischer. Their stories over. My own just beginning.

What I have striven for all these years has always remained tantalisingly just out of reach, through no fault of my own. I need to put that right. To claim what is mine. To ensure that whatever difficulties the chess authorities and other manifestations of the State have caused me in the past, they do not hold me back much longer. Magnus Carlsen has no way of knowing what is coming his way. Uneasy is the head that wears the crown!

There is no reason why the world champion elect should not enjoy a night off, but what is unfolding in this municipal park is somewhat painful for me to watch. It seems that they have not thought any of this through. I will grant you the bonfire has been shaped like a tepee, just as is advised. I have looked closely, and it is clear it has been properly positioned within a shallow pit, but the wood is too damp. That is the problem.

In true British fashion, one of the yellow vests is peering at the lifeless stack by torchlight while two others look on. The radios attached to their belts all crackle away, but no one is doing anything useful. The lack of fire at a bonfire is not a problem they seem to know how to solve.

I sense a growing restlessness in the crowd. Somebody yells out, 'are you nearly ready yet mate?' I notice all the yellow vests have the words Round Table emblazoned on their backs. I am not entirely sure what this signifies, or its relationship with the State, but I can only worry about a certain number of problems at any given moment.

I tell myself it does not matter what a couple of officers at the hostel happened to say. If their judgement was any good, they would presumably have been in better jobs. It is hardly worth thinking about. A few happy hours at a fireworks display, even one as bad as this, is the least I deserve. There are plenty of other places I can spend the night. London is my town, and this is my time. It is not as if there has been any real harm done.

I take a sip of the warm mulled cider, enjoying the heat as it trickles down my throat and into my stomach. I have visited the plastic Portaloo once or twice since my arrival, without incident, so I suppose that is something. My feet are sore, and my back is stiff from carrying my rucksack. What else is there, other than a little drink, to keep a man ticking over? I can feel good health coursing through my veins. I light a cigarette and drag on it contentedly.

I remember a night around this time of year a long time ago. More than half a century ago I would think. It was not like this. The four of us in our garden along with some neighbours. I cannot remember who built that night's fire, but I doubt my father would have been up to it. It was early in the evening, a few hours before we were due to get the festivities underway and I could see a similar problem, albeit on a smaller scale, to that which the organisers face tonight – the thing was never going to burn without a little extra help.

I did not tell anyone what I had done, but it worked. I remember the blaze with real pride. A terrific effort that the whole family enjoyed. My mother with us in the moment, my father's ineffectual beaming somehow just right, the warmth from the yellow and orange flames toasting our skins. Rockets and Catherine Wheels spraying brightly-coloured sparks through the night air. A happening on the edge of magic. A feeling of togetherness that I did not experience all that often back then. A night to remember, even if ultimately it did not end well.

My solution tonight will be a little more orthodox. I am itching to help, so I duck under the plastic taping that is meant to keep the paying public from the action, stumbling a little, as anyone might. I pull myself up without anyone seeming to notice and walk toward the man with the torch. He looks a touch alarmed as I approach. I would guess he is in his forties. He has an air about him that I often recognise in those who see themselves as successful. Some might say confident. Others stupid. Perhaps it does not matter. I am sure he will be glad of my assistance.

'Please get back behind the fence, sir,' he snaps. 'This is a restricted zone. Only trained members of the Round Table are allowed in here.'

'Well, I am hardly going to burn, am I?' I say. 'I just thought I might be able to help. I am something of an expert in these matters you know.'

'How so?' he says irritably.

I try flattery. 'We might well be the only two people who really understand the situation,' I say. 'The point is, the fire isn't going to catch without a little jollying along.'

'What did you have in mind?' he asks, I think somewhat guardedly.

'Paraffin and fucking petrol. Lots of it. That will get things going. If you have any spirits, they might also pep it up a bit, if need be. We could use what was left over for a celebratory toast!'

I reach into my coat pocket and pull out a packet of Zip firelighters. 'I bought these from a garage on the way here, in case you were having difficulties. I'm quite happy for you to use them for a small fee, provided I get to chuck them on. I can't really say fairer than that. What do you think?'

'You must be out of your fucking mind,' he says. 'That's the last thing we need. Paraffin and petrol? Are you mad? Your firelighters would do precisely fuck all. Have you any idea how

15

many people are waiting for us to get started? I haven't got time to talk to a nutter.' He calls over to a colleague and without knowing quite how, I find myself being led back to the public area. I should have better appreciated that some people are overawed by the prospect of having a drink with me.

Just another fucking idiot, I fear. This is what happens when you show people up. A few more minutes of my wisdom and his colleagues would have mutinied and put me in charge. How much happier they would all have been, had they entrusted the proceedings to a man who knows. I shake my head and put the firelighters back in my pocket.

When it comes to a knowledge of fire, I could have told them about the thin layer of red-brown oxidized ash beneath our feet. There since the first century, when Boadicea quite understandably burnt the city down. Without recourse to the internet I could have enlightened them as to how many times St Paul's had been reduced to dust. I could have given them a window on the city from the Hadrianic fire through to London's burning bridges, Crystal Palace and the Blitz.

The paying public would probably have found a monologue like that more satisfying than a normal Bonfire night. Presumably someone would have recognised me. I would have been happy to talk chess and sign a few autographs. That none of this is now going to happen is entirely the organisers' loss.

Still, I am reluctant to allow the State another victory, without considering further whether there is a way for me to take the stage. To seize my rightful place as the master of ceremonies. How long would I really need? A minute tops. Even if they have been foolish in not purchasing any paraffin or petrol, my firelighters are terrific. I would be wary about using more than half my packet, but that should be enough. I could throw them on, strike a match and then bask in the warmth of both the raging inferno and the cheers of the crowd. We would all laugh together at the useless organisers who I had shown up so completely.

Surely it should be possible to give them all the slip if I take them by surprise and run at the bonfire at speed? I tried to work with the Round Table, so who could blame me for now going it alone? I must trust my instincts. It was a mistake to try and collaborate.

Every chess player is an island, we do our best work alone. I get myself ready. Firelighters in one hand, box of matches in the other. I duck under the plastic tape for the second time. If I do not look at anyone, they might not notice me until my work is done. This could be a special moment.

I start to walk quickly towards the bonfire, and nobody stops me. I have judged the situation perfectly. How Guy Fawkes could have used a man of my initiative. This is going to be glorious. If there was any justice, I would most likely be awarded the world chess crown for my services to fire, but there is a lot about life that is far from fair.

I am about halfway toward the bonfire and perhaps have allowed myself to be overly distracted by visions of glory, as two members of the Round Table are approaching me – their hapless leader, who is clearly determined to stop me receiving my due reward, and one of his sidekicks.

I try and run, and almost hear the crowd cheering me on, but it is no good. Someone blessed with a mind like mine possibly never stood a chance of outrunning much younger State agents, at least without putting in a bit of training that I have not had time for. So that I fall face-first in the mud is academic.

I roll around a bit for form's sake and shout, 'I've been shot, I've been shot,' but neither of the officials seems convinced. They just stand there, looking at me, but I can see what strikes me as looks of relief on their faces when I stand up and tell them that I am all right now.

'I fucking told you,' the leader says. 'You are a danger to yourself and the public. We cannot entertain people who continually try and breach the restricted zone. I am going to have two of my team escort you from the park. If you return any time during the rest of the evening, we will have to call the police. I would strongly suggest you get some professional help.'

His face is red with rage and I notice that a vein is throbbing in his forehead. He is clearly miles out of his depth, but what the State lacks in brain power at the junior officer level, it makes up for in muscle. Two more agents join him and then another two. I am grabbed roughly by the arm and find myself being marched toward the gate, unable to understand precisely what has happened.

I tell them that I am struggling to breath and one of them says to 'take it easy.' I am not sure whether this is directed at me or the thugs and goons that make up the State's Round Table team. Either way, they wait for a minute before continuing to march me forward.

I feel exactly as Guy Fawkes must have done when he was arrested. Saddened that I have been thwarted, but more so for those who will now not get to enjoy the fruits of my labour than for myself. I am surprised that the spectators do not protest. Perhaps I am not quite as famous amongst the general public as once I was. Possibly they do not fully appreciate the full extent of my gifts.

Even if everyone else has lost far more than me, there are no winners on a night like this. I have the consolation that when I am the world chess champion, no one will even care that I did not get to light the fucking bonfire.

2. A Whopper

The journey back into central London took far longer than I had envisaged, and this has curtailed my choices. I stare at yellow and black masking tape which stretches across a large crack in the restaurant glass. Underneath the Open sign is a warning that the premises are monitored by CCTV.

I look up and see a small camera peering down at me, but I have no way of knowing whether it is working. The bright glare of fluorescent lighting is too sterile to be considered welcoming. I hesitate, but it is now or never. I am like a moth near a flame – I take the risk.

I push the door, surprised by its weight. No one steps forward to bar my way or even looks up. More fool them. What happened last time has doubtless been forgotten. The staff come and go. It is not somewhere people choose to work for long. I curse my previous caution. It is just a case of knowing how to do it. Street smarts I think they call it. Own the space. Leave no room for doubt. I blink as I adjust to the brightness of the strip lighting. I have as much right to be here as anyone.

The place has the feel of a Moscow café from 1977, with its

tattered floor and cheap décor. It smells of chip fat and poly-ethylene and the stale defeat of people with nowhere else to go. I am not like them. Not really. At least not for much longer.

My chest is a little wheezy. The effects of the walk and the cold. I hold my left arm with my right hand so that it does not shake. I know how to make the most of myself. I need to urinate. I need a cigarette. I need more than all this and it is coming. But first things first. Get some food in. Find a table. Wait out the night. London does not sleep for long. Her fire might dim but it never goes out. Light always follows darkness. New beginnings always await.

Tomorrow I will be meeting Gabriel. Our disagreement is unfortunate I grant you. It is entirely his fault, but it has become a distraction. All it takes is for him to see things my way and everything will be resolved. I know he is deeply embar-rassed by his behaviour, even if he hasn't quite admitted this yet. It is surely time to let bygones be bygones and to focus on getting me back to the very top. He wants that for me as much as I want it for myself, in his own understated way. A certain lack of visible empathy, a family trait I suppose.

I imagine things are always difficult between brothers. At least in a family like ours. I have rehearsed my lines. As ever, I have a good plan. Both for tomorrow and what will inevitably follow, as we put together a team of top grandmasters to assist me with my world title challenge.

I visualise Gabriel's future apology and warm embrace and it makes me smile. There is much to prepare, a lot to look forward to. I feel a sense of anticipation, but it is all for the morning. Tonight, I am free just to be me. The world can wait.

I hear the sound of a saxophone crackling through the cheap speaker behind the counter. Gerry Rafferty's 'Baker Street' – the dream of buying some land and finally settling down as seductive as it is dangerous. I am worth more than that. Much more. People like me stand outside the space others convince themselves is the real world. We put ourselves out there in a way that the conventionally bound rarely do. The rewards can be great, but so is the pain. Still, take away all that and there would be nothing left. I might as well be dead. No, the quiet little town was never for me. At least, if it was, I was never brave enough to give into it.

I think I might have had a drink with Gerry Rafferty once or twice, God rest his soul. He could never really keep up with me, but he always enjoyed the crack, even if he was always a little star-struck in my company. We most probably talked about his music and my chess, but I don't recall the specifics. If I am honest, I do worry that my memory is a little hazy at times.

Drink becomes a less forgiving companion over the years, but I tell myself it matters not. My capacity to assimilate chess theory is essentially undiminished – plenty good enough for Magnus Carlsen. When everything else is dust, my chess will endure. I sometimes resent that Gerry Rafferty's new morning, metaphorically, came about before my own, but I know that I am heading toward the light.

I must have been daydreaming – the server is talking to me, asking what I want to eat, and not for the first time, if his tone is anything to go by. I hesitate and then order a Whopper meal, which consists of cheeseburger, fries and a lemonade, sorting out money that does not take much counting.

The mulled cider has made a significant dent in my finances, not that I was properly thanked for my generosity by anyone from the Round Table. The coins are flecked with fragments of tissue paper from my pocket. A bronzed one pound, two fifties and a few twenty and ten pence pieces. Two rather tired five-pound notes, doubtless stained with cocaine from someone else's London. It is more than enough. I hand it over as reluctantly as the server accepts it. Legal tender cannot be denied.

I momentarily feel slightly dizzy. It is just the contrast between the heat of the restaurant and the cold of the night. My body has been through enough for me to gauge that it is nothing more serious than that. It will not take me long to adjust.

I pick up a black tray, restaurant insignia etched in the plastic, part obscured by a dried in stain. I take an extra cup, and as I wait for my order, I stare at the clock on the wall that says it is 11.30 pm, framing the hour in block green digits. I am not even tired. I suppose I always was something of a night owl.

The prospect of food is cheering, even if I do not really eat. It is my choice. I get what I need. As with most things, the idea is always better than the reality. There are some cans in my bag. A hip flask too. My pocket chess set with its playing surface worn smooth. My books. A few clothes. Photographs. The folder that my comeback depends on, where I will also record my story. Time will show that I am the real writer in the family. A pack of wet wipes. Playing cards. A few low denomination poker chips. A printout of Gabriel's email. A box of matches. A few spare firelighters. The fake ID that occasionally comes in handy. Not much to show for all my years on the planet, but my worth can in no way be measured through an assessment of my meagre possessions.

I find it ironic that the supposed number one and two chess players in the world are also in town. Doubtless both currently dozing in luxury hotel rooms. They do not know they are born! Magnus Carlsen and Fabiano Caruana. Their world championship match underway in Holborn. Carlsen and Caruana will be contesting a mere twelve games. A far cry from the 1985 marathon between Karpov and Kasparov, abandoned after forty-eight games.

I imagine I am not the only one who saw my influence in Karpov's play, when he stormed into an early, apparently unassailable lead. The way Garry mimicked my style when he fought back is probably even more obvious to most. Frankly I always thought Garry should have been a little embarrassed on that front, but he lacks the emotional intelligence to recognise he is a mere imitator.

Those in the know would likely rank Carlsen and Caruana at two and three, if they were aware of my imminent comeback. At least, if they really understood these things they would. The work I have undertaken since I was last competing makes it inevitable, whatever the precise ins and outs of my previous track record. The best will always out. Demonstrating I am the true world champion, not Magnus Carlsen, has a kind of inevitability about it.

As I wait for my food, I look through the window at a couple kissing underneath the lamppost across the street. The bulb is flickering cold white light, on the verge of failing, and they are only properly visible intermittently. She has placed her feet on his and he is gently rubbing the back of her coat. I turn away, not wanting trouble.

As the server returns, I look at him properly and see the spots on his brown forehead, the badge that says Amal. Two stars on it. The gap where a third might one day go. He has bags under his red and puffy eyes. His hair is lank, and a bolt has been sheathed through the helix of his ear. I dislike the way he looks at me, as if I could be anybody.

For so many years, this has been what I have been reduced to. Hiding, running, living in the shadows. Even when Bobby Fischer urged me not to make the same mistakes he had, not even that was enough to spur me into action, and so I have been stuck in this London of backstreet eateries and cheap hotels that someone like me was never meant to endure. Gabriel's flat and the house in Coventry the briefest of diversions. When the money has run short it has been either the hostels that will still have me, the park or places that stay open all night like this one. London often rejects its finest, but I know my time is close.

3. A very near miss

A few young people, always the worst, are giggling loudly at a corner table. They seem to have no awareness that their voices carry. I'm keen to sit as far away from them as possible.

A girl in the group in a short black dress catches my eye and then turns away abruptly, clutching the arm of the boy who is next to her, and he glares at me. His teeth are crooked despite his braces and he has an angry looking rash of acne on one cheek, a thick chain around his neck. I notice his nose is a little bent. I pretend that I was looking over them, at the clock on the wall, all along.

The first few bars of a new song begin to play, and I worry that I have inadvertently entered a torture chamber. It's one of Keith's numbers. I shout that for fuck's sake they should turn it off. That a man like Keith should never be allowed on the radio. I stick my fingers in my ears, but I can still hear the fucking thing, so I clamp my hands fully over my ears instead and start to sing myself, just to blot out the terrible noise.

I hear Amal shouting out from the back to ask if I am all right, and I take a deep breath and try and compose myself. When I am world champion, they certainly won't be playing

Keith's music anymore. Just thinking this seems to do the trick. Pop singers are a funny bunch. What did Prince sing? Something about in the centre of fire, there is cold. If he really thought that, I am amazed he lived as long as he did.

I try to refocus. Like all chess players I will be judged against both those who went before and those who will walk the earth long after I've gone. I am disappointed that more chess books have not already included me as an honorary world champion, given my illustrious achievements.

What was it I read Magnus Carlsen said when asked who the best player of all time was? Himself. Three years ago. The arrogance of a true champion. When the time comes, he is going to prove to be a formidable opponent.

He would not have been able to offer up many names before volunteering my own. How funny that would have been! To hear him describe Tennessee Greenbecker as an historical figure, and then to be confronted by me in flesh and blood. The thought makes me chuckle.

Objectively there was Bobby and now there is Tennessee, the two greatest players there have ever been. Please do not give me a Kasparov or a Carlsen. Magnus knows this really. I would not be surprised to learn that he had wanted to acknowledge my standing but was held back by the State.

Magnus is not the only top chess player to be somewhat lacking in grace and warmth. Chess players are generally a prickly bunch. Korchnoi was always hard work. My difficulties with Wengrower and Dubrovnik are well documented, and Votov was also challenging. He had the capacity to hate as only true greats and complete nonentities ever can.

Once he thought I had pushed in front of him in the coffee queue, during round four of the Hastings event. We were stood on the cheap lino by the serving hatch just outside the playing hall. I was up in my game against Phil Page and he was losing to Michael Wengrower. Perhaps that had put him in a bad mood. It might be that he had come to realise what everyone else already suspected, that his, in my view, overstated talent, was not going to take him all the way. That a new generation of players were emerging who were going to surpass him, taking his dreams of winning the world title with them.

More precisely, that the world championship was now beyond his reach because he would never be able to win a match against me.

That said, he was a truly combative individual and it is also possible that my imagined slight in the coffee queue was enough to make us sworn enemies. I offered my apologies for any offence caused, but he held up both his hands and shook his head, fixing me with a look of cold contempt. I realised too late that he viewed my apology as a sign of weakness, more damning perhaps than the original incident. We were now officially done. What was worse was that he had broken my concentration.

As I sat back down at my board, I could not get the exchange out of my head. I had turned down an earlier draw, but then lost the thread of the game and when I offered a later draw Page said no before continuing to grind me down. When I lost, I went out onto the street and wept, my agony compounded by the fact that Votov had somehow managed to hold the draw against Wengrower. There can be no crueller mistress than chess.

I hated Votov as much as he hated me after that, but Hastings was not the end of it. Several years later, he saw me stumble and crash to the floor in the conference centre where we were both playing in some Open event. It was not obvious that there would have been a step down between one part of the playing hall and the other. It could have happened to anyone.

'The man is a fool,' he exclaimed to all in earshot, laughing loudly and pointing. 'He's pissed out of his head.'

Despite what the press wrote, I had not been drinking, and certainly not enough for that to have had any bearing on what happened. A drunk would not have been able to remember the moment so clearly. To be able to recall with such clarity the basic errors in the design of the step.

I comforted myself by thinking back to our previous game, that had taken place with no handshake and without a world being exchanged between us. I had been victorious in a complex knight ending, where he should have drawn but went astray right at the end, the hard work all done and then ruined by his stupidity. I knew it was I who had the last laugh.

When I read soon afterwards that he had died in a car crash, I was delighted. In my view one of those rare occasions when the State got something right.

The story of my descent to rock bottom and subsequent rise again will add to the lustre of my comeback. It has been twenty years, but I have lived with my chess set and the games in my head, much the same as I always did. My knowledge of London's fires and what it means for things to burn. None of what has happened has made much difference to who I really am.

I stand by my choices, albeit, I know my decision to return is not risk free. Carlsen and Caruana will not be a problem in themselves. I can match them over the board. I have reserves of toughness aplenty to draw on for the fight.

Still, a lot of other dangers remain. The State. The past. Who I am, and who I might be? Sometimes I fear that I am not quite what I once was. Time is always the trickiest opponent. I do recognise that. A chess player's competitiveness and harboured grudges must in part be a 'raging against the dying of the light'.

As I place my food on the plastic tray and look for a table, I survey my fellow patrons. The restaurant is not overly busy. In a corner a prostitute with streaked blonde hair fiddles with her food and picks at a burger. Her face is pretty, but tired. She is wearing blue jeans with holes in the knees, purple pumps and a faded denim jacket that seems a little too big.

I notice a ring of thorns tattooed on her left wrist and a simple silver pendant with engraved initials on it around her neck that hints at story I am never going to know. Her eyes are pale blue and clearer than I might have expected. She half reminds me of someone, but I put the thought out of my mind.

Sitting opposite her is a guy who might be her pimp, might be her boyfriend, might be both. His waxed jacket and bright white trainers look expensive, but there is a certain weariness in his voice, as if all this was not quite the plan.

A homeless man in the next booth from them is playing with the sachets of sugar and salt, building a granulated white castle on the Formica table, singing softly to himself. I have seen him here and in other such places before, but I have learnt to instinctively keep my distance and he never seeks company. He digs out a cigarette and starts to smoke it. Everyone pretends not to notice as the scent of tobacco permeates the restaurant.

He knows what I have also learned. Whatever the law might officially say, the State often turns a blind eye to the regulations in places like this. The prospect of the cliental inadvertently going up in smoke something the bastards are reasonably relaxed about. This level of indifference sometimes makes me angry, but equally it is handy when I feel like a cigarette. Besides, it also shows that those in authority are more sympathetic to fire than they generally let on.

The State will always wish me harm. Actively so, which is what distinguishes me from the rest of the patrons. The English Chess Federation. FIDE. The British Government. They are all one and the same. The Soviet Union might have been the first to understand the power of chess in society as a propaganda tool, but they were far from the last.

What was Fischer – Spassky after all, if not a battle between two differing ideas of society? Capitalism versus Communism writ large on sixty-four black and white squares. It didn't matter that Bobby and Boris were hopeless ambassadors for the systems they were meant to represent. Neither State was going to let a trifling little detail like that get in the way. At least not back then.

Is it any wonder it all proved too much for Bobby? That he did not play again for twenty years? That he came to hate and fear America just as much as he did the Russians. The more time has passed, the more I have realised the depth of his foresight.

It is not as if I really have a choice. I only feel truly alive when the chess clock is ticking and the patterns on the squares in front of me are dancing in my head. Very little else gives me the same feeling. Nothing else, that does not involve a flame.

It is like unlocking a complex riddle, that is beautiful and for a few moves might only be for me, until ultimately all becomes clear and appreciable to the talentless fans and hangers-on. Often, my opponent only understands when it is too late to alter the course of events.

No, nothing can surpass the feeling of weaving magic into cold hard combinations on the board. Creating game by game another part of chess's story with me at its centre. Let's be honest. The feeling that comes when an opponent has been humiliated, their ideas destroyed, cannot be bettered. There is no higher calling than to crush a man's dreams, and to then hold out your hand for him to shake.

I examine my food. The beaded bread of the bun, the slabs of meat and salad and golden cheese within. The fries glisten with grease in their cardboard holder. More varied in size and shape than at the real chains, smelling faintly of antiseptic. I sip the lemonade through a plastic straw and feel the bubbles at the back of my throat.

I know I'm going to have to look after my body as well as my mind if my comeback is going to work. I tell myself that while tonight this food is just the price of somewhere to sit, soon I will be eating properly again. I will need carbohydrates in my system to defeat Magnus Carlsen.

Intuition. I always know before I know. Can sense danger before it has a definite form. Things can change so quickly! Something is not right. Even the youngsters are suddenly a little quieter. I have allowed myself to become far too complacent.

The tread of a footstep, the solidness of a voice. Authority. The State. This can only be bad.

The police officer says good evening to Amal, and I am frozen at the counter when I could have been safely sat at a table if I had just got on with things instead of daydreaming about Bobby and Garry and Votov's demise.

This has the potential to be a disaster. My rucksack might as well be radioactive. Are they going to try and seize my folder? I can't wholly discount that they might want me for other reasons. There are a lot of agents and their motives vary. I hear a crackle on his radio, see the handcuffs in his belt. Think. Think. Could he have followed me here? Unlikely, unless he wanted to offer apologies on behalf of the Round Table.

If there was any justice, the police would be here to take my statement regarding the officials who assaulted and possibly even shot at me, but I know that all branches of the State work in unison and this is never going to happen. One of the many reasons the Establishment does not get as to why people voted for Brexit.

Did the restaurant recognise me after all and call them? It is possible, but not enough time has passed for that. Surely my entirely natural reaction when Keith's song came on can't have elicited this response? The State knows it's already won on that front and is determined to play his fucking songs, whatever representations I make.

I try and pull myself together. To use my brain. As I have said to amateur players for so many years, don't guess, calculate. Always make the most precise assessment based on what you see, not what you think you see. You must be concrete in your approach. It is true that chess is a game of perfect information, in that all your opponent's pieces are visible, and life is not really like that. I am one of the few who excels equally at both, I suppose.

Taking my own advice, I do the calculation. What could be pinned on me, not that they necessarily need anything specific. Could the girl in the street have complained about me looking at her? No, not enough time has passed. I don't see how that could be a crime anyway.

Remember that what distinguishes exceptional chess players from the merely good is an ability to hold their nerve. After a certain point, everything is psychological. The incident at the hostel? Seems unlikely. Wouldn't something have happened on that front already if it was going to?

The fact that I have paid for my food will be on the CCTV, so there can't be any comeback there. Although of course, they could wipe the tape. Perhaps it is a Russian plot after all. It is late and I might be a little more tired than I thought. I haven't drunk all that much, but perhaps what I have has slowed my brain just a touch.

When you don't know, do nothing. Unlike chess, I can wait for the State to make the next move. Just freeze. Stand where I am, calmly, deep within my own thoughts. A normal man about to enjoy a late-night meal – and why not?

'Are you all right sir?' I hear him say.

I look again and there are two of them now. He is big and blonde, heavy set, his gut attempting to spill from his shirt and not quite succeeding. His flies not properly fastened. He has a small scar on his neck and takes care over every syllable, as the stupid often do.

She is smaller, fiercer, with eyes as hard as a Moscow winter.

She adjusts the plastic strap of her watch and I notice the top of what must be a heart tattooed on her skin underneath it. The hairs on her lower arm are thin and downy. She exudes airs of scepticism, boredom and indifference to her fellow man in roughly equal measure.

He does too. I would imagine this is something the State teaches police officers as part of their basic training. There is an authority to both I grant you. Not the sort of people who run the world, but here in this place they could certainly make things run.

'Yes, quite all right,' I hear myself say, very much on guard.

The police officer's conversation with Amal continues and I head to a seat at an empty table, hoping for the best. The place is very still. I am not the only one who is somewhat perturbed by the presence of Her Majesty's finest. The man with the bent nose is staring intently down at his phone, one peaked hand on his forehead, obscuring most of his face. The prostitute and her pimp are holding hands and staring intently at their table. Londonbeat's 'A Better Love,' is playing and the patrons are pretending to listen.

'Usual is it?' Amal says and the policeman nods.

When it arrives, I see they've ordered Whopper deals, but with coffees instead of lemonade, and sealed with the lids to take out.

'Parked around the corner, did you?' Amal asks.

'We find it's generally easier that way,' the blonde one says, and the three of them laugh as if in on a joke that I don't get. Is this all an elaborate ruse to lull me into a false sense of security before they pounce?

Possibly, possibly, but no.

Amal puts their food into two separate brown paper bags. They take them and turn and head back out onto the street. A few minutes later I see their car pulling away, blue light switched off, aimlessly waiting for someone else to harass. This sort of nonsense makes me glad I'm no longer a taxpayer.

4. Meat and potatoes

I unfold the tightly creased quadrants of Gabriel's email and read it again. A few days in my pocket, it smells of tobacco. A tea stain roughly the shape of Africa shades the middle of the paper. A minor spill. I had hoped he would write again. Morally, I could not have replied to his previous emails, but this time I was ready.

Yes, he is full square in the wrong, but I am prepared to be pragmatic. To let everything go, for the greater good of my comeback. One of us had to be man enough to get things back on track.

This whole email, social media world has left me behind. It was not really a part of how things were when I was in my prime. I did not grow up with it. But it is not age that makes me wary. Nor is it a result of any temporary funding issues on my part. I could have full access to all the money in the world and I still would not touch a mobile device. Those who do are fools unto themselves. If that means everybody, I rest my case.

Who would want to give away so much about what they buy, where they go and how one vapid train of thought leads onto another? They said that John Updike never had an unpublished thought and it was not entirely a compliment. I imagine he would be considered positively reticent by modern day standards.

So far as I can see, the world is drowning under a welter of banality, ignorance and rage. People think such devices are soulless, but rather they are a window into the soul and one that I would not want to open. Normal people just don't have the cognitive ability to see this as I do.

It is important not to make things too easy for the State. You might as well volunteer to wear an electronic tag as carry a mobile. Of course, the internet itself is bad enough, but what can I do? There are certain things that draw me in.

The internet café I sometimes frequent is warm and dark and smells of curry and electronic circuitry. A faint tang of oil and heat and stale air. Theoretically you can stay a long time for not much money, surrounded mainly by Chinese and Asian surfers, who chat away in many languages but never English.

The downside is that it is run by a Muslim. Not a problem of itself, but alcohol is strictly banned and that does lead to me being thrown out on occasion. They also frown on smoking, for reasons I have never fully understood. I may or may not be barred at present, I sometimes lose track, but either way it is a detail that is usually sorted out if I return with apologies and the right money.

My chess playing site of choice is the Internet Chess Club, or ICC as we players call it. Gabriel set the account up for me and my handle is GreenB. A mistake perhaps, as the quality of my play has sparked rumours that GreenB is indeed Tennessee Greenbecker, but a consensus has developed in the chess community that it most likely is not.

Still, I relish the air of mystery (and perhaps wistful anticipation and excitement) this has created amongst the more
die-hard of my fans. It has sown something of a seed. There
would of course be a problem were Carlsen, Caruana or
Kasparov to analyse my games on the site, which is why to
be on the safe side I rarely utilise any of my newly developed
opening novelties. They stay safely secret and neatly written
up within my folder. Not that I need them anyway, not to win
game after game against the hacks and 'patzers' I encounter.

I like the shape of the electronic pieces just as much as those
on a solid board. The way they glide so smoothly, under the
guidance of a mouse. The names of the players and their associated flags, shown as clearly and as cleanly as they would on
any display board in the grandest of tournament halls. The
clock that counts down your time, glowing red when under
ten seconds.

My fellow players are not in my league, but many will share
my sense that there is nothing better, no other more interesting
way to waste a life than playing chess. I once read that having
access to the ICC was for most chess players as tricky as it
would be for an alcoholic to have a bar installed in their front
room. The ICC and a bar! What could be more like heaven?

I read Gabriel's email once again.

T.G.

*I think you might accept that recent events have come as a shock
to both of us. I did not like to see you in the state you were in. This
isn't something that is going to go away you know, but I am here
to help, just not in the ways you continually demand.*

Yes, you are still my brother. Yes, I think we should both now know what is important. I just need you to understand that it is simply not realistic for me to keep subbing you. Mum's books have long since stopped bringing in any real money. Your chess has never exactly been a money spinner either, has it? I can only be expected to fund so many bedsits.

Some of what you have done with my cash constitutes a betrayal of the highest order. It always seems to be left to me to clean up your mess and I have had enough of it. Most would have washed their hands of you long ago. I must also think about Ginevra. Your behaviour has put her through a lot too.

Understand, I am simply not prepared to put up with your ridiculous requests, pipedreams and general haranguing any longer. That does not mean I can't help in other ways.

If you want to meet sometime soon in The Red Lion, let me know.
Your brother

He always was one to flap. In my experience his grip on the facts rarely aligns with reality, and whatever he is mithering about now is unlikely to be all that important. There was only ever one bedsit, so whatever precisely happened there, he's clearly not making sense on that front.

The weaker brother obviously. Not just on the chess board. Open to manipulation in ways that generally work to my advantage. He is only frustrated because he wants me back in the saddle delivering on my greatness. I suspect his email is his idea of tough love. All else is flotsam and jetsam. Gabriel is annoying but time is short, and I am sure we will get everything sorted out. Until then, there is nothing to do but wait and to study some chess.

I reach into my long overcoat; the same one I wore in the Candidates Final all those years ago and feel for my copy of Bobby Fischer's *My 60 Memorable Games.*

The cover is deeply creased. The lettering on the front in gold. I don't need either set or book to play through these games. They are all in my head, the patterns and rhythms as natural to me as breathing. Yet I have noticed in places like this that you are more likely to be left alone if you appear occupied. Now I am seated I will start by playing through Game 8 from Bobby's book. Fischer – Keres 1959, which he has titled 'Meat and potatoes.' One maestro admiring the work of another.

Fischer refers to Alekhine, a former world champion and undoubted victim of the State in the preamble to his write-up. A salient lesson for us all. In disgrace following his support for the Nazis in World War Two, Alekhine was preparing for a title match with Botvinick when he was found dead in a hotel room in Portugal. He had choked on a piece of meat or had a heart attack, it was said. As if anyone would fall for that. It is obvious he was murdered. People who are choking get up and move around. They are not found slumped on a table, as he was.

All the rumours surfaced in the end. That he was discovered on the street and his body moved to his desk. That it had been a takeout by the Soviets who were reaping revenge on Nazi sympathisers.

Forget the stuff about his liver and the depression, I know the truth. It's all out there and written down. You don't have to look very hard for it. They say it is still a mystery, but it isn't really. That's why I'm so wary. Why Bobby was too. We understood better than most that they were out to get us.

Brilliant chess players are always a target. We represent something that the State will forever fear. Our ideas are too profound, our ability to move men so powerful, that those in authority are never going to leave us alone if we are deemed not to be on the side of the status quo. History may not exactly repeat itself, but as Mark Twain said, it often rhymes. I'm sure you don't need me to tell you that the great Paul Morphy did not really drown in his bath.

Even the conspiracy-theories, were themselves a part of a deeper conspiracy. It had nothing to do with Alekhine's Nazi sympathies. It was always obvious to me that his death was the work of the Soviet chess authorities. The young and meticulously prepared Botvinnik might have been well fancied to win against an ageing drunk, but why take the risk?

Bump Alekhine off, set up a tournament instead and install Botvinnik that way. Chess takes a certain ruthlessness, but perhaps only people at my level properly understand that. We players and officials are all the same. We will do whatever it takes.

Alekhine himself was no exception. He had previously managed to maintain the upper hand when under threat. You might have heard the story about him, Capablanca and the Russian peasant?

Go back a decade or two to when we find Alekhine in happier times. Alekhine and Capablanca, the great rivals of the 1920s and 30s. Capablanca the stronger player, but insufficiently prepared for his title match with Alekhine. He liked the ladies and the finer things in life too much. The social scene. His film star looks. Capablanca's play so brilliant I can forgive all that. But it cost him against Alekhine, who on winning was canny enough to avoid a rematch.

So, think how it must have been, late one night, when during a tournament they were both playing in, Capablanca hears a knock on his hotel door. He opens it to find a shaken looking Alekhine and an elderly gentleman standing there. Capablanca has an important game the following day and struggles to hide his obvious annoyance. He assumes a trick, an attempt at sabotage, or that Alekhine has been at the bottle again. There is just no reason for Alekhine of all people to be stood outside his door.

Capablanca makes to shoo them away but they will not budge. Perhaps a heated exchange follows, I don't know, but in the end Alekhine is able to tell Capablanca what has happened.

He explains that a peasant had knocked on his door earlier in the evening and promised that he could force checkmate in any game of chess after just five moves. However hard he tried, Alekhine could not get him to leave, so he finally ushered him into his room and pointed to his chess set. Lo and behold, five moves later Alekhine was checkmated. He asked the peasant to do it again and he did. And again – Alekhine's whole world order now falling apart before his eyes.

Perhaps he wondered if he had drunk more than he had thought. Perhaps at some desperate level, this was what he hoped, better than the alternative for sure. There was only one place to go, to the man he hated above all others, precisely because Capablanca was the only person he could look on as a peer. As Kasparov said years later, about his despised rival Karpov, I would not go to dinner with him, but who else can I talk to about our games? He took talking to me about his play as a given of course.

Eventually, Capablanca sighed and asked them to come in. He sat at his own board, opposite the peasant. Alekhine standing nervously, watching on, both wanting and not wanting the trick to be repeated.

The light is gloomy and Capablanca's hotel room is cold, but the chess board is the only thing that matters. The heavy wooden pieces, with bases of green felt, the squares of brown and white, the two greatest players of their generation, and this strange fellow with his crazy assertions and yet... The peasant moves first and five moves later Capablanca is checkmated. Then again and again.

In the years that followed, both masters told this story to friends and contemporaries. The punchline was always the same. When asked what they did next, they would both say, well we killed him of course.

I always think people misunderstand the tale. In many quarters it is assumed that it was a joke, but I am not so sure. It might not be literally true. If a forced win could be found in five moves, either I or the computers would have unearthed it long ago. But I do believe Alekhine and Capablanca saw someone, felt that chess and their place in it was threatened, and did what they needed to do. That's the kind of ruthlessness necessary at the very top of anything. Bobby is the only one who understood this as I do.

Of course, like Alekhine, Bobby was also a Nazi sympathiser despite being Jewish. Just another contradiction in him. It never caused us problems personally. Look at the record. He was always unfailingly polite to Jewish players like me and Tal, he said he just didn't see us as such. I always told him that his admiration for Hitler would not have saved him, but he would glaze over, much as he did when people tried to convince him that the Kasparov and Karpov games weren't all fixed. I give you that much, Bobby was a little confused toward the end.

5. The safest form of contraception

I am putting off deciding whether to risk trying to urinate again. I rummage in my bag for one of the four cans of White Ace cider within it. I curse that there aren't more, but those I've already drunk, along with the mulled cider at the Bonfire, have served their purpose in keeping out the cold. I plan to open the can discreetly under the table, but I can see no one cares, so I openly pour three quarters into my empty cup and top up with a splash of lemonade.

I drink it down in one hit, feeling a wave of warmth and wellbeing wash over me. For a moment I am entirely in my own world of apples, sugar and possibility, but the feeling does not last, so I pour the remains of the can into the cup and drink it neat.

Gabriel says that this is a problem. That if I'm serious about becoming world champion I'll have to kick the drink, but he would, wouldn't he? I don't believe it was the skimmed milk diet that worked for Alekhine in his re-match with Euwe, I just think it was that he was the better player. He did not lose the first of their title matches because of the drink either, he was a touch underprepared, that was all. The impact of alcohol on cognitive prowess is something that is often overestimated. Gabriel is less convinced, but what would he know? He can't play chess to save his life.

My stomach is now filled with cider and I do not want any food. Perhaps later. If you don't want it, you don't want it. I can no longer deny my urgent need to piss. I am going to have to try and go and hope for the best. I tell myself that things were fine earlier in the evening at the Bonfire. That I am most likely worrying too much. That I have let others plant a seed of doubt in my mind. A typical Establishment plot I should have seen coming. I must believe in myself.

It is always tricky when there is nobody to guard your stuff and your seat. In the end I leave my coat, book and rucksack, but take my folder with me, and of course the cigarettes. I push at a badly fitting wooden door and find myself standing in the gents.

The toilet wall is tiled green and white. I avoid looking in the mirror. There is a metal tray urinal and two cubicles, both empty. There are warning posters on the toilet wall about STDs and how if you don't book a minicab it is just a stranger's car. Something from the Samaritans saying that if you are up, they are up. Graffiti ingeniously implying that Theresa May's withdrawal agreement is the safest form of contraception.

I cannot risk someone else coming in and urinating next to me, so I head to the cubicle and piss a long stream of red streaked urine into the lightly skidded bowl. At least it came out easily enough. Yet again I have been worrying about nothing. My waterworks are in good working order. I would not be surprised to learn that they are the best in the country. My judgement is always superior to others. Things only ever go wrong when I let people mess with my head. I imagine I am not all that far from my physical peak.

I put the lid down and get out a cigarette. I like the feel of the match on the box, the spark of blue and yellow, the smell of sulphur, the softness of the smoke that fills the air. I think sadly to the Gunpowder plotters. The way their stars simply failed to align. How much they would have valued being able to strike a match like this, as the culmination of their life's work. How different things might have been. We would all be so much richer, morally and spiritually, had they succeeded in their noble dreams.

I cough a little on the first drag of my cigarette, but then it feels good. That and the drink have brought my system back to life, have made me whole again. Here I am in a restaurant with more cider in my bag and food on the table just waiting for me. An illustrious past to remember and an exciting future ahead. It may well be that I am the luckiest man in London.

Sitting on the toilet seat, I open the folder, which is going to be key to my future success, and flick through some of the handwritten pages. It is a green ring binder, neatly split into sections with dividers of different colours. I have been working on this for a long time and it is all in there.

Section one (purple tab): my notes on Carlsen, Caruana and Kasparov. What I have learnt from many hours of intensive study of their play. Section two (blue tab): an assessment of some of the others who appear to be near the pinnacle of today's game. Aronian, Kramnik, Nakamura. I have a keen understanding of how chess has evolved in my absence. The level of accuracy today is impressive I grant you, yet modern-day play, in the main, lacks imagination. You can see the influence of computers; it is all a touch mechanical. They see, but I am not sure they necessarily feel.

I am from a different era, will bring back a swashbuckling romanticism that has not been seen on the chess board for a very long time. My opponents will not know what has hit them, hopefully not literally – such incidents are firmly behind me.

Section three (yellow tab): the opening innovations I have worked out ready for my comeback. It is possible that some of these ideas will put my previous most famous novelty, The Greenbecker Gambit, into the shade. Section four (red tab): is where I log threats from the State against me, together with other risks. I will make a note of tonight's happenings in the restaurant, recognising it was most likely nothing, just in case a pattern later emerges that I am yet to identify.

Section five (orange tab obviously): is where I record my observations on London fires and what can be learnt from them. Section six (green tab): notes on my current day-to-day situation, which will doubtless be used in future biographies. It is where I am scribbling right now.

I have resolved to properly record these moments for posterity, when everything seems at its darkest, but triumph is so close. A portrait of the chess player as a misunderstood genius, something like that. After I am done with Carlsen I will tidy the notes up into an autobiography. That could be a good early money-spinner, before the product endorsements and all the rest start properly flowing in.

I increasingly feel the need to tell this story, though I would have seen such a project as sentimental when I was younger.

Even now, I worry that it shows I am not as focussed on my chess as I should be, but there is, I think, space for both. In many ways they are one and the same.

I contentedly smoke another cigarette before my need for another drink and to get cracking on Fischer - Keres becomes too much. I leave the cubicle to head back toward my table.

On the way out of the toilet, despite my best intentions, I catch a glance of myself in the large rectangular mirror that hangs above the sinks. The glass is in two panels, a brown gap where a third once was reminds me of a mouth missing a tooth. A fluorescent light bulb above, amplifies the effect.

The truth is I do not like what I see. My hair sticks up a touch and my brief efforts to pat it down with water make little difference. My beard is all grey and bushy, yet somehow does not properly obscure the droop in my jawline. I brush some stray cigarette ash out of it and tug at a knot, but the effect is much the same. My stomach sticks out more than I think it should. I fear I look like a balloon, but it is probably a trick of the light. My trousers and shirt both look a little stained.

The only piece of advice my father ever gave me that reso-nated was that men should never wear light-coloured trousers. He might have had a point, but my trousers are dark enough for the stains to blend in until they are barely noticeable. It is hardly my fault that blood leaves more of a trace than urine. Somehow, I just look *older* than the person I know myself to be.

Perhaps we all look a little older these days and I am being too hard on myself. Besides, it is late, and I have not had a shower for several days. A mirror cannot capture an aura and I know mine is strong. That counts for more than the superficiality of the moment. I have always appeared impressive to others. I should know by now not to doubt myself. There will be ample opportunity to tidy myself up before I take to the stage, and it might well be that looking a bit rough and ready works to my advantage, leads others to underestimate me. Who would have the last laugh then?

I'm not saying there aren't going to be challenges ahead, but my belief in myself has been restored. A real chess player needs the optimism to be able to turn any situation around. There are cards for various prostitutes tacked to the mirrorless section of the wall. As I head back to my table, just to help tidy the place up, I pick one up and put it in my pocket.

6. A fucking useless father

The lad with the bent nose and the glasses is staring at my things but turns away hastily as I retake my seat. He could be a State agent I suppose, but it seems unlikely. He looks blankly at my ring binder as I wedge it back into my bag.

I look at my food, but it's still no good. I just don't want it. I pick at a cold chip and from a sense of politeness take a single bite of the burger, even though no one cares. Certain things are ingrained into us from childhood. Too much has been from mine, I know. I reach for another can and drink this one straight. It is crisper and purer without the lemonade and it goes down well. It is time to get to work on Fischer - Keres.

It starts with the oldest opening in chess. The Ruy Lopez, named after the sixteenth century Spanish Priest Ruy Lopez de Segura, who recommended that the board should be set such that the sun shines in your opponent's eyes. I have no need for such a ploy, but the opening itself endures – the king's pawn forward two, the knight to f3, the bishop to b5. White has central pressure, rapid development and a myriad of follow-up plans and variations to choose from, some which run thirty moves deep or more.

I pull out my pocket chess set, which is of the peg variety, and I move the pieces into their well-trodden holes, placing the white knight and bishop onto squares that feel as natural to me as breathing. A player at my level does not need a chess set to visualise these games, but it is late, and I don't see why I shouldn't do what I want with my things.

Chess always seems so fresh for me. It is like a fire that still has many hours to burn. The hundreds of thousands of games I have played, and yet usually I am as enchanted now as when my father first taught me back when I was five. He did play a bit himself, much as he did most things in life, which is to say badly. I despised his general uselessness. His inability to grab the world by the scruff of the neck and to make something of it.

All those years as a mid-ranking official at the council. The suits he wore that made him look like a librarian. His serious looking briefcase filled with meaningless papers. All of it made a mockery of by the non-job he did and the non-money he earned. The only status he had was by proxy, first through my mother, later through me. He was someone's husband and then someone's father. That was all. What was worse was that it never even seemed to bother him.

He would come home from the office. Tired. Tie slightly askew. Prepare the supper while my mother finished off her writing, or as I came to suspect, pretended to finish her writing so that he would do the cooking. He always looked a bit like Philip Larkin. Balding, spectacled. Tall. Unreadable. A trace of something Eastern European in his accent. The details were hazy. He had been born here. His parents had fled to England not long before his birth. He would never say where from. Not exactly.

Jews have been friendless in many places, he once told me. An uncle had been shot. A cousin raped and killed. Just what happened. The world is not what you think it is, he once said. Something I already knew. His parents had purchased a passage to New York, but the boat brought them to London. Another trick. More benign than some. Apparently, they did not even realise the deception immediately, and by the time they did it was too late. They were here, then he was and finally me.

Chess was his only activity outside the house. The weekly club night his one and only hobby. He would always come home and shower then change into fresh but similar clothes before heading out. He was not a strong player, but still it was something. I know it mattered to him, which is why I try not to be too scathing about his inadequacies at the board, as hard as that is.

He was in the local club D team or some such. His reliability and his car both worked in his favour. He was always happy to drive his teammates to matches and back home again. There were many more clubs in those days of course. From the bus drivers, to the civil servants, every workplace, town and village seemed to field several teams. A lot of it has gone now. The people have died out, the working men's clubs turned into luxury flats or car parks. League chess today a shadow of what it once was, but of course interest in me could change all that.

In terms of my own development, there is the story and then there is the real story. Most chess players have them. Kasparov watched his parents fail to solve a chess problem in a newspaper and despite never having played before instantly pointed out the winning move. Capablanca looked on as his father and a friend played and then beat them both.

We all of us, or nearly all, claim to have been instantly brilliant. Seirawan admits that he was awful with a capital A in the beginning, but he always had too much integrity to reach the very top.

My official story is that, having never set eyes on a chess piece before then, I beat my father the first night we ever played, won the club championship the following year and was recognised as the best six-year-old in Europe soon afterwards.

The truth was almost like that, which is more than close enough. It took me four months to beat the old man. He had bought me a plastic chess set for my fifth birthday. A strange gift for one so young, and I had welled up with tears when I had pulled off the cheap wrapping paper and seen that it was not the Meccano I had been hoping for.

His track record with presents did not improve in the years that followed. Some men might have been better at such things, but I blamed my mother, a woman who was always physically present and mentally absent for every terrible gifting choice he made. Once a chest of draws. Once a woman's bicycle with a basket on the handlebars, so tall that when I sat on the saddle neither of my feet were anywhere near the ground. By then it did not matter, I had eyes only for chess. I was supplied with all the books about the game I needed by a growing array of fans and supporters, keen to bask in my reflective glory and no doubt determined to bleed the life out of me.

All that was in the future though. Back then, I threw the box at him and the lid came off, pieces scattering everywhere.

He started to cry as he often did, then I cried some more. We yelled to say how much we hated each other, Mum shouting from the other room that we should keep the noise down as she was trying to write – the usual extent of her interest.

He bent down on his hands and knees and picked the pieces up. I stood there watching, intrigued by the shape of the chessmen. The noble look of the knights, the bishop's visors, the pointed turrets on the rooks. I sensed there might be something to this. I started to help him pick the pieces up, and soon we had found them all and he had set the board. He asked me if I wanted to know how the pieces moved and I found myself nodding.

He was like the guide who knew a few words of a foreign language, but it was enough to get me started. The whole point of chess is to trap your opponent's king, he tells me. It doesn't matter what the material balance is. If you can attack the king and it cannot escape that's checkmate. The end of the game. Checkmate I whispered. The end of the game.

Over the next week or so he got me to practice moving each of the pieces until it was second nature. He showed me some basic checkmates and tactical ideas. We would play games like king and eight pawns versus queen. But I was itching to play for real, and then we did. He won easily, but every night, as soon as he had got in from work, I would beg him to play again. He would usually put me off until he had eaten, and then we would sit at the tiny kitchen table, plastic chess set between us, as slowly, slowly I figured the game out for myself.

Perhaps it was the only time in our relationship when we were relatively at peace with each other, were conspirators in a common purpose. He would steadily drink glasses of cider as he played, and I would work myself through thin slices of bread and butter.

Beyond the basics he was not really any good. He knew the rudiments of his openings. The need to develop, the power of the centre, the basics of pawn structure and a handful of tactical motifs. I will grudgingly admit his early teaching did give me a certain foundation, but that is as far as I will go. I would have worked it all out without him. He was a dilettante. He had no real depth of understanding behind the opening moves he had been taught to parrot. His middlegame plans were rudimentary, his endgame play astonishingly bad. I did not know all this at the time, but even when one victory for him followed another, I somehow suspected.

My breakthrough came gradually. First, I would be winning a game and he would start taking longer to move. He would stare at his drink, while I fidgeted with excitement and anticipation. Then somehow, I would always manage to go wrong, and he would win. I would be devastated. It felt as if someone had stabbed a stake through my heart. I have never been renowned as a particularly good loser, but who would want to be known for that? I remember after a particularly unlucky loss, storming into my bedroom and slamming the door shut, swearing that I would never play him again.

The next night I was back.

Over the following few weeks, I gained and squandered more winning positions, and then finally we reached an ending where I had just a king and he still had his king, pawn and bishop. He didn't know it, but I could see from the geometry that it had to be a draw, given my king position meant that his pawn would never be able to queen.

That first shared point foreshadowed what was coming. Soon I was winning game after game. In his book, *Searching for Bobby Fischer*, Fred Waitzkin writes that his son Josh, the chess prodigy (albeit not one compared to me) did not want to keep on beating his father. I think that lack of desire to pummel someone when they are struggling is in part why Josh did not make it. He clearly lacked the basic humanity inherent in any decent chess player. I would happily have kept on destroying my father for years to come, but instead he decided to take me to his chess club.

They met in an adult education college every Friday. I remember the white brick of the walls with the water pipes that were never silent, always hissing and gurgling the whole evening long. All you could hear was the ticking of the chess clocks, the occasional muted conversation at the games end and the movement of the water around the building.

I remember the brightly coloured posters advertising various courses. Ways out of this suburban world, a pathway to something better. The vending machine offering a range of hot beverages, chocolate and crisps. The gents toilet with its huge enamel urinals, remnants from an earlier age. Most of all, I remember the chess sets. Large Staunton style wooden pieces, ancient wooden boards, some a little faded perhaps by age, perhaps by the many journeys that had been played out on them. Proper equipment, far removed from the plastic pieces, not even weighted, that you will find in most chess clubs today.

Of course, they did not want me. Why would they? Few chess clubs would cater for a six-year-old. They did not have the foresight to recognise my genius. Yet it seemed my father had some standing amongst that group of men. (They were all men.) For all that he was boring and small and defeated before he had begun, though few knew that in those days, he brought in most of our money. My mother's books did not actually sell back then. Albeit, that was why we never had anything. Yet amongst this group, my father's social skills and ability to articulate were well above average. He was surprisingly persuasive. He insisted that I be allowed to play. That is something he did do for me I suppose, although he probably had his own more selfish reasons.

I was asked to play against one of the club's weakest members and promptly demolished him. I played somebody a little stronger and the same thing happened.

It took a while after that. I had to be taught how to play with a clock. The League Committee held special meetings and much earnest debate followed before I could play in actual League fixtures. I did actually lose quite a lot of these to begin with but looking back I was naïve, and it is highly likely that my opponents were cheating.

I was the club junior champion rather than the club's actual champion that first year, which was something of an honorary title as there were no other kids on the books. I was not nationally recognised until I was eight and there were many struggles to be had after that. It matters not if the official version of my CV is a touch embellished as to the instant nature of my brilliance. What matters most is that my brilliance was ultimately indisputable.

The one thing I do acknowledge is that I am going to have to hold my concentration better to make my comeback work.

My mind does tend wander more than it did, but still I have capacity to spare.

The clock says five fifteen now and it's only me and Amal and the homeless man with his towers of sugar and salt left in the place. I guess there must be someone in the kitchen, but I can't see them. While I have been daydreaming, someone has thrown away my food, unless I ate it and returned the tray on automatic pilot, it's hard to be sure. I need the toilet again and another smoke.

Soon night workers from the Underground will be arriving, new staff starting their shift. Soon, but not yet. There is still time to finish my night's work. I know the analysis inside out. Bobby is too good and leaves the Soviet delegation in no doubt that he is indeed the real deal.

I can imagine the whispered conversations. The chess administrators and government officials recognising that this brat is a major problem. Unlike me, he is rude and lacking in social skills, but his actual play is astonishing. It was obvious to every KGB Agent from the very beginning that he threatened the hegemony of Soviet chess. That they need a plan to stop him. Bobby was always wise to it, just as I know that the State has now turned its attentions to thwarting me instead.

Bobby liked the game with Keres a lot and we talked about it more than once. Tried out some different ideas that are not in the notes of *My 60 Memorable Games*. I think we were in New York, when we made a few discoveries that I am not going to share. They are noted in my folder. Just waiting for me to incorporate into my play when I return.

I must have dozed again because the next thing I know, I am nudged awake by a blonde woman whose badge says her name is Imogen. No stars yet. She is young and she presses into my arm quite forcefully, making me jump. I keep my wits about me. Instinctively knowing she is not a policewoman before I even properly register that she is a waitress. I'm generally pretty good at discerning things like this. It is 7.30.

Imogen places a black coffee in front of me. Have this on us, then time to go she says, walking away before I can respond. I can't imagine why she would think that I would want coffee at this time of the morning. I reach into my bag but find I've drunk all the cider. Not good, not good. I check my pockets for money. A few pounds left. Not ideal, but it will get me something to sup from the off-licence before I meet up with Gabriel. I feel quite rested and ready for the day ahead. All in all, it has been a good night.

7. Leaving the kettle on was no accident

I contemplate the coffee that Imogen placed in front of me. I drink it down with a grimace. Feel the poison trickle into my system, the bitterness of the cheap coffee beans catching the back of my throat, the drying aftertaste of caffeine on my tongue. All far from ideal but needs must.

I stand, a little dizzy, before everything rights itself. I look around one final time. It is all London Underground workers breakfasting at the end of the night shift now, before presumably going home to their families. People for whom time is more precious, more pressing certainly, than for the night crowd. I am the bridge between the two groups, the man capable of spanning both worlds. I can fit anywhere and nowhere.

London is truly a crowded space. It is not just the drifters and the workers taking turns in cafés. I feel the weight at my back of previous generations who have walked these streets, conducted their business within the city walls, lived lives of hopes now long forgotten, played with fire one way or another. But perhaps nobody ever really goes. We just all shine a little less brightly in the end. Blend with other memories, souls and stories, on the ash heap of time, become just an echo or a whisper of things gone before.

The conversations had. The clandestine affairs plotted, the betrayals and the heartbreak, the triumphs and disasters. All those things that seem so important before they are lost. I have always been sensitive to ghosts, but today the thought of them does not scare me. I am not a religious man, but I do believe we are all a part of something bigger. Besides, how else to explain my talent? It must have come from somewhere.

Too many people make the mistake of trying to understand London's history by studying its writers and artists, its politicians, entrepreneurs and engineers. Only an enlightened few think to study its chess players. An even smaller number understand that the key to knowing London lies not in word or brick, or even chess moves, but rather through a study of her fires. It is arsonists from Boudica to Guy Fawkes, and those brave souls whose names have been lost to history, that are most in need of thanks.

I think to the Ratcliffe fire of 1794. The kettle of tar left unattended until it boiled over. The flames spreading to the barge filled with saltpetre. The explosion that destroyed more than four hundred and fifty buildings. It really must have been a terrific sight. I wish I had been there to see it. The worst destruction of London between 1666 and the Blitz in a conventional telling. London's biggest opportunity for re-birth in mine. The man who had to pretend leaving the kettle on was an accident is a hero to me. I appreciate the gift he gave. His seeming act of destruction helped London build toward a better future.

I head out of the restaurant into early morning London.

Breathing in the fresh air. The cold is invigorating. There are no leaves left on the trees now, just a mulch of brown and gold on the pavement, coated in frost. Some of the shop windows are all ready for Christmas, spray painted with snowflakes and dressed in tinsel and multicoloured lights. Plastic trees for sale. Signs counting down the days to the 25th December, still weeks away. We are forever looking forward, never content to live in the present. I am no different. It is the way we all are.

I breathe out and watch the steam from my breath separate and fade away. Time is passing. 2018 nearing its end. Enough of it left to still be my year.

Being on the move again re-connects me with my body, makes me notice it in a way I did not while sitting down. My shoulder feels stiff from sleeping on the table, neck a touch cricked, rucksack heavy on my back. My toenail is pinching. My bladder, as ever, does not feel quite right, but I am getting used to ignoring it. I know I cannot really need to piss, so I try to convince my brain to override my nervous system's faulty signal.

Perhaps it takes a minute or so to find my stride with confidence. No more. My constitution is pretty much as good as it has always been. The vagaries of the night no real impediment to someone of my strength. A few minor aches and pains are neither here nor there in the scheme of things.

I have had all the sleep I need, and it does not take much air for my head to feel as clear as the day I beat Frederick Hamlet, to reach the World Candidates Final. It is ridiculous to think that was my last significant victory. That when it became obvious he could not stop my pawn storm and held out his hand, that was as good as it was going to get. The State-manipulated disaster against Dubrovnik was still in my future. As were the years that some might consider to be a waste.

The match with Hamlet took place in Amsterdam. Our relationship was reasonably amicable as these things go. Deep down he knew I was the stronger player. I was desperate to beat him of course, but there was more to it than that. The games we played were interesting. They absorbed me completely.

I enjoyed those two weeks. I would swivel in my seat and turn my gaze to the large electronic display boards that framed the position in silicon at the back of the stage and think, I made this, I am a part of this. Yet the matches you win can leave you feeling somewhat cheated. Whatever I do, it never feels enough. I remind myself that I am a survivor and winner both.

I am sure I must look pretty good to those who pass me right now. My face feels fresh from a quick splash of water at the restaurant sink. I have even taken the opportunity to pat my hair down, and except perhaps for the dash of charisma that I inevitably exude, the wattage of stardom, most likely appear indistinguishable from the city workers making their way to offices and desks, coffee shops and meetings, PowerPoint presentations and endless email.

There is plenty of time before I meet Gabriel both to watch and to think, the two things I am best at. Watch, think, then make the right play. That is what all my success has been based on.

Around the corner from the restaurant, I pause to buy some White Ace, just to tide me over. Blue and yellow signage missing several letters proclaims Singh's Twenty-Four-Hour Newsagent and Shop, nails sticking out around the wooden board to prevent it being used as a staging point for anyone wanting to climb onto the roof. Wire grill in front of the window, a plastic refuse bin on the pavement outside overflowing with bottles and discarded remnants of takeaway food. A family member standing guard outside.

I nod at him and he does not respond as I push on the door, which triggers a low groan from some electronic device attached to it that sounds a bit like a ship's foghorn running low on battery. Just their way of warning the staff that another customer has entered.

It is like stepping back into the 1970s. Tatty peeling floor tiles and prominently displayed offerings of cigarettes and pornographic magazines; the smell of spice, tobacco and tin. Somewhere that never really sleeps, but never fully wakes either. I know it well; this is on my patch. I could picture the shelving with my eyes closed. The bottles and cans in every colour from the greens and the whites through to the browns and the gold. Pictures of apples and hops and grapes adorn the labels. Images of vineyards and blissful autumnal scenes. Rising suns and beautiful women, arrows, harps and polar bears. There are ring pulls and screw tops and corks. And all of it screams drink me, like something out of *Alice in Wonderland*.

The food shelves have been designed for those who eat as an afterthought. Pot Noodles past their sell-by date, large bags of rice, a range of tinned spam, a good supply of liquorice. This is my kind of shop. Its emphasis on vice, base needs. Alcohol will suit me fine.

Shaggy's 'It wasn't me,' is playing on the shop's sound system and I find myself swaying a little to the beat. Annoyingly, there are family members posted everywhere. As well as the guy on the door, another fixes his stare on the shelves, which makes it difficult to steal. Hardly sporting, but increasingly the way of the modern world.

My remaining coins will run to three cans of White Ace and a packet of roasted peanuts. Enough to tide me over until the pub opens, a more than reasonable breakfast. I don't have many cigarettes left, but I must make a choice and elect to string out those that remain. Cigarettes are still easy enough to cadge, easier than alcohol at any rate.

These days of my money not going far enough will soon be over. It is not that I really need Gabriel's help with my chess comeback. Just an unfortunate accident of timing on the cash-flow front, that's all. Let's face it, none of the other contenders for the world title are beating a path to his door seeking assistance and advice.

What is he really? A hapless architect who designs rabbit hutch-sized houses for modern estates, most likely built out of recycled cardboard. It would not take much for the whole fucking lot of them to go up in smoke. Albeit most are so badly put together, they would likely fall down of their own accord, faster than any reasonable man could properly douse them in paraffin and strike a match.

There certainly can't be any real money in the architecture game, so essentially Gabriel lives comfortably on the proceeds of my chess career and my mother's books in a house that, according to Zoopla, is worth well over a million pounds. He will be shocked when I tell him that I know this, and he will feel morally bound to hand over a large sum of money on the spot. I know exactly how he thinks.

I am sick of Gabriel criticising without ever giving me any credit for all the cash I did make at one point. Another facet of his moral superiority. We have never been close. Perhaps I have never been all that close to anyone. Well, hardly anyone, but difficulties with Gabriel are not my fault. I do not wholly lack empathy – it must have been difficult for an idiot like him to grow up with a genius for a brother. My chess talent. My mother's vanity projects. The shadow she cast over all our lives. My father's uselessness. It did not leave all that much for Gabriel.

I do not like to talk about it, but ours was hardly a childhood of bike rides and picnics and building dens in the woods after school. The best days of your life? Don't make me laugh.

I remember once walking back from the bus stop, down our boring road, past the phone box and the house with the rusting cars on the front lawn. The low-slung row of local shops. A grocer, a post office, a garage that was soon to close, a hairdresser where we got our pudding basin cuts. Very good value my father would say, but of course he did not have to endure the teasing that inevitably followed.

Uniform red brick houses with different colour doors. The ten-minute walk we did every day. There and back. There and back. In all weathers. A ragtag group of local children who took the same bus. Mainly friendly with Gabriel. All either hostile or indifferent to me for reasons I know not why.

It was late February and the world still seemed to be bleached of colour and bathed in cold. I just wanted to be in the warm, with my chess, far away from school and everything that went with it. We were nearly home when Michael Halfpenny ran up to Gabriel.

'Is he your brother?' he asked, laughing, running circles around me, even though he knew full well who I was. Sticking his tongue out. Spitting at me. Pawing at my face. Pulling my tie. Grabbing my genitals.

I tried not to cry. Tried to avoid showing weakness. Waited for him to stop. What else could I do? I pretended it did not bother me, wiped his spit from my blazer as if it was no more than a stray piece of early blossom, barely noticeable. Nothing at all.

It stayed with me though. Still does. The irrationality of it. Yet another problem that logic cannot solve.

I remember Gabriel said no, I was not his brother. Left me to my tormentor. Made no attempt to help me. Always one for an easy life. The path of least resistance. He denies that this ever happened, so he is a liar too.

All families are the same. It is just how it is. Yet blood is still thicker than water after all.

I pause. Breathe. Bring myself back to the here and now. To the future. This is a different world. What has gone before does not matter. I am firmly in control of my own destiny.

I had planned to hold onto the cider for a bit, but now I think, why not? I reach into my bag, pull out one of my newly purchased cans, flip it open and drink deeply. Immediately I feel better. Warmer, more grounded. Properly back in control.

Today is destined to be a key staging post in my journey. I have already achieved great things and more await. I look out on London as one of the most celebrated men in the city, even if that is not universally appreciated. Soon I will be back in my rightful place, leaving all hint of sadness behind me.

8. Writers are frauds

Families. Who would want one? Perhaps it is the unfortunate memory that has found its way into my head. Perhaps it is the cider that has made me nostalgic. I don't know. I feel a little wheezy and have plenty of time, so I pause to sit on a green bench. It has a metal plate screwed into it in remembrance of Tess Archer – *Wonderful mummy, wife, sister and daughter. 1971 - 2014. Sit here awhile and think of Tess*. A bunch of flowers taped to the bench's arm, just on the turn.

I rummage in my bag for one of the photographs I keep in a zipped compartment. I do not look at these all that often, but right now for reasons I cannot fully articulate, it seems important. Something to do while I take a moment's rest and smoke one of my last cigarettes. My foot always feels better with the weight off for a bit.

Too many people I knew died young. Andrew, a fellow junior player was killed in a car accident on the way to a chess tournament at the age of eleven. I'm not sure why the State judged him such a threat that they chose to murder him at such a young age. I feared for a long time that they had got the pair of us confused and had in fact been planning to kill me. They could hardly have judged him the better player and there is no other obvious explanation. I suppose it was a fortunate mix up.

I went to Andrew's funeral. It was the first time I had been in a church. Afterwards we all ate stale cheese and tomato sandwiches and salt and vinegar crisps at the pub across the road. You've done us proud with this spread, love, one of the mourners told the half-cut landlady to general murmurs of agreement.

I remember my father sitting next to me. Holding my arm. He looked at me and said, 'Whatever you do, just be careful. That is all I ask. There is only one of you.' He obviously knew that I would always be a State target, but that was the best he could come up with, in terms of practical advice. The man was completely useless.

Later there was Mark, the arbiter and secret alcoholic who allegedly drank himself to death in his thirties. He apparently could not admit that he had a drink problem. Some people knew and some did not. It is hard for a purely social drinker like myself to get my head around it, but there it was. It did not occur to me until much later that it was just another Establishment cover story. He had undoubtedly been poisoned.

More recently the State has become ever more brazen. An emerging Russian player allegedly died when a game of parkour went wrong and he fell from the twelfth floor of a Moscow block of flats. The State must have been laughing its head off at the ease with which it got away with that one. He was just practising his hobby. Oh please.

I always try and avoid upper floor windows, cars, and when

71

possible, I will only drink from a can I have opened myself. Just the usual sensible, everyday precautions.

The photograph I am looking at is in black and white, a little greasy and grainy. I stroke it with my fingertips. I remember the day well. All its false narrative. The attempt to frame us as something we were not.

There we all are, in the formal dress of the period. Gabriel and I with our locally cut pudding basin haircuts, kitted out in black suit jackets and shorts, thin ties, his straight, mine not. My mother and father sitting behind, him with his hand on Gabriel's shoulder, wedding ring reflecting the glare of the flash. He wears the knitted jumper and tie he always wore. I don't think I have any memories of him in any setting where he was not clad in a cheap tie, always solid red or solid blue, top button on his collar undone.

In the photograph he has that smiling, half apologetic look I remember so well. He never had it in him to take control, to assert himself, to tell the world to go get fucked.

My mother stares into the middle distance with a look that is hard to discern, so nothing new there. White pleated summer dress, some sort of academic-style tweed jacket over the top of it, hanging stiffly on her shoulders. Making slightly more of her breasts than she probably envisaged. The whole day a chore to her no doubt. Taking her away from her writing and her reading, forcing her back to a realm where the rest of us exist. A world of actual people with real needs.

Whatever her level of perception on the page, and she does seem to have pulled the wool over the eyes of some, none of it ever spanned over into her actual relationships with actual human beings. Or more precisely, with Gabriel and me. Just the way it was. We were never more than something for her to endure, if we were lucky. Anyone can be a mother, she once noted in one of the interviews I did away with. The truth is though that they can't.

I have seen the letters where she writes of the boredom and sheer drudgery of it all. I am sure the publisher only put them out after her death as a way of getting at me. The washing and the cooking. The playing. The mundanity of a world far less interesting than those she could create in her head and translate onto the page.

A lot of writers complain of the drudgery of the everyday, but in a way that lets you know that they are in on the joke. That while they write these things, in reality they are *terrific* parents. That was not how she was. People say I live in my head too, but perhaps she drove me there. Either way, there is no comparison between the things we have made. My brain has created some of the finest games of chess that have ever been seen. I have been imaginative in many other ways. What did she make? Memories I have worked hard to erase. A few books that are not very good. She was nothing. Nothing at all.

Back at the time of the photograph I had already surpassed my brother on the chess board, as well as intellectually in every other way. Of the four of us, I was the one with the true talent, even if this was never openly admitted. Still, Gabriel's resentment and bitterness toward his more gifted little brother was always there. Even if he would never have had the balls to hit me himself, he was always happy if others did. To align himself with those at school who both wished and did me harm. If he had to sacrifice me, to join the 'in crowd,' well that was a price he was more than willing to pay.

I think it was only later, as evidence of my talent racked up, that he came to be more accepting, and for a while respectful. At least before the wheels fell off. Ultimately through the ages, those who lack genius are drawn to those who truly possess it. That is how it is with us. He will be happy to help me now. It is just a continuation of his previous less than successful efforts. Between us we will make this all work.

Perhaps it was reading the inscription on the bench that did it. Perhaps just looking at a picture of people now gone was enough to trigger the memory, but I find myself thinking to my mother's funeral. I did not want to go, but Jewish deaths leave little room for contemplation and I was swept along by the suddenness of the event. Had I been in the middle of a chess tournament it would have been easy to avoid the wretched thing. Everyone would have understood that.

The funeral was forty-eight hours after her death. It would have been sooner if the coroner had been more competent. I argued for a cremation, but that was always going to be a non-starter.

Various from the literary world in attendance. The dreadful extended family in all their glory. Doubtless still more there to catch a glimpse of me, fresh from my victory in the Global Open. To rub shoulders with a man then in the world top ten and on the brink of going higher.

I am reasonably certain that I saw Martin Amis smoking a cigarette at the back of the group of mourners. Heard him, just as my mother's coffin was being lowered into the ground, explaining to someone as to why he had had to dump Julian

Barnes's wife for a new literary agent. Writers are all smokers. I have noticed that. It is the only way to be of course.

Then there were the others. The dreadful Irish novelist, who could not quite be dismissed as no one understood a word that she wrote. She had come to visit fairly often when we were younger. Her and my mother would sit in the garden for hours, drinking whisky from the bottle. If we were lucky, they would give me and Gabriel money to buy chips. If we weren't, there would be nothing. Kindness was the overarching theme of her writing apparently, in so far as anyone could tell.

The whole bunch of them were the same. Writers are all frauds. Just know that. Do not believe a word that any of them ever write. They all have an agenda. They are all in the employ of the State. At least with chess players you occasionally know where you stand.

The huge Jewish cemetery in Rainham, with its marble monuments stretching in every direction, was all of stone and loss. So functional, so organised. How we Jews do death when left in peace. The tap to wash your hands under on leaving. All the other connotations that accompany such an act. No flowers allowed. Just solitary pebbles left next to the headstones.

The neighbouring plot to my mother, occupied by a seven-teen-year-old male, the inscription declaring that his parents will grieve in anguish for all eternity. Two empty spaces on the other side of his grave, waiting for the day when they will join their son in the soil. Still, the day was my mother's, not theirs. Down she went into the earth joining my father, her body barely cold, not that she was ever warm.

A stroke they said, although I always suspected there was more to it than that. One minute doing a reading in Hampstead.

The next, she had collapsed on the floor, piles of her new book on the table casting a shadow over her body. People gasping. Six separate calls placed summoning an ambulance. A doctor in the audience trying to resuscitate her.

Perhaps the State realised that I was considering exposing her and decided to act fast. That was my first idea, but only partly right. It was certainly a State-sponsored assassination, but the reasons for it were most likely more mundane. I was obviously being sent a warning. At that time, my chess had made me too well known, too celebrated, for them to take me out directly. So, they killed her instead as a shot across my bows, perhaps not realising that I despised the woman and was grateful to them for their actions.

I don't know exactly how they did it. A poisoned dart or something in her food perhaps? These matters are not difficult to arrange. Besides, just because I cannot explain the method does not invalidate my reading of the act.

It always offended my very being that Gabriel suggested that my reaction to our mother's death was just another way in which I made everything about me. As if I would ever do that. I have always been regarded as someone who takes very little interest in themselves. Gabriel said I was talking nonsense, had no grip on reality, that things were clearly worse than he had thought. I tried to be conciliatory by suggesting that if it wasn't a State-sponsored hit, it might have been a publicity stunt that had gone wrong, but he would not even meet me halfway on it.

I was angry to begin with, but I could tell that he shared the same misgivings I had. The way he refused to properly discuss how my mother came to be slumped on the floor of the fucking bookshop was an obvious give-away. He was doubtless trying to alleviate my burden by not letting on. He did not want me to worry about the danger I faced from the State. That was most probably it. He was my brother after all.

As we threw sods of earth onto the coffin, I felt only exhilaration. If I wasn't allowed to burn her, I was fucking well going to enjoy burying her. It felt terrific that not only was she dead, but I was still alive. Participating in this ceremony seemed to confirm the impossibility of me ever dying, of falling into the ridiculous trap in which somehow you allow others to lower your body into the grave and cover you with soil. No one is ever going to do that to me, I promise you.

On top of this feeling of immortality, there was an extra personal sense of delight that it was my actual mother who was dead. That finally I was free of her. That she was now nothing and I was still everything. That my pass for the world still worked fine, thank you very much, while hers did not. That is why we go to funerals, I suppose.

We went on from the cemetery to eat bagels and cheese with cousins we only knew well enough to be sure we did not like. Just like any other family, when confronted with death, we fell back on ritual and habit. The traditions of the service. The routines of food, small talk and the observation of time shared. There is nothing else. None of the writers and hangers-on had been invited, not that they were missing much. Stilted conversation and crumbs picked off the good china. The silent speculation as to who might go next. The only event that would bring this grouping back together.

They were a miserable bunch. None of them had amounted to much. Howard, who had been a chemist before being jailed in somewhat mysterious circumstances, now apparently reha-bilitated. He had a scar on his neck that he would never talk about. Every time there was a knock at the door he would not exactly jump, but perhaps stiffen a little.

Benjamin, the good Jew, with all the right Jewish literature on his bookshelves. He would absent-mindedly pick at the boil on his chin and then pretend that he had hadn't and take another bite of his pickled egg. His house was close enough to London to be worth a packet, but it was a soulless place with thin carpets and tired walls that needed a lick of paint. The shelving was cheap. Metal units that you might more readily associate with student digs. He fussed around ineffectually, managing to irritate everybody with his overstated politeness.

Helen his wife, who had always had a reputation for being highly strung, made most of the food, retreating regularly to the back porch to smoke and swig vodka from a miniature bottle when she thought no one was looking. Keith played a few songs before departing early in a chauffeur driven car that I imagined at the time he had hired just to show off.

Gabriel and Ginevra sat on the sofa, picking at their bagels and cheap sunny tomatoes with the air of creatures warily watching out for predators. We had our usual arguments. Who would be buried in which plot? Great Uncle Bernie's will – again. He was gay. First a ballet dancer, then a tailor. He had lived with Saul in a house painted pink, then when Great Uncle Saul had died, Bernie made a new will and left everything to our father, who he had barely seen. Many years later it was still a thing. We re-hashed it all a little, for forms' sake as much as anything.

Standard arguments aside, I felt everyone else treated me

with the reverence that was my due, not just from being the son, but because of my exalted position in the chess world. It was a terrific time in my life really. Perhaps I have never felt happier than I did that day. Close to the peak of my powers. So certain that things would work out. I smugly crossed off the minutes until I could be free of the lot of them, ready to continue with what seemed back then to be my unstoppable ascent.

9. Rats with wings

I watch a few pigeons pecking for crumbs by the bin. Big fat grey creatures, rats with wings. An extraordinary array of greys and greens and whites and browns in their plumage. Even the mundane becomes complex, beautiful, if you look closely enough.

One bird is missing a foot, but it keeps on with its task just the same. Another shits right in front of my shoe and I realise that I am getting sentimental in my old age. I should have stamped on the fucking thing while I had the chance. I do need to focus on maintaining some sort of edge.

The river is calling. I always like to take the air and the walk will bring me close to the Red Lion, just up from the Houses of Parliament and the Westminster Tube. It is a bit of a trek and I will most likely need to pause to catch my breath from time to time, but no matter. There is no rush. This is my London.

A woman in a smart suit is engaged in an animated phone conversation. It seems to be some sort of lovers' tiff. 'You always say that,' she says angrily and as she hangs up, she spits a wad of chewing gum onto the pavement. She does not seem very happy and I wonder if I might be of assistance, but I think not, I don't want to get distracted. Drawn into other people's issues. Focus is important.

Now is as good a time as any to consider where Carlsen might have the edge over me. Basic stamina would be an obvious consideration. He seems to just wear the kids out in the final hours of play. To turn half-points into victories through sheer force of personality. That is something I need to consider further, and it is already noted in my folder.

Look at it another way, his fortitude has never been tested in quite the way that mine has – I think it is unlikely that he has ever slept at a train station or dozed on the Formica of a restaurant table. His usual opponents, with their snappy suits and social media accounts, are not real warriors. Little more than computer nerds, most of them. I have a depth to my endurance that others do not. Ideally, I will need a training camp to just put myself back into peak condition, but it could well be that the street has been the best preparation of all.

Openings is another area to consider. Here I think Carlsen's approach plays entirely into my hands. He is not a theoretician in the way of a Kasparov. Rather, he is more of a slow burner. To some degree he avoids mainline theory and just aims to get a position. Something to work with later. Remembering opening theory is the one area where I am not as sharp as I used to be, I do sense that. The depth of my general understanding is such that it might only be an issue against the very best, but if Carlsen isn't playing the critical theoretical lines, then it is not a problem. More fool him!

Equally, many of the new ideas I do have will work well against the vanilla setups Carlsen likes to adopt. I feel my good humour rising further, he does not stand a chance, it is almost as if I have won already. He can count his lucky stars he is playing Caruana right now.

As I approach Westminster, I pause for breath outside the Tube station, just resting my legs for a moment. I take in the sandwich boards asking if I know who Jesus really is, the earnest followers who are handing out leaflets, seeking new disciples, but they leave me alone. The Tesco's with its crown of barbed wire.

I rummage in my bag and bring out a can of cider, my folder and the plastic pot I sometimes use to supplement my income in such places. There are more and more women doing the same thing these days and I find that people prefer to give to them. Yet another field where being a man is a disadvantage, but no matter, sex is not key to any of this.

I drink the can down and feel a new surge of energy coursing through me, my senses sharpened, everything good. I know Gabriel will deliver, but it is true that it never hurts to have a bit of extra money in your pocket.

Ideally, if I can stand the first round, that might be to my advantage. It would demonstrate that I am already set, that I don't really need his help, am in fact doing him a favour by continuing to involve him in my enterprise. I am good at thinking things through like this. Always looking ahead.

For now, I know exactly where to sit, just far enough away from the entrance to the Tube such that they are unlikely to move me on, but close enough that all the commuters will pass by me. Perhaps it is being a little bit older than I once was, I don't know, but I increasingly like the sensation of just sitting and letting myself be. Feeling at one with the city around me.

Entirely free. The moment belonging to me and no one else.

I plan to study some middle game tactical motifs, just by way of sharpening myself up, but I look at the first one in my folder and my mood sours. My mind wandering almost immediately. This is something I really am going to need to work on, but in the circumstances, it is understandable.

The position is one of my own. A tactical blunder I made many years ago that unfortunately still gets reprinted regularly in magazines and journals. It was in a London tournament that nearly destroyed me before I had even started. A total disaster, the whole thing.

The UK Masters. I was twelve or thirteen I suppose. The finest player of my age on the planet. Undoubtedly a world champion in waiting, which was why the foreign press was always so dismissive of me, sometimes barely even alluding to my many triumphs, or not writing about me at all.

It was an invitational all-play-all, involving seven of the world's top twenty and me, the great British hope of the future. There had been warnings. Some felt the event would be too strong, that brilliant as I was, I was not quite ready. I knew it was all jealousy, people trying to hold me back. I still believe that, but I had not counted on the forces of the State that were at work.

The first round was all right. I played Florentian Gambaccini, the Italian ranked number eight in the world. A tall, thin, hawk-like man in a crumpled suit who fussed with his cufflinks throughout.

I had the white pieces and played the London system, rapidly building up pressure with the classical formation of pawns on c3, d4 and e3 and my dark squared bishop activated outside my triangle of central pawns. It was not often seen at the top level in those days and Gambaccini did not find the best way through, leaving me clearly in the better position. Then I ran a little short of time, got nervous, was not entirely sure of the best way forward. So I offered a draw and he said yes. I was delighted to be off the mark, but I had clearly underestimated what the chess establishment would throw at me after that.

In the next game, I was black against Michael Wengrower, the world number thirteen. A huge bear of a man, with a thick black beard, who never seemed to wash or change his clothes and as a result always stank, mainly of the tinned sardines he seemed to live on. Such worldly things did not trouble him, or his acolytes, who always seemed to be in attendance.

When we shook at the beginning of our game, he clasped my hand tightly and gave me a look of pure hatred. Leaning in close, exposing me to the stink of rotting sardines he whispered in his strong Russian accent,

'I will kill you, you cunt,' before leaning back in his seat and giving a half-wave and a smile to the spectators.

He put me off, pure and simple. He knew he could not beat me fair and square, so he chose to resort to mind games. Being a child was no excuse, I should have been mentally tougher. As it was, I made a near beginner's mistake on move twelve, hanging a piece to a simple queen check, leaving the game lost.

Wengrower replied to all my subsequent moves instantly and spent most of the game chatting with the spectators and my fellow competitors. I could see them all laughing. At one point, Wengrower mimicked my look of horror when he had snapped off my knight. He slapped his own forehead in mock despair and laughed loudly. When finally, I could put the inevitable off no longer and resigned, he leaned in once more to shake my hand.

'You were really shit,' he said, leaving the board before I could say another word.

It got even worse after that, but it took me a while to figure out the root cause. Of course, my opponents were working collectively against me. I did not blunder again, but whatever I did, I kept losing. If I ever got into a good position, I would go wrong. If my situation was poor, I was crushed without mercy. Long games, short games. Some theoretically interesting, some not, it did not really matter. Nothing went my way. The result was always the same. It was not until round five against the English number one Adrian Mottram that I realised what was going on.

I was the better player. It was clear that he did not know what to do, how to steer the position into more favourable territory for him. Then he went to the toilet and did not emerge for some time. I needed to go too, and I think I already had my suspicions by this point. I found him standing outside the gents, deep in conversation with Michael Wengrower.

I was sure they were talking about the game. That Michael was coaching him. I screamed and the arbiter came running, doubtless fearing that I had been some subjected to some form of physical attack, which in a way I had.

I tried to hold back my tears as I explained what had happened. The arbiter looked uncomfortable. The whole event had been set up to introduce me onto the world stage and it was not going entirely to plan.

'I don't need Michael's help to beat this idiot,' Adrian

said, setting the scene for the years of animosity that were to follow between us as I went on to surpass him as England's number one.

Michael just laughed.

'We were talking about our summer holidays,' he said, stretching his arms out and pretending to be an aeroplane.

This was a bit rich, I doubted that Michael had ever taken a holiday in his life. I always remember the story of the Egypt Masters, where on a rest day the players were taken on a tour of the Pyramids. Michael and a number of others refused to get off the bus, preferring to stay in their seats studying and playing blitz with each other on pocket sets.

In their position I would have done the same but if anything, that just further underscores my point. It should have been obvious that he was lying. It was not until later that I realised that the arbiter was in on it too. It was a powerful lesson for the future, if extremely difficult at the time.

We all headed back to the playing area, but the inevitable happened and I lost, neither of us making any pretence to offering a handshake at the end. The arbiter avoided my eye when I handed in the scoresheets. I lost in the final round too, ending up with a solitary draw and six straight losses.

I developed a speech impediment that lasted for many years and for a long time after, my dreams were filled with games of chess in which queens and rooks would tear through my defences. My king would have no squares. Tactical ideas that appeared to be flawless turned out to be anything but. If I was in an overwhelming position as white, the pattern in my sleep would change and I would suddenly have the black pieces and lose. And all the time, Michael Wengrower would be in the background, laughing and slapping his head and stretching his arms out as if he were an aeroplane.

It did take me time to recover. Yet it was also the most formative experience of my early career. It showed me that I wasn't just trying to take on individual players, I was up against a system that hated and wanted to destroy me. And not just the Russians, it went deeper than that. The UK establishment too. I must have seemed to them to be a modern-day representation of the peasant Alekhine and Capablanca had come across all those years ago. The man with the capacity to upset the apple cart, to destroy the comfort of the status quo.

Those who say I am paranoid don't realise how very well attuned I am to the threats I face. I could not have been beaten as I was by normal means, even back then, when I was nowhere near the player I am today. They were all out to get me, right from the start. Wengrower, Mottram, Korchnoi, the whole lot of them. If they had not all been working together, I would have won every game.

10. The fourth estate

My train of thought is interrupted by a lady who has squatted down on the pavement to talk to me.

'Hello,' she says. 'Are you all right?'

I am immediately suspicious and on guard. Most likely another do-gooder with an empty life, who thinks they can fix mine. I seem to attract any number of them these days. They have their uses, but I also must consider whether this might all be some sort of police trap. A sting operation. I don't know. Anything is possible.

She is perhaps thirtyish. City suit. Kitten heels. As she adjusts her foot, I notice the label from the shop is still attached to one of the soles. Her hair is dark brown, expensively cut, even if I am no expert in such matters. She smells of cigarettes and perfume and her light hazel coloured eyes are deeply earnest. Not pretty exactly, but well turned out.

I grunt non-committedly, reminding myself she could be anyone. A State agent spying on me. Someone from the Prime Minister's office or even FIDE. Conspirators come in many guises. My best guess though, is that she is none of these things. Westminster is the sort of place that allows people like me to hide in plain sight. The agents of the State may be everywhere, but round here they have other things to worry about.

The Queen. The Cabinet. I might not even make the top ten list of subjects of interest in this square mile. That's just logic isn't it? Partly why I like the centre of town. Even if I understand why others consider I do myself a disservice in thinking other potential targets rank higher than myself.

'How long have you been here for?' she asks.

It also needs to be said that I am deeply cautious about talking to women in general these days, but the cider has had some effect and while my guard is not entirely down, I think I can risk it.

'About twenty minutes,' I say.

She looks surprised and then re-frames the question.

'How long have you been on the streets for?' she asks, looking at me earnestly.

'Since about 7.30,' I say.

'I'm Jasmine,' she tries, and I see her thinking about offering me her hand, but then does not, giving me a half-wave instead.

I notice that her nail polish is bright red, but peeling, one digit just naked nail. It is not exactly erotic, but somehow humanising. I wonder if she might in fact be a very skilful agent who is trying to lure me in so that she can denounce me. My instinct is that she is as harmless as any woman can be. She certainly seems to be drawn to me, which is understandable.

So, I tell her,

'I'm Tennessee Greenbecker.'

I wait for a reaction.

'You're not related to Judith Greenbecker by any chance, are you?' she asks.

I do get this question occasionally and it is always baffling, as to how people could have heard of my mother, but not of me. I must hand it to the semi-literate publishing house that puts out my mother's books – they do seem to be quite good at promoting her, all these years after her death.

All those friends in the literary community, most of them as talentless as she was, still banging away on the radio. The newspaper articles about her that are used as kindling by most readers before the ink is dry. The fact that her books, such as they were, are no good, is almost beside the point. Propaganda is everything.

I sit there, quietly. Very still. Mothers are difficult to escape from.

'Are you all right? I mean really?' The woman who calls herself Jasmine asks. She takes a deep drag on her cigarette and watches as the smoke she then exhales disappears into London's chilly air. She half raises an eyebrow and opens out her small hands to emphasise the gesture.

I am stumped as to how to answer. The question has given me pause. There is something in her tone that makes me think. Is it possible that I am, in fact, not all right? But I banish the thought as quickly as it arises. Just another sign that my mental toughness is not quite what it was in my prime. That I need to be careful who I listen to.

'Are you all right?' I enquire and she is surprised, taken aback a bit.

'I think so,' Jasmine says. 'In so far as any of us ever can be.'

We sit together and I ask if she happens to have a cigarette. Just the act of asking makes me realise how much I am craving a smoke. It is doubtless a lack of nicotine that has disturbed my equilibrium.

Jasmine reaches into the tailored pocket of her suit jacket and pulls out a packet, before extracting and handing me one of her Marlboro Lights. This isn't really going to do the job but is better than nothing. I gesture for a light and she hands me her lighter. I flick its head, enjoying the sight of the sparks, my cigarette first glowing and then properly taking. I put the lighter in my pocket, half surprised to find that even with such a weak cigarette I still enjoy the first drag of tobacco my body has felt deep within it for a good half hour.

Jasmine hesitates for a moment as if a thought was forming, but then replaces it with another one.

'If I give you some money, do you promise not to spend it on drugs?'

'If I gave you some money, would you?' I ask gruffly.

'Point taken.'

She sighs but does not hand over any cash. She is weighing something up, but it is hard for me to tell what it is. She seems to have time on her hands, which for someone dressed as she is, in a city like this, is difficult to account for. The only explanation is that she must be fascinated by me. I wonder if her interest might be professional as well as personal. She certainly seems to be asking a lot of questions.

'You don't have to live like this,' she now offers. 'There are places. People who could help you get back on your feet. I could help you, point you in the right direction.'

I say again that I've only been here for twenty minutes. She smiles and it is as if we are locked in one of those chess games where the way forward is not entirely clear to either side. Both waiting for the other to make a pawn thrust or do something else that changes the structure, crystallises an imbalance, points, perhaps, to a path forward.

'What does your day hold?' I ask.

I am surprised by the question as soon as it is formed. People would interest me more if they were more interesting. It must be the cider and the morning and the knowledge that my plans are progressing so well that has made me more affable than usual. Bolder perhaps. I am generally wary of women who might be trying to seduce me, such that they can either then have me locked up or thwart my path to chess glory in some other way. Still today I think, where's the harm?

Jasmine hesitates. 'Well, I'll be working on one or two of my projects. I'm a writer you see.'

I sigh. I really hate writers. At least my own books are based on my expertise. Those who write for its own sake are just attention seekers. Writing leads to nothing but pain for those around the author. I should know, but my experience is hardly unique. What was it they said about Karl Ove Knausgard – another overrated Norwegian? His second wife had a nervous breakdown because of the way he wrote about her in one of his early *My Struggle* books. So of course, he then wrote in detail about her breakdown in a later one. Nothing any good ever comes from writers and writing.

'I'm a journalist really. At least, until I finish my novel.'

Given my previous with the fourth estate, journalist would normally be even worse in my eyes than her being a writer, but the timing today strikes me as fortuitous. A sign. Only a very skilled journalist at a top newspaper would have had the foresight to approach me so carefully, with just the right amount of respect and flattery.

I can tell by the way she dresses that she is very successful. I always knew I was going to have to go public with my comeback at some point. It would not surprise me if Gabriel had set this all up for me to get the ball rolling.

'Is this my brother's doing?' I ask her.

'I didn't know you had a brother,' she says, but I can't tell whether she is telling me the truth or not. I suppose it doesn't matter and I can always ask him later.

She takes out a cigarette and I offer her a light, which she seems to find funny and we both sit there smoking her cigarettes.

'I'm writing something at the moment about London. The real city, one removed from tourist attractions and over-priced days out. The people like you, who manage to survive, despite everything that gets thrown at you. The indifference of society. Life on the margins. I must be honest, that was partly why I approached you.'

I laugh loudly and slap my thighs with my hands. I must hand it to her. She is good. I wonder how long it took her to create that cover story. She must have practised her lines a thousand times in the mirror. That's what top journalists do. Even if her use of the word 'partly' gives the whole game away, we both know what is going on really, but I am happy to humour her.

'So, I'm a research project, is that it?' I say. 'I know there is enough in me to keep a dozen writers and academics fully occupied for years and years!'

'No, no, I genuinely wanted to find out if you were all right too,' she says. 'It's just that I could see you were an intelligent man with a story. I thought you might make a great subject for the Article I am writing.'

I laugh again and shout, 'Yes, Yes, Yes!'

What I find funny is that her cover story is so amusing because it could almost be true. It is perfectly possible that I could be asked to give an interview on London life, from her gutters to her fires. Jasmine is very skilful to position everything like this, in case other journalists who might try and steal her exclusive are listening in.

I'm sure I read somewhere that there are more bugging devices in London than there are rats. The press has most likely been staking me out for weeks. Jasmine doubtless also wants to get the price down, and of course that's something we can sort out later. She has a certain wisdom to see everything so clearly.

'I am very busy today, but if meeting up will help with your 'research,' I would be happy to do so tomorrow. I know exactly what you want. There aren't many stories quite like mine,' I say laughing and winking at her.

She looks a little worried but nods and hands me a card with her mobile number. Even for someone of her standing, this is clearly a very big gig. We agree a time and a place – the Breadline café just off the Strand tomorrow. If it is meant to be, it is meant to be. We will see.

Then Jasmine gets up to go, handing me £20 and the rest of her packet of cigarettes. I take it as a down payment. It is no less than I deserve. I can spot a fan a mile off.

11. Unicorns

Jasmine's will not be the first literary project I have been involved with of course. A life like mine has inevitably made its way into print in many ways. My games feature in books and magazines in a variety of different languages, all of them serving to exploit my genius while lining the pockets of others.

I recognise now that I should have written more myself. Although I will never admit this to Gabriel, the truth is I was just too intimidated by my mother's success. If the sort of banality she churned out was what people wanted, somebody as innovative and original as me never really stood a chance.

Even Bobby, who rejected endorsement opportunity after opportunity, including the offer to promote a famous brand of car on the grounds that he did not drive it, was more astute than me on this front. *My 60 Memorable Games* must be the best-selling chess book of all time, although how much of the money Bobby saw, I cannot say. One book like that and you should be set.

My 60 Memorable Games caused him issues of course, such as when John Nunn bought out an error-filled reprint which made Bobby so angry. Nothing is ever straightforward. Nothing is pure. I make a brief note in my folder that John Nunn is not to be allowed to re-edit any of my own works.

What have I got? Gabriel's hack job, published in my name, always did all right. *Greenbecker's Glories*. Fifty of my most famous demolition jobs, including my game against Dubrovnik, where the Greenbecker Gambit was seen for the first and only time.

My primer on queen verses queen and rook endings, *When Major Pieces Collide*, was never a big seller, but does have a certain cult status. I couldn't get any takers for my exposé on Michael Wengrower, the cheat and the charlatan. Some nonsense about libel laws.

My book on gambits would outsell anything published to date by a factor of ten, but I need to keep that under wraps until I retire. They are the weapons that will bring me the world title, but because of that, in a financial sense they can't help much right now.

The truth is my folder contains enough material for most likely two brilliant technical chess books and a more mainstream biography of my wilderness years and beyond. I can see film rights. Spin-offs. A computer app where all comers can take on a program wired to mimic my style of play as best it can. Frankly why I bother to employ Gabriel as an agent when I have ideas like these is beyond me.

Big Ben strikes eleven and it is time for me to begin meandering toward the Red Lion. I open the last of the new cans of cider, when a policeman approaches. He is very young, I would guess perhaps nine, and because things seem to be going my way, I feel no fear. I can see him for what he is.

He asks if I am all right and I assure him that I am perfectly fine. It momentarily crosses my mind that Jasmine might have filed some sort of complaint against me, but I think not. If the lighter had not been a gift she would have said.

'You know you can't drink here, sir,' he says.

People are starting to watch. *The Big Issue* seller has stopped trying to drum up business and is following the action, though is pretending not to. His face as lined as an ancient map from years of tobacco. Orwellian almost, with pale white skin and hair fiercely cut.

A couple of suits have looked up from their phones. I have an audience that I can sense hates the State as much as I do. This game is one I do understand how to play. I know exactly what needs to be done.

'Rest assured Officer, I quite agree with you,' I say. I lift the can to my mouth and down it in one, before handing it to him. 'No more drinking' I say, basking in the smattering of applause that has possibly broken out.

PC Matthew Haydon, according to his badge, although I know many of them use false names these days. His black shoes gleam in the sun, his white shirt is crisp, silver buttons sparkle. I wonder for a moment if I have misjudged him, if the State is even more dangerous than it once was, but it seems not. He looks me up and down with as much dignity as he can muster. His expression like that of a child caught with his hand in the sweetie jar.

'Just move along please sir,' he says.

I assure him that I will. Someone of his age was never going to recognise me and that's okay. I have won again.

I sling my rucksack back on and eat my peanuts as I walk through Westminster, a critical business meeting in The Red Lion before me. I like the tang of salt in my mouth from the nuts, the way it lingers after the initial sweetness of each mouthful has passed, the feeling of grease on my fingers. I truly am blessed.

This is my city, with its bright red busses and underground tunnels, its drunks and prostitutes and fellow chess players. The Houses of Parliament and London Eye. Madame Tussauds and London Bridge. Its layers of ash and soot that I am in tune with like no one else.

As I walk, I pass a family, father pushing a buggy, a tiny restless child within it, wriggling somewhere between wake and sleep. Just figuring whether to cry, as if still not entirely sure of this world and how things in it are meant to work. Various bags and other detritus are crammed in every flap and storage area the buggy has at its disposal. Nappies, bottles, changes of clothes, what looks like a packed lunch wedged into the netted area below the seat. A large plastic water bottle is already half empty.

They are clearly out for the day. Seeing the sights. The child dressed in a pink romper suit, covered by a yellow blanket. A pristine white bobble hat on her head. She will have no memories of this occasion. Maybe the others will remember and tell her all about it in the years to come, perhaps this here and now will drift away into nothing. I have no way of knowing where any of this might come to settle within the broader narrative of their family life. Whether it will ever warrant a do you remember?

The baby is not more than a few months old. So perfect and yet somehow so helpless. An older child holds the mother's hand and tries to distract her from her phone. I can hear her asking if unicorns are real. The mother does not really engage, is somewhere else altogether. The father indicates that they might be. No one knows for sure; I hear him say.

The group pauses for a moment and the father reaches into the buggy to adjust the sleeping position of his younger child, who has begun to protest a little more loudly. He wipes a pool of dribble from her chin, dabbing oh so gently, with the skilled air of an artist. He kisses her forehead, a reflex action driven by the heart, not the brain, and straightens up.

The older girl has been looking on watchfully and she smiles at him. He smiles back. Whatever else they remember from the day, I know this moment will soon be lost to all of them, but not to me. Who is to say how many fragments of our own lives are forgotten to us but remain lodged within the memory of strangers?

I am not even sure why I will remember it, but the act of thinking the thought has made it so. The baby, now more upright and comfortable, has properly fallen back to sleep. Now the four of them go on and I know this will be the only moment from their lives that I will ever witness.

I pull myself together, relieved that Magnus Carlsen will never know that I showed a momentary weakness. I was always with Solzhenitsyn. We might have discussed all this more than once. Any man can, from a biological perspective, be a father. It is no great achievement, nothing special. A refuge for the talentless who must fill the void with something. Being a mother is different of course. There is an important distinction to be made there. Stands to reason.

The fans who continually salute me for the joy my brillian-
cies at the chessboard have brought them are all the family I
need. It might be a little superficial, I grant you, but for men
of talent it is always the same. The mind can play tricks, but
other people and conventional choices are the last things we
need. I suppose the odd fleeting sense of loneliness is a price
all truly successful people must pay for our gifts. I tell myself
that I do so willingly.

12. An unfortunate nickname

It was not far to walk, and I see that while I have been musing, I have made my way here on automatic pilot. I can home in on a boozer as easily as I might a weak square on the chess board or an isolated pawn.

I push my way into the pub, trading the smell of autumn and exhaust fumes for the dark wood and history of the Red Lion. Places like this are always a sort of coming home for me, even if I no longer like the weak apple juice they serve, or the people who choose to frequent them. It is a remembering perhaps, something like that. The memory of things that once were, possibly what I once was... I don't know.

The camaraderie, the chance to escape. Nowhere else is as forgiving as a pub. Where else offers the same opportunity to begin again with every glass?

In the voices at the bar I hear the echo of drinking sessions long gone, the urgency and the laughter, lives being lived that little bit more fully than they otherwise might be. That feeling of complete clarity and exhilaration that can only truly be found with the right amount of drink. There is no other way to still the beating march of time. Much of my life has been spent in pubs and bars and it hasn't all been bad.

I see him almost immediately. I feel much like I do at the beginning of every chess game. Focussed, ready, able to deal with whatever comes my way. I know I am stronger, that in this, as in every other encounter, I will prevail.

Gabriel is sat at a small table close to the entrance, just on from the door that has the word lavatories embossed on it in black and gold. In such a spot it would be difficult not to notice him. He never seems to quite understand that a quieter corner would make it harder for the State to monitor us, but this is a point I have been making for years now and I am resigned to him never comprehending it. I suppose I will take on almost any risk for a free drink and a bit of funding. I always back myself to outwit any affiliate of the State who wishes me harm.

Four mirrors with engraved patterns hang on the green wall just in front of him. I wonder how many reflections have been caught in these panes of glass over the years. Whether a trace of them somehow still lingers?

On the wall behind, I see pictures and notes on William Pitt the Younger and Benjamin Disraeli. I look up at John Thirkell's history of The Red Lion. He declares that every Prime Minister up until Edward Heath has been here, including Sir Winston Churchill and Clement Attlee, as has Charles Dickens.

I silently contemplate where my own achievements rank relative to these men. Churchill possibly has the edge, but I most likely trump Attlee and Dickens. People will still be playing through my games long after Dickens has dropped out of the literary canon and Attlee's welfare state has been wholly abolished. So many Prime Ministers of a later vintage have reached out to me over the years, but I have always been canny enough to keep my distance.

Gabriel has some froth and fuss concoction in front of him. Most likely a cappuccino. It takes me a moment to heed my sense that something else is not quite right – beyond the abomination Gabriel, with his twisted sense of logic, has decided constitutes a drink.

He sits there fiddling with a beer mat as if arranging his pieces at the beginning of a chess game. Tense and grumpy looking, but that isn't it. Damn – she is sat next to him, looking at a menu. I should have guessed this might happen. That she would somehow get her snout in my trough.

Ginevra makes things trickier. Bobby Fischer once told me never to trust her. Just from the way I described her he was certain she was a Russian agent.

She will always egg him on. Tell Gabriel that I am no good. Suggest spurious reasons as to why he should not give me my money. Yet she knows full well that she did not always hate me. That things between us were somewhat different once. All of that now lost to the fog of more recent practical calamities.

Still, what difference does it make? Look at the evidence. I am a future world chess champion. A truly celebrated individual. As an opponent she is hardly in my league.

I resolve not to let her get to me. I am a man who need only sit at a tube station for a few minutes before I become the focal point of the national press. I draw people in. I continually make things happen. I doubt anyone could say the same about Ginevra.

Gabriel waves, but cautiously, reluctant to show anything

that might be taken to resemble warmth. He has the sorrowful look of a schoolteacher who has been disappointed again. He will not meet my eye, and I begin to wonder if this might all prove to be harder than I thought. Although it could be that he is being discrete. Perhaps he has finally learnt something after all, despite my earlier misgivings.

This place is often as full of Russian 'tourists,' as it is civil servants and low-grade politicians. There are spies everywhere. Still, they most likely follow me wherever I go, so I might as well be here as anywhere.

Ginevra is also judiciously nursing a coffee. She does not look at me. Her jowls are heavy, and I cannot look at her without thinking of a mother hen. The person I once met all those years ago, when Gabriel somewhat sheepishly bought her home, has morphed into this. The lines on her face caked by expensive makeup. She wears several heavy looking copper bracelets and there are rings on every finger, doubtless all funded by my money. She always was insecure.

How would Gabriel have ended up with her if it were otherwise? Didn't she tell me once that she knew that she had chosen the wrong brother? I was tempted back then, but I have always been wary of the risk women pose.

Bobby Fischer's worst tournament showing came when he was rumoured to have become heavily involved with a prostitute during the event. He went out of his way to warn me not to make the same mistakes. Stick to the chess Tennessee, he might have said, you will find it easier that way. Good advice, as most of Bobby's always was. I know he only ever wanted the best for me. Over the years I have tried with varying degrees of success to try and avoid becoming distracted by the fairer sex. Especially in this era when it appears that even to look at a woman is to risk jail.

Ginevra finally looks up but makes no move of acknowledgement. Getting me sorted was once her project, even, much to my chagrin, relatively recently. I know those days are likely past. Too much and not enough has happened for anything to make much of a difference now – Gabriel was so stupid in telling her some of the things he did. It is all his fault really. I consider whether I should shake his hand, shake her hand, but they make no move and I find I have sat down before I have fully processed my social instincts.

Gabriel is wearing a blue and white check shirt that looks expensive, grey suit jacket with black jeans, gleaming mobile phone in silver case resting on the table. His hair is white, and you can see his age, but he is lean and trim. It is doubtless easier to be slim when you do not have genius to carry around with you. Clean shaven. Insufferably smug. That fake air of authority that has irritated me since childhood.

Still, the bags under his eyes are perhaps a little heavier than I remember. I detect a degree of strain that I do not normally associate with him. It is clear he is not wholly comfortable with any of this and that can only be to my advantage.

I know his game. He is going to blind me with science. Invent problems that do not exist in order to paint a false picture of things. I am resigned to him throwing some examples of my conduct back at me. As if the past has any bearing on the future! Families! Who would choose to be a part of one?

I take a deep breath. Remember my match temperament. Few would be able to see all this as clearly as I do. Being so many moves ahead inevitably works in my favour. Play it long, play it long. Focus on the main prize. A simple truth will always out a complex lie. He is robbing me blind and I will not be cowed out of what's mine!

'How are you Terrence?' Gabriel asks, with the weary air of one who does not really want to know.

I freeze. Stock still in my seat. There is no question of him getting anything if he chooses to insult me like that.

He looks across the table warily and I stare back, getting my bearings. His opening is a low blow, but a primitive one. I will try and ride it out.

'Terrence?' he says again.

I let out what I hope is a suitably bitter laugh, but it is possible it sounds more like a howl. I consider punching him in the face and leaving. That would certainly be satisfying. A few years ago, I suspect that is exactly what I would have done, but I am much wiser now.

I bang the table with my fist and shout 'fuck,' several times, which I am sure has the effect of calming everything down. Gabriel knows I hate this nickname. Have done ever since we were kids, when it was the only weapon he had to wind me up. What's in a name some might say, but what else do any of us have? Terrence means nothing to me.

I say nothing further. Narrow my eyes. Sigh. I consider whether it would be to my advantage to start to weep. Quite possibly, but it would take a lot of effort. I can see he is not going to budge either. We are deadlocked.

Finally, Ginevra speaks. 'Oh, for God's sake. How are you Tennessee?' I am grateful that the angry look she shoots is at Gabriel rather than me.

Gabriel grunts. I sigh. My honour has just about been satisfied. It is time to move on.

'I need a drink,' I say. As the words come out, I realise the extent to which they are true. Perhaps I am more stressed than I thought.

I idly wonder how much alcohol I have drunk in the course of my life. A hundred thousand units? A million? More? Enough to knock out any number of horses, I shouldn't wonder. Still, I am lucky that my constitution has soaked it up without complaint. The more I think about it, the more Churchillian I appear.

'Yes of course you do, it's always the bloody same,' says Gabriel archly, causing people to look over in our direction. 'Do you think just for once we could have a conversation without you being pissed out of your head? Assuming you aren't already?'

I stare back at him. Aiming for something between hurt and dignified. Silence is a powerful weapon for those who know how to use it. I see that he might be able to wait, but she can't. Watch and wait. That has always been my way.

'It's your life,' Ginevra says reproachfully.

I think I hear Gabriel say, 'what's left of it.'

I wonder to what extent the two of them have planned this out. How many nights have they spent together in bed, plotting against me? I can't imagine that they would have much else to talk about. Then I notice the way that Ginevra is looking at Gabriel. Expectantly, challenging, and he seems to withdraw a little into himself, much the same as my father might once have done.

Now I clearly hear Gabriel say under his breath that we

all need a bloody drink. I can't help but think that they are already off track. We have not even started yet, but I sense I am already winning. I had no way of knowing that this would be so easy. They just need some gentle guidance from me, and all will be well.

'Ready for a drink,' I say.

Gabriel catches the bartender's eye and points at his coffee cup. The man is all talk. An empty blagger, unable even to follow through on purchasing himself an alcoholic beverage.

'Well, I'll have a pint of cider,' I say and Gabriel shrugs. I feel like telling him that the average pint of pub cider has roughly the same alcoholic content as a glass of mineral water, but I decide against. Despite probably knowing this anyway, I suspect he would take the point the wrong way.

Those who do not have my gifts rarely appreciate the part alcohol plays in refreshing the soul of the talented, the way it numbs the brain just that touch, such that life away from the chess board can be lived.

People like Ginevra have minds so lacking in suppleness that they might as well have already been pickled in formaldehyde. In which case the choice of a coffee or a vodka makes little difference, albeit I know which I would make, were I to be so singularly ungifted.

In normal circumstances I would insist on watching the barman pour my drink to ensure that he did not poison it, but today I can't be bothered. Part of me would like to drop dead just to spite Gabriel. Then him calling me Terrence just now would haunt him for the rest of his life.

I doubt he could carry the guilt for his years of neglect and unreasonableness. If they poison me, they poison me. Beside the State are so used to my vigilance in such matters they are most probably not geared up to spike my cider right now. I laugh and shout 'more fool them!'

'Well you came,' Gabriel says, ignoring my triumphant cry. I know he will be silently marvelling at the way I have managed to defeat those who wish me harm, without even doing a thing.

'Don't I always?'

'No.'

He pauses and I wait for him to say more but then realise he is not going to.

'Why wouldn't I come? We have a lot to plan. Time is pushing on. I've been giving this all much thought, but it does need one or two things from you, just to get things moving. The moment for me to take on Magnus Carlsen is drawing close.'

'Still on about your bloody chess,' Gabriel says, with the jealous air I have come to expect. Anyone else would have fired him years ago.

'You can tell us about chess, but we need you to understand that we have other things to talk about. It is time for a bit of honesty. We want to make sure you are looking after yourself. You know what you were told. We also want to be clear that we simply can't keep on giving you money.' I don't know why, but Ginevra looks at Gabriel rather than me when she says this.

My pint arrives. I suddenly worry that I might have been ridiculously overconfident. I sniff it warily. It smells all right, but of course not all poison is scented. I pour a bit onto my wrist, so I can smell it properly, and accidently spill a little on my trousers.

'Not fucking this again,' says Gabriel.

'Fine, why not just admit you want me dead,' I say.

Ginevra looks at Gabriel. 'Please,' she hisses.

'Oh, for fuck's sake. Do you want me to try it?'

'I think that's probably wise,' I say. 'If I died now the chess world would never forgive you.'

'Just out of interest,' he says. 'Suppose your theory is correct and your cider is poisoned. If I drink it, wouldn't I die? Have you considered that?'

If I was not somewhat wedged in my seat, I would be rolling around the floor with laughter at that one. 'Don't be fucking ridiculous,' I say. Trying to stop my slides from splitting with mirth. 'It's not as if anyone would ever want to kill you.'

He rolls his eyes and sips my drink. 'It's fine,' he snaps and brings the glass down on the table with a bang.

He always was paranoid, but I decide I will give it five minutes before drinking any of it myself. Then I realise I can't wait and take a first sip of the weak-as-water piss that passes for cider in hostelries up and down the land.

Still, with the cans I have already had this morning I feel a surge of contentment, notwithstanding my unhappiness that Gabriel has stolen some of my pint. I need to suppress the thought that a brother like him would drive anyone to drink.

13. The wayward chicken

'It's always the bloody same,' Gabriel says. 'These ridiculous games all the time. You stink, you drink, you talk about plans that are never going to go anywhere. Never any hint of what you have put us through. Never any comprehension of the damage you have done.

'All those years, I sent you money for your bills and living expenses and what did I eventually find? That you were essentially living rough and pissing the lot away on drink and cards. How dare you take me for granted like that? I would have been in my rights to never see you again. The troubles you have caused this family are beyond belief.'

I lean in, just as I would at the chess board when poised for the kill.

'It wasn't your money. The only thing the old witch we were unfortunate enough to call a mother had going for her was the ability to make pots of cash. You've only ever given me my share. Most likely not even that. You've had your tongue up the arse of her publishing house for so long now that I'm sure they've worked with you to see you pocket most of it, leaving me a few scraps to keep me quiet. I am going to hire a private investigator one day and then everything will come crashing down around you! How do you like that?'

'Let me try and explain this for the millionth time,' Gabriel says with something of a groan. 'Mum died in the 1990s. She wrote twelve books during her career, only two of which are still in print. Last year her total sales were in the mid-hundreds. Yes, she is still sort of famous, because she was bloody good at what she did. She's just not a commercial proposition anymore. I am not telling you anything you don't already know.'

All nonsense. As usual Gabriel has missed out certain key facts in order to create a misleading picture of reality. I hate it when people do this.

'You don't even mention the film,' I say triumphantly. 'Where did the millions go from that, I wonder?'

'Yeah, it was made for BBC2. They showed it twice. In 1984. It was not exactly 'Gone with the fucking wind,' Gabriel says.

'All writers are millionaires,' I shout. 'You've funnelled off the fucking lot. How else would you be able to afford a million-pound house in Putney? Even one that is a bit dark inside, I grant you. You didn't think I would know about Zoopla?' I smile broadly, I've got him now I'm sure, but it seems he does not know when he's beaten.

'Let me explain. There are two points you entirely miss. First, we bought the place a very long time ago. Years before London property prices went crazy. Secondly, I have this thing that is called a job. I know you scorn such mundanities, but it is how normal people pay for things.'

'It's not much of a job is it?' I say as gently as I can. 'People say that the houses you design are so shit, that by the time they've finished building an estate, it's already falling down. I know you were never much good at anything, but seriously Gabriel, it hardly constitutes an honest day's work does it?

'I would imagine most people like to go to bed at night without the need to wear a hard hat in case the roof falls in. You can't earn much from such poor-quality stick drawings. For once just be upfront about where you really get your money from.'

Inexplicably, Gabriel looks very angry indeed, but Ginevra rubs his arm and tells him to remember what they said. Still more evidence of their fixation with and continual plotting against me. He stares at the ceiling and counts to ten, before sighing and ignoring the charge. Comprehensive proof that as ever I have been right all along.

'The truth is, Tennessee, I am ready to retire. We're going to have less coming in. I just don't have money for you to waste anymore. Besides, you've left me completely at the end of my tether.'

I am somewhat taken aback to hear Gabriel own up to his inability to cope with the real world. But before I can respond, Ginevra is speaking.

'It's not just that is it? What did Gabriel do when you ended up in hospital and the truth came out? Did he disown you? No. He tried to find another way to help by putting you up in a bedsit, which he paid for directly, even though we were both furious. He said it was obvious you couldn't look after yourself, that he was the only one left, and it was his duty.

'I tell you Tennessee, he has really gone above and beyond. We both have. He even got you out of London to try and help give you a better chance of recovering. It turned out you couldn't even be bloody trusted with a chicken. Even after that we let you come and live with us, for all the thanks we got. No one could ask any more of us.'

I hoped I had forgotten about the bedsit, and am momentarily surprised that Ginevra has not, but she always did worry about the wrong things. I suppose her basic point is true. Although I fail to see how I can be held responsible for the loss of a wayward chicken.

And it wasn't exactly the big favour that Ginevra is making it out to be either. The bedsit in Coventry was the least Gabriel could do after my near-death experience. I'm sure he got the place to ease his own conscience rather than out of any genuine desire to help me.

I did also wonder at the time if Gabriel might have joined forces with the State to thwart my ambitions – Coventry is the most obvious of locations to bury a man's dreams. I never quite believed that it might be better for me to take a break from London. Did Gabriel think the charms of the Coventry Oak would prove too much, alluring as they were? Was it all a cunning plan to ensure that Magnus Carlsen never faced a challenge from me?

Well, it seems probably not, but it is a testament to my sharpness that I considered all the possibilities. Besides, at that time I had no place else to go, so what could I do?

St Ives Road was very tricky, mainly because the place had a mind of its own. Within days of my moving in the sink was piled with dishes and newspapers covered the floor. It was difficult to walk around the room without stepping in the metal tray of a discarded takeaway curry or on a grease-stained fish and chip wrapper. I slaved away but could not seem to make a dent in the mess.

The chicken was my attempt at home cooking, at finding a different way to survive. Somehow it got mislaid under some other things when Gabriel arrived to see how I was getting on, just as I was searching for it with maximum intensity.

The fire was genuinely not of my making. After we had abandoned the search and headed to the pub, certain things on top of the cooker caught fire. It was hardly my fault that the gas ring somehow turned itself on. I will admit, it was a bit of a shock for the pair of us when we returned from a swift half at the Oak to see the place ablaze. I did always tell people that the conventional domesticity of everyday life was not really for me.

Besides, we sorted it all out with the help of a portable fire extinguisher and one or two firemen. It was nothing really, but it did render the place somewhat out of action. Fortunately, my folder was undamaged, which was the main thing.

I mentioned something to Gabriel along the lines that setting fire to a house in Coventry reminded me of Larkin's poem about calling for the bombs to rain down on Slough, but it was most likely too soon for a joke.

As we were leaving, a neighbour came around to complain that the smoke from the fire had asphyxiated the ferrets he kept in a cage at the bottom of his garden. He was quite rude about it. Hardly neighbourly in the circumstances, but that is what happens in the provinces.

As we drove back to London Gabriel only uttered one thing to me the whole journey. 'I really think you might be a bit depressed,' he said.

In the circumstances I chose to say nothing. He was right though. As fires go, this one had been something of a disappointment.

After Coventry, I did stay with Gabriel and Ginevra in their London flat, but as you can imagine, the pair of them were impossible to live with. Always fussing about this or that. Never quite providing me with the funds or the space necessary for someone of my talent to flourish. Gabriel continually on at me to go and see a doctor.

We had an argument about a tomato soup stain on a white carpet that proved to be the final straw. It was entirely their own fault. The bowl had slipped from my hand. I had not wanted the bloody soup anyway, but they insisted. Had they ever been prepared to turn a few more fucking lights on, I would have been better able to see what I was doing. It is hardly my fault that they chose to live like moles.

The soup made a stain like the pooling mass of blood from a bullet wound to the head. The way Ginevra reacted; you might have thought I had murdered someone. Talk about making something out of nothing. There were one or two other incidents of course, but nothing worth mentioning here.

14. Burning bridges

I did manage to get some chess work done while I was in Coventry, in those rare moments when I took a break from my domestic duties. I was mainly working on closing out winning positions, which might seem like a funny choice, but I had learned from Bobby's experiences in his comeback match with Spassky.

I had begged him not to play of course. I said to him,

'Bobby, everyone thinks you are a chess God, but if you play again people will see that you are now a man.'

He knew I was right, but what choice did he have? We would talk about it late into the night. Some thought it was because he wanted the money. The influence of that girl who was credited with coaxing him back. I knew from our conversations that having turned his back on the chess world for so long, he was simply ready to play again. He had made every other choice imaginable and it was the only one left to him.

He told me that I was a good friend. That he appreciated my counsel. Then he went ahead and played anyway. I am less interested in the impression he might have made away from the board. It is what he did to his legacy over the sixty-four squares that worries me more.

All too often he would be ahead and find himself unsure as to how to best wrap things up. It cost him points. It made him look ordinary. In the end, despite the rumours that Spassky had been carrying him, he did win the rematch of course, but somehow, brilliant first game apart, he wasn't so hot.

The more I have thought about it, the more cognisant I have become of the differences between Fischer's position and my own, and what that might mean for my comeback. I have never had quite the same level of leverage with FIDE, the international chess governing body. Fischer did have one advantage over me, in that he had actually been world champion. Just one extra hurdle for me to overcome. I know Bobby regretted the fact that he would not live long enough to see me crowned as his rightful successor.

'Are you still with us?' Ginevra snaps, rudely interrupting my train of thought. 'I think we are all just a bit tired and hungry,' she continues more diplomatically.

It is as if the heat of some of the exchanges have drawn the fight from her. I guess she still likes me a bit really. I know my personality makes me hard to resist.

She looks at Gabriel.

'We've all said what we wanted to say. It is a lot to take in. Why don't we have something to eat?'

I sigh. Very well, if it is going to take them filling their faces to get me some money there is no harm in me playing along. Perhaps I might even relent and decide to give him one last chance to be my agent. I am sure he would be grateful for that.

I gaze at the section of the menu that outlines the 'Hand Crafted Pies'. Ginevra orders a Steak & London Pride, which has caramelised shallots, button mushrooms and thyme baked in. Gabriel goes for a West Country Lamb & Wild Mushroom, and I settle for a Hampshire Game, which the menu assures me comes with 'Mrs Owton's bacon & fig, red wine & junior gravy'. I try to disregard the somewhat alarming warning that it may contain shot – it is not as if I am planning on eating any of it, so I suppose it does not overly matter.

Gabriel places the order and says that we will all have the seasonal vegetables and triple cooked chips as accompaniments. At £15.50 a pie it is hardly cheap fare, but of course Gabriel is paying. He wouldn't have suggested eating at these prices if our finances really were that bad.

'Have you ever wondered why the King allowed so many wooden houses and shops to be built on London Bridge?' I ask by way of making small talk. 'The way I see it, he must have known what he was doing. Plenty of people advised him of the risks. I think he just liked the thought that it would most likely all go up in flames in the end.'

'What is it with you and fire?' Gabriel snaps.

He was never the quickest on the uptake, so I spell it out for him. 'Let's face it, other than St Paul's, nothing else in London has burnt down as many times as London Bridge. It must have been an amazing spectacle. I honestly think the planners should be more sympathetic towards permitting wooden structures. If they do burn, it's great to watch and kind of cleansing don't you think? You know what they say, burning is what bridges are for!' I laugh.

'Absolutely no one in their fucking right mind ever says that

Ter, Tennessee,' says Gabriel. 'You are utterly obsessed. I've told you so many times that no one wants to hear your thoughts on London fires. They might get entirely the wrong impression. At least, I hope that is what they are getting,' he adds.

I think of highlighting the fact that today's planners are not so different from their predecessors. How else do you explain the choice of cladding on modern-day tower blocks? Still, I say nothing. Gabriel just hasn't got the right sort of imagination to fully appreciate an insight like that. I bet when he designs a building, he does not even stop to think through the aesthetics of how best to make it burn. Another reason why he has never been terribly successful.

I wonder if he is remembering that first incident with the school bike-shed. The feeling of joy I got when, finally, the wooden shack with the corrugated tin roof properly caught and I stood back to watch the whole rotten structure belch black smoke. They always say the first time is the best.

The cause of the blaze was never determined. There was no CCTV in those days, and I had timed things such that there were no witnesses. It is true that one or two asked what I had been doing at school so early and why I had been there to raise the alarm, but no one ever suspects the child from the chess club. They did not think to look through my bag, with its now empty can of petrol and boxes of matches. Gabriel always knew the truth though. He never said a word, but he most probably admired me for it.

It turns out it isn't that which is on his mind.

'Your antics completely ruined this time of year for me,' he says. For a moment I think Gabriel might be about to

120

hit me. He is leaning forward in his seat. His nose inches from mine. His face puce. His breath smells faintly of coffee and marmalade.

How dare he!

'We are not going to go through that again, are we?' I shout.

'Keep your voice down, for fuck sake,' he yells back.

'Boys, please,' says Ginevra pleadingly.

We lower our voices, but it turns out we are going to go through this again.

'Have you any idea the damage you did? How hurt mum was when she realised what you had done? You were as bad as the bloody Nazis.'

I am not having this. Everything that happened was at least partly for Gabriel's benefit, the ungrateful bastard.

'Did you not have a good time?' I yell. 'Was it not the best bonfire night ever, at least to begin with? Just give me that. Do not make a fool out of me. At least give me something.'

'Terrific,' he says. 'Absolutely terrific. A truly wonderful night. We all marvelled at the way the fire burned. You know, it is possible we might have still had fun either way, but yes it was a good bonfire. Why was that though? What was the secret? Tell Ginevra what you did.'

'I'm not sure I actually *did* anything,' I say. 'I just gave the thing a little assistance. I was thinking of everyone else really.'

'What did you do?' asks Ginevra. 'Why haven't I heard this story before?' she asks Gabriel crossly.

Gabriel looks at me, as if to suggest that Ginevra's reaction is somehow my fault. Honestly, he needs to take more responsibility for his choices. I'm surprised he has managed to stay married for all these years, if this is how he carries on. I suppose

I always was the more responsible brother. More fool Ginevra for not realising I was the real 'keeper.'

'I saw the wood was too wet,' I say. 'Dad was never going to be up to it, and I doubted anyone else had the intellectual capacity to make things right. I just added a bit of paper to the mix. That's all. Most likely page one advice in any Boy Scout manual, I shouldn't wonder.'

'Tell Ginevra what paper it was,' says Gabriel.

'Just one or two books, nothing special. I'm not even sure I was looking particularly when I picked them out. I was just focussed on helping everyone have a good time.'

'All mum's personal first editions. Every single one she had, she said you might as well have been burning her.'

'Well, I'm not entirely sure that would have worked. That's just the sort of typical, self-obsessed nonsense that writers come out with all the time. She always had to bring everything back to her. The books were easily replaceable.'

'They absolutely, bloody weren't and that's not the point anyway.'

'Well, why don't you go out and buy some replacement fucking copies now? It sounds as if we could do with the fucking money!' I shout.

'You know she was devastated. It took her months to get over it. Not even what you did, but why. It was all to show her how much you hated her. What kind of son were you really?'

A waiter approaches. I half-expect him to ask Gabriel and Ginevra to leave, given their disgraceful behaviour, but instead he issues a more general instruction for all of us to quieten down. I nod at him apologetically and turn up the palms of my hands to demonstrate that I understand his position. I wouldn't be surprised if the pair of them ultimately end up being barred. Still, no matter, what is family really, other than an outlet for a lot of screaming?

In my experience, it is best to let Gabriel get things off his chest. He has been this way for years. He is like a chess player who storms into an attack without properly developing his pieces. Ultimately, when faced with a player of my skill, his initial thrust will blow itself out leaving the wreckage of his position at my mercy. He knows full well it was the least she deserved. None of what she did to us goes away just because he pretends it did not happen.

The food arrives and I pick at my pie. I like the steam that is released when I cut into the pastry, the smell of the meat and gravy, but inevitably I am not hungry. It is just how it is. Gabriel and Ginevra eat in a silence that I suspect they find more disconcerting than I do. When they are finished, we will get all this sorted.

I touch my rucksack with my foot, can feel the outline of my folder within it. All is well, all will work out. What's a few old books between family? It does not sound like anyone much would want to read them now.

Gabriel puts down his knife and fork and reaches into his suit jacket. He hands over four envelopes, which is the least he can do seeing as his house is currently the forwarding address for my mail. I put two in my pocket. The other two could be something official, legal or perhaps medical? I never know whether items like this should be read or burned.

For now, I opt to lightly crumple them both into a ball which I throw under the table. Then I decide that I may have been too hasty and pick up the scrunched envelopes and place them in my jacket. I don't want to look like I have rejected Gabriel's peace offering out of hand.

Gabriel looks irritated, his food clearly not soothing him as much as we both might have hoped, but he does not say anything. Most likely because he appreciates the gesture I have made with the envelopes.

Balling the paper has reminded first my hands and now my body that I have gone too long without a cigarette. A man needs what a man needs, but I worry that if I head through the door for a quick smoke that might bring the meeting to a close with none of our business done. I decide to press on, to make my play. What have I got to lose?

'I'm nearly ready,' I say. 'I'm sure of that. I'm seeing the board better than I ever did. There are things I know about the game that Magnus Carlsen clearly does not. All it is going to take is for the challenge to be issued. He won't be able to say no. To do so would be to show his fear and he won't want to do that.

'All I need is a bit of money to tide me over. Somewhere to set up base and to spruce myself up a bit. Finish my preparations. Reach out to the powers that be. Get it all scheduled. Perhaps we could host an invitational tournament or two to get the ball rolling. It's in your interests to help.

'You've done amazingly well in the past on a 10% cut. Look at your house for goodness sake! I'm prepared to offer the same terms again. I think a twenty grand advance would do for now, so long as we meet up again soon.'

Despite everything, I am still offering Gabriel the chance to be a part of my rise to international superstardom. That's brothers for you.

I can see him thinking about things, taking it all in. Unsure quite what to say. Perhaps he knows I should have asked for more. He hesitates. Looks at Ginevra. Looks back at me. His look could be confused with one of annoyance, but I know it is more likely to be excitement. One last hurrah. A chance at the title. An opportunity to be a part of that. Who could resist?

Perhaps he simply can't believe his luck that I still want him to be involved.

15. An incident with a toilet roll

It is no good. I really do need to smoke. I need the toilet too. I decide to leave him to think it through. I will just have to hope that the offer is so enticing he will know it would be madness for him to walk out. I am sure that is the case. He needs time to get his act together. He always was ponderous when it came to calculations.

I climb the steep wooden stairs, walk past the glass frontage of the upstairs dining area and through the toilet door that has the word gentleman embossed on the heavy wood. I head for the cubicle, lock myself in and sit down.

I like the peace and quiet of the toilet, so far removed from the bustle and confusion of the street. A place where no demands can be made of you. Where no one can interrupt your train of thought. It is just me and the silence and a faint smell of bleach.

I think the absence of any real alcohol or nicotine I have endured would be ruinous to any man's health. I look up at the cubicle window and don't see a smoke alarm. No warning light blinks back at me. Perhaps it is worth a shot.

I pull the packet that contains my remaining cigarettes and lighter from my pocket. I sit on the Johnny, trousers round my ankles, and find I urinate easily and triumphantly. It is hard to imagine that anyone ever thought I might have a problem in that department!

I smell the richness of the tobacco through the cardboard and plastic wrapping, try and ignore the picture of a blackened lung and the warning as to my imminent death on the front. If I don't exhale hard and if I wave what smoke there is away with my hand, well, even if there is an alarm it would hardly pick that up.

I flick the lighter and bring a cigarette to life. Draw deeply, hold the smoke within me for as long as I can. Breathe out gently, smoke barely even noticeable. My body feels as if it has been released from purgatory. Is suddenly at peace.

I will certainly need to make it a condition of my return that we can play somewhere that allows me to smoke freely and throughout. I am sure that Magnus Carlsen will have no objections. I would not be surprised if he enjoys our match more in such a scenario, perhaps with a pint or two thrown in.

I reach into my jacket pocket and pull out the balled-up envelopes. I smooth them out, cigarette gripped in my mouth, prior to tearing them open. They are not what I was expecting. The first is from a hospital, but it is incomprehensible. Something about Stage 4, whatever that is.

I put it back in my jacket and open the second letter. The words on the top suggest that I have been summoned. Must appear at a certain date, already in the past. This has the potential to complicate everything. A last desperate throw of the dice by the powers that be. I do not need to read the details. Whatever is stated will not be true. It is all trumped up.

There is only one logical course of action. I reach for the lighter and set fire to a corner of the missive. Just a corner. As a statement of contempt for all that it represents. I will blow it out in a moment, and no one will be any the wiser.

But somehow, I miscalculate. The flame takes hold more quickly than I anticipate. It is burning my hands and I drop it on top of the toilet roll and in seconds that has caught fire too.

A somewhat noxious smell in the air. A lot of smoke. I can't see clearly enough to make a definitive judgement as to what is happening. I need a cleaner, brighter light, so I take the packet of Zip firelighters from my pocket, break a couple off, place them on the floor and stoop down to bring them to life with my lighter. Rather than bringing further clarity, this turns out to be something of a mistake.

Just when things couldn't get any worse, a smoke alarm activates, and the building starts to wail. I hear patrons starting to make their way down the stairs and out onto the street. General pandemonium of the sort that in my experience often afflicts those who don't know what they are doing around fire.

I was never convinced the 'Hand Crafted Pies,' were a particularly healthy option. If some of the patrons end up not getting to finish theirs, I will have done them a favour.

Someone is banging on the toilet door.

'What's happening, what's happening?' he shouts. His accent sounds Eastern European. I can tell that he is quite young. I think I hear fear and excitement in his voice in almost equal measure.

'It's nothing,' I assure him, as calmly as I can, spluttering through the smoke, which is seriously irritating my lungs, making me wheeze. 'Nothing to worry about at all. Somehow your toilet roll has caught fire, that's all. Things like this happen all the time.'

Admittedly, the atmosphere in the cubicle has deteriorated and my trying to speak has brought that home. I gasp and stand, pulling my trousers up, before emerging coughing from the toilet stand, affecting a look of bewilderment.

The waiter is trying to size me up. Is this an accident or a deliberate act on my part? Is it something or is it nothing? Unfortunately, he spies that the toilet roll is blazing and that the fire has somehow spread to the nearby linen cupboard. I can tell he is impressed.

Other waiters emerge from the smoke bearing fire extinguishers, yelling at me somewhat rudely to get out of the fucking way. I am escorted down the stairs and out onto the street, blinking in the light. The smoke alarm ringing in my ears, wailing like a cat on a hot tin roof. I feel a touch dizzy. What on earth could have happened to cause all this, I find myself wondering.

There are crowds of people. Evacuated punters. Passers-by. A lot of talking and pointing at some curtains on the first floor which seem to be on fire and belching smoke through a window. They were very ugly, and any self-respecting landlord would of course have replaced them long ago.

I see Gabriel and Ginevra standing together, an island of two in the broader melee. My rucksack is at his feet. They had been good enough to bring that out for me, which is something to be grateful for, I suppose. The waiter who has led me out tells me to wait where I am. That people will want to talk to me. That the police are on their way.

He has seen me looking at Gabriel and asks Gabriel if he knows me. Gabriel almost nods. The waiter asks Gabriel to keep an eye on me while he helps his colleagues sort things out, and this time Gabriel nods properly and says, 'Oh God,' under his breath. He does not meet my gaze.

As soon as the waiter has turned his back, I can see Gabriel contemplating a decision. Working out what happens next. Evaluating our choices.

'What the fuck...' he starts to say, but whatever was intended to follow he decides to keep to himself. 'Just walk with me,' he says.

I am too hot and fragile for all this. His suggestion strikes me as a massive inconvenience, but then I am an obliging sort of person. We start to stroll, cautiously at first and then more confidently. Nobody challenges us. I am too breathless to walk all that far or fast, but in no time the Red Lion is in the distance and we are free of the nonsense and false accusations that might otherwise have been put Gabriel's way.

He is fretting to Ginevra about having paid for the meal on a credit card. That they might be able to trace him. A guilty conscience if ever I saw one. Families are always something of a liability. I mention the warning the waiter gave him to be quiet and he tells me to fuck off. The pressure of the situation is clearly getting to him.

'You've made your choice,' Ginevra says to him. 'Just understand, this is the last time.'

He nods and we keep walking until we find ourselves by the river, standing watching the boats making their way up and down the Thames. Pleasure crafts and tugs. An ageing ferry being towed, most likely on its way to a scrapyard further down the estuary. A rusting barge, the lettering spelling out her name half worn away, but I can still make it out.

Destiny.

'We shouldn't have done that,' I say. 'Just because you feel guilty about something.'

Gabriel looks back at me with an expression that cannot be taken for anything other than rage.

'You wanted to fucking stay?' he says. 'You want to go back and tell them all about it? Be my fucking guest.'

I see his point. The more I think about it the less obvious it becomes as to which of us is to blame, or whether what happened had anything to do with either of us. If the worst comes to the worst, I'll happily vouch for him.

Gabriel stands, holding Ginevra's hand.

'It's only now that I see it,' he says. 'I've given you the benefit of the doubt for far too long. God knows what my denial has cost other people. We've tried and we've tried, but you are incapable of even eating without setting fire to something, and I've had enough. You are a danger to yourself and everyone else. The only person who does not see this is you. There is no money left. There is nothing more we can do for you. The end.'

'You still want to be a part of making my comeback happen,' I say.

'No,' he says shaking his head. 'I've done all I can, and when I say no more, I mean no more. I have nothing left to give. Go fuck yourself.'

He reaches into his pocket, and for a moment I think he might pull out a gun and shoot me, before resolving not to let myself become paranoid. Rather, he produces an envelope stuffed with money. I would guess perhaps £500 judging by its bulk and the sheen of the notes.

'Take this and fuck off,' he says. 'We're done. This is the last of the money. No more emails. No more plans. You can't be helped. You are beyond help.'

I half expect him to reach out and shake my hand, but he does not. My first clue that he does not really mean what he says. The pair turn and leave me standing by myself, by the river, with my rucksack and a bundle of money. I count it. £600, in ten and twenties.

When he has calmed down, I know he will resolve to make everything work, to do a better job in discharging his duties.

I now have money in my pocket, which was not the case even a few hours ago. History will most likely judge me an unsung hero for my role in preventing The Red Lion from going up in smoke. Everything is still on track to end well. From my point of view the meeting could not have gone better.

16. Urgent maintenance

I sit on the bench, looking out across the water as afternoon blurs into evening. A seagull circles overhead and in its screech, I hear the call of the sea. The ocean that will keep on just as it always has, many millions of years from now, slowly grinding rock into sand. Washing some things away altogether, leaving a trace of what has been in the changing contours of the cliff, the evolving shoreline.

A red and white pleasure boat makes its way through the gloaming. She is as much of glass as of iron. Most likely on a standard tourist route. Westminster and the London Eye, then on past St Paul's and the Tate Modern, Tower Bridge, finally the glittering temple of modern money and human folly that is Canary Wharf.

I see a young girl standing with her father, a little removed from the rest of the passengers on a corner of the stern. I wonder where their lives will take them. How things might look in three years. Five. Twenty. It is impossible to know. No one does. From my perspective twenty years has as much practical meaning as a thousand.

I guess from their body language that she is asking a question. Perhaps she wants to know how many times St Paul's has burnt down. Not that he could most likely tell her. In 675, 961, 1087, 1666 and a near miss in the Blitz. If anyone also suggests 1135, know them for a fool.

There is a chess tournament in Golders Green I could look in on, but I am not sure if that would be fair to the other players. It would also give Magnus Carlsen too much of a clue that I am on the march again. Word would reach him faster than I could pick up my king's pawn and place it on e4.

So, I will not be so reckless. Just as I will ignore the voice in my head that is urging me to put my new money to work in a casino. A few really good hands and I would be free of Gabriel for good. I certainly have the talent to make myself very rich very quickly, but in my experience the State is skilled at ultimately thwarting me, and the truth is I am not really in the mood.

I feel dirty from the fire in the Red Lion. In need of a wash and a rest. It is time to regroup, but my options are not brilliant. My usual hostel is of course out of the question, although frankly I doubt that they will be open for business anyway. For a moment I feel uneasy as I think back to what happened yesterday, but there is no point worrying about any of that. It is ancient history I am sure.

I do have money in my pocket. I could afford something a little grander for a night or two. It is tempting, but I must be careful. I cannot know for sure when Gabriel will have calmed down enough to bankroll me further. It is hardly as if he is wholly rational in his thinking. It is as well to be prudent.

There is somewhere else I know. I don't really like the place, but it will do. I have the capacity to study chess wherever I happen to be. Besides, who cares if I sometimes stay in establishments not worthy of a man of my status? Nothing lasts forever.

I take the Tube for a few stops. I sit next to a woman who is wearing a business suit and white trainers. A baby on board badge on her lapel. Large red headphones cover her ears. I can hear her music seeping through. 'One Night in Bangkok' my all-time favourite song.

There are some who think the musical *Chess* is loosely based on Fischer and Korchnoi. I might well have had a laugh with Tim Rice about that more than once. It is my story of course, even if disguised a little at my request, to throw the State off the scent. It must be a sign. An omen. Everything is going to work out well. I laugh out loud for joy and slap my thighs hard with my hands. I am going to tell the woman the song is about me, but she has upped and left before I have composed myself.

A couple of stops later I get off the tube myself and trudge to the Happy House Hotel. It is not much to look at from the outside. A big property at the end of a shitty street, with large tower blocks looming above it. A part of London where those with no money are herded by the wretched State.

A board that hangs by the gate is missing several letters. The wooden windows, once painted red, have faded to brown, and even from the road you can see they are rotten. A stain runs down the brickwork from a top floor water pipe that is still leaking. I notice that there appears to be a tree growing out of the roof of the building. Something the maintenance team has presumably had on their list to sort for a while.

Takeaway food debris, cigarettes, cans and needles all litter the path to the door. A swastika has been etched in the wood of the door frame and half-hearted attempts to rub it away have not been successful.

The front door is dark green, with peeling paint and a long piece of sodden cardboard held in place by masking tape, covering what was once a glass panel in its centre. A handwritten sign says that the bell does not work and 'those making enquiries,' should knock and wait.

I chuckle as I push the door open and step into a dark hallway with an unmanned paper-strewn reception desk at the far end. I walk toward it. There is a silver bell to ring for attention, but then I think that it would be prudent to check things out. To ensure that the State has not anticipated that I might make this move. I need to know that I will be safe here.

I sit down in the battered old dark blue fake leather armchair behind the desk and start to look through some of the paperwork. It feels natural enough to light a cigarette, seeing as I am basically in charge. I drag deeply and feel a sense of contentment rising inside of me. This is what it feels like to run an empire! To be master of all you survey!

I look at some of the documents. The check in book on the desk. Names. Dates of birth. National Insurance numbers in a few cases. A handful of DHSS referral letters. A leaflet, that they haven't got around to putting up yet, warning the residents not to do drugs in the toilets. A hardback A3 notebook is the maintenance log. Someone has scribbled, 'everything is fucked!' on the first page in red biro.

None of this is really what I am looking for. I scan through a few folders for any police notifications, lists of wanted men; but all I find are more details of boring check-in records. Guidance on how to steal Tennessee Greenbecker's opening secrets has most likely been circulated to every hotel within a hundred-mile radius, but bizarrely I can't seem to find such a document here. It is possible no one is on Reception because whoever should be here is studying it right now.

It was certainly clever of the State to try and lull me into a false sense of security by not leaving anything suspicious for me to discover.

Still, I am not easily fooled and resolve to keep an open mind. I look for evidence of bugging devices. There is a small quantity of what looks like crack in one of the draws of the desk, but it is not my poison and I leave it alone.

The bell rings and I look up, somewhat startled, but quickly compose myself. A man is standing at the other side of the desk. He has a greasy crew cut and a mouth full of gold teeth. A large tattoo of a dragon on his neck. He wears a threadbare blue duffle coat that is missing some of the buttons, his jeans are muddy and do not fit him properly. He has a rucksack a bit like mine, even if it cannot possibly contain material remotely as important as my chess folder.

'Do you have any rooms for the night?' he slurs, leaning his weight on the desk.

I can tell he is drunk. Most likely drugged up too. Frankly I do not like the look of him. This may be a shithole, but we still have certain standards to maintain.

'I am afraid not,' I tell him and then feel bad as he looks a little crestfallen. 'Urgent maintenance work going on, you understand.'

'The council said to come here,' he tells me. 'They said this was the place.'

He pulls a piece of paper out of his pocket. I can see from its worn look that he must have read it many times. He stares at me determinedly. Menacingly even, which just goes to show how right my initial instincts were.

'The council!' I say. 'Well what did you expect? I doubt there is anyone there who knows their arse from their elbow. How many times do you think we have told them not to send more people here?'

I can see him hesitating. My confidence has left him unsure. All the world's a stage, it is just a case of knowing how to work it.

'I tell you what,' I say. 'I know just the place. This is where the council should have sent you.'

I take his piece of paper and scrawl out the name of the other hostel for him. You never know, it's possible that they have patched things up by now. Who am I to say that they will not have re-opened?

'Mate.' he says. 'This is miles away.'

'Yes, yes' I say. 'That's Theresa May for you,' I add knowingly.

He can see there is no answer to this. He stands there for a moment, unsure what to do. Then he mutters his thanks and turns and leaves. I am always happy to help.

I go back to rifling through the desk draws again, just to make sure that they do not have a secret dossier on me hidden in a sealed compartment, when I hear a yell.

'What on earth are you doing?' someone shouts.

I am on the verge of telling him that this is my hotel and I will do what I want, but I sense this might be the wrong answer. I can see he recognises me. I decide it is better to be conciliatory.

'I did ring the bell, but nobody answered. I thought I heard a mouse in one of the drawers. I was just checking that out and having a rummage around for listening devices, but I think we are all right. All good and shipshape! Very happy for you to take over again. My shift is over now, SIR!'

I stand, click my heels and give a friendly salute to set him at his ease. I go back to the customer side of the desk and gesture that he should take the chair again. Leading with confidence is always the way. People appreciate that.

He takes his seat, sighs, scratches his head. I know he would be grateful that I moved our dubious potential patron on, but I decide not to tell him. He needs to feel that he still has a role here after all.

He is white. Fifty something. Blue NHS glasses, one of the spectacle arms secured to the frame with a sticking plaster. Both lenses a little greasy. There is a 'pools coupon' in the pocket of the once white, now grey shirt he is wearing, sticking out above the V-neck. A small stub of black pencil protrudes from the pocket. I can tell immediately that he would not know a top chess player if one hit him in the face, which I have no intention of doing.

I just want a bed for the night. An opportunity to have a quiet drink from my newly replenished stock of cider. A cigarette or two from the forty I have just bought. My clothes might be a little sooty now, but I am sure it is nothing a quick rinse in the sink will not fix.

He seems to slip into automatic pilot, assures me that the sheets have been freshly cleaned for my stay. His voice is higher in pitch than might be expected. Weedy. Runtish almost. A hint of Brummie in the accent. Sometimes I think that no one is truly from London. No one quite fits here. Not really.

I hand over some of my cash and he takes it without comment. Just perhaps the merest flicker of acknowledgement in the half-nod of his head. He licks a finger and runs it through the wad of fives and tens before stuffing them into his trouser pocket. I try not to think about the dent this transaction makes in my reserves.

'There is a bathroom down the corridor from your room. There is a payphone on the landing. I'm not sure what else you might need. There's a kettle. Absolutely no smoking. We don't do breakfast.'

I know, not that it matters. There can have been few more pointless inventions since the beginning of time than breakfast. With its croissants and assorted pastries, its runny eggs and burnt sausages and cheap baked beans that bleed pale orange sauce onto your plate, its sickly grapefruit and inedible cereals. Whatever guise it comes in, just the thought of it makes me want to heave like little else. A cigarette and a swig of cider, that's the breakfast of champions, nothing else comes close.

17. A moment of optimism

So, two nights it is then. Enough time to get my bearings. To plan what comes next.

I pull my rucksack onto my back. The lift is out of order so I climb the three flights of stairs to my room, wheezing more heavily than I would like. It is all hard-tiled floors and walls of peeling cream paint. It reminds me of my old school and for a moment, I think I can smell Brussel sprouts, toilet freshener and the vague feeling of apathy and defeat institutions always bring out in me. The cloying indifference of a life I no longer live.

One day the planning laws will doubtless change and this place will be burnt to the ground and, given the location, the relative proximity to central London, turned into luxury apartments that people will pay a fortune for. More fool them!

I twist the key in a stiff lock that finally yields and pull the door open, revealing a space that for now belongs only to me. I step in and switch on the light, irritated by the sound of the music that is seeping through the wall.

The room is narrow. The single bed has a rough brown blanket over it, perhaps from an army supply store. One pillow. A folded grey towel not much bigger than a flannel resting on top of that. By the bed is a small table with a digital alarm clock, a kettle, a basic looking television remote. Across the room, a bulky television on a plastic stand. A hard, wooden chair.

The floor is of thin blue lino with a once white rug in its middle that when I push at with my foot reveals a dark stain beneath. A chipped white sink, stained yellow, with a plastic cup wrapped in see-through plastic resting by the taps. The sink could do with a mirror above it, but who cares for such things? There is a wardrobe with four coat hangers, a few shelves beneath them lined with tabloid newspaper. I look at the dates. Mainly from the 1970s. Better times, even if the newspapers now smell only of dust and finished lives.

There is a metal framed window that opens stiffly on its hinges when I tug at it. I light a cigarette and smoke looking out onto London through the cold and the mist of a freezing night, that unlike last night, is unambiguously all of winter.

I can see the lights on the horizon spreading away from me into nothing. Some reds and greens, but mainly the white sheen from tower blocks, and behind every light there is a story; out there everything you could imagine is, at this very moment, happening to someone. Partnerships that will last for decades are being formed and others are ending. First sex. Last sex. Winners and losers. Births, deaths. Literal and metaphorical. Everything is universal in its way.

Yet that is not entirely true. Not everything is on a loop, being duplicated in different parts of the city over and over. No one else is planning a chess comeback to rival mine.

What I want most surprises me. Is unusual but is perhaps a product of a night in a café and the minor fire I have just survived. The lack of recent comforts. What I want is a shower. I take my coat and suit off, admiring the cut of the cloth once again. It may be a little old now, but like a fine wine, an expensive garment only ever improves with age. It marks me out for the success story I truly am.

I hang my clothes on the brown coat hangers. Everything stinks of smoke, but it is nothing some air won't fix. By the morning, they will be as good as new.

I will unpack later. I can always change into my spare suit while I sort this one out. How can a man with a change of clothes and money in his pocket ever be confused with someone who is on their uppers?

I sit on the bed in my underwear and drink some cider, for refreshment. A small pick me up, nothing more. I plan to urinate in the shower but find I can't wait that long, so I piss in the sink, and am satisfied by how easily I manage this, even if my urine is still streaked with blood.

The voices of the couple next door are, suddenly, louder than their music.

'Just tell me the fucking truth,' the man says. His tone angry and insistent.

'I already have, I really have,' the woman replies, a hint of desperation in her voice. At some level already resigned to what is coming.

Then there is a scream. Something, perhaps a cup or a lamp smashing against the wall. More likely the radio, as the music has stopped and all I can hear now is sobbing. I stand in my room with no idea what to do. Someone else does. There is a knock at their door. A woman's voice asking if they are both all right.

'We're perfectly fine,' the lady next door assures her. 'Everything is fine. Absolutely fine, there's no problem at all.' Her voice is soothing, reassuring, there is nothing to see here.

The other woman sounds doubtful but what can she do? A few more banalities are exchanged, and I hear her walk away. Everything is quiet.

I would guess the woman in the next room has played this part many times before, the battered partner who convinces everybody that all is well. Perhaps even convinces herself. Almost... But what can I do about it? It is not my world. They are only next door, but it might as well be another universe.

There have been other times in my life, in different circumstances I grant you, when I have lamented the fact that nobody could reach into my world to rescue me – seen Gabriel and my father act as apologists, pretending that our lives were one thing when they were another, allowing my mother to continue to flourish because it was just easier that way. Who created the most compelling fiction in our family is a question without an obvious answer. There are too many walls around all of us, both physical and metaphorical.

I strip naked. With one hand holding the towel together around my waist, I clutch my room key within the ball of the other and stride purposefully down the corridor. I pass a startled mother and child walking toward me from the opposite direction. She puts her hands over her daughter's eyes and backs away, draws herself as close to the wall as she possibly can as we pass. I do not get it. Has she never seen a man in a towel before? I am perfectly decent. Perhaps she is working overtime to suppress her natural desire for me. I know that my raw masculinity must be extremely attractive.

Her daughter cannot be more than four or five. My guess is they have been housed here by the council. Temporary DSS tenants until who knows when. Searching for a better life, a better way of living. Not yet quite found. Perhaps it never will be. Even so, I wish her mother had the basic courtesy to respect my privacy and my boundaries. Does she not understand how tiring it is to live in a world where everyone seems to want something from you?

I go into the shower and lock the door. It is a small bathroom really. The toilet is missing its seat, the dark green bowl a little stained, but I have seen worse. There is half a bar of brown soap on the basin. The bath is a different vintage. Newer, but perhaps not much. It is a different colour to the toilet. Primrose yellow. It makes no sense but is often what you find in places like this. The bath has no plug and there are white plastic shower tubes attached to the taps.

The shower nozzle rests on top of the taps, dripping slightly. Not brilliant but it will do the job. The shower curtain is missing most of its hooks and has a thin layer of mould that half obscures a pattern of flowers and a golden sun that has clearly seen significantly better days. I do not want the curtain to touch my skin when I am showering, so I rip it off its remaining hooks, scrunch it into a ball and throw the wretched thing into the corner of the room.

I hang the towel on the metal hook behind the door, stand in the bathtub and pick up the shower nozzle. The base of the bath feels sticky on the soles of my feet. I look down and notice how yellow and gnarled my toenails are. Nothing a bit of powder wouldn't quickly fix I'm sure. My ingrown nail has made the surrounding skin red and puffy, but it only really hurts when I think about it. One day I will track down a competent doctor who is not a State agent and it will be the work of a moment to get it fixed.

It is difficult to ignore the room's faint aroma of drains and other people's sweat, to say nothing of the tang of soot and perspiration on my own body. I twist the tap and cold water comes out, first in a trickle and then a gush. The tubing is not wholly watertight, some escapes between the attachment and the tap, a bit more leaks from what appears to be a small hole close to the nozzle, but it does not matter. The shower still works and while it starts out cold the water gradually warms up to a point. I rub my face, my hair, my chest and a torrent of black soot drains off me.

It is like being reborn. Everything can be washed away, forgiven, nothing is impossible. My body is soothed and reinvigorated by the water. It is impossible to feel this good and not be well, of that I am sure.

I rub soap into my skin, into my hair. A stream of black water running off me, down the plug hole, and into London's sewers. I suck my stomach in. It only sags when I don't concentrate. Few are blessed with a physique as good as mine.

Finally, the water runs completely cold and then gurgles and stops. I must have drained the tank. I stand in the tub, still foaming under a layer of soap as rapidly cooling droplets fall from me onto the floor. No matter, I was nearly there. I grab my towel and scrape off some of the bubbles, dry myself, wrap the postage stamp of material back around my middle.

There will, perhaps, be some evidence that I have been in the room after I leave, I grant you. The bathtub is now black with soot. A considerable amount of water has spilled onto the bathroom floor, and possibly through it if the yells from the room below are anything to go by. Not that that is any concern of mine. Still, it will be but a trifling job for the next user to spruce things up a bit.

I walk back along the corridor to my room, leaving a trail of water and padded footprints behind me as I go. It reminds me of being lost in a maze. The water like breadcrumbs, showing a path, a possible way back. Or at least a way to keep going.

I sit naked on my bed and in a moment of optimism touch myself, but nothing happens, and I wonder whether I should just leave it or whether I might look to be a little more creative. Have I not earned something from this day?

The card I picked up in the café toilet is still in my trouser pocket. It is a tempting thought. I walk over to the chair I have hung my clothes on and pull it out. A picture of a pretty girl. A telephone number and an instruction to call her. I wonder if just looking at it might do the trick, but it turns out it doesn't.

I consider the phone number. The seductive gaze of her eyes. The bloom of her youthful body. There are so many nutters out there, I know she would really appreciate spending time with someone a million cuts above her usual clientele. A man of my talent might well end up getting it for free. A racing certainty if, it transpires, she is a chess fan.

I find myself walking up and down, trying to supress the impulse, but it is impossible now the thought has formed. Part of me says that this is crazy. Unnecessary at least. Bound to end in trouble and disappointment. Fortunately, that is not the dominant voice I hear. I am more man than mouse. A raging stallion. I do not see the harm in at least calling her and talking business.

I pull some clothes on and walk to the phone on the landing. A man is using it, so I must wait. It is the sort of equipment you don't much see these days. Grey and bulky. A wire between the receiver and the phone that is wrapped in thick plastic. A dial to twist rather than buttons to press. It has a half dome-like booth over the top.

'The time is right,' he says. 'We should be together. I'm your balm pot. I need you.'

He is old and fat. Bald on top and his remaining hair is greasy brown, streaked with white. Large, fleshy face covered in salt and pepper stubble. He wears a blue denim shirt and brown suit trousers held up by red braces that seem to accentuate the heft of his stomach. Battered and stained desert boots on his large feet. He gestures with one hand as he clutches the receiver with the other. His movements strangely feminine and fussy. I can tell by his expression and the way he continually moves his weight from one leg to the other that he is not hearing good news.

'Well, err, I could get you your own room here if you like,' he says. 'I have the means to do that.'

I suspect this might be something of a stretch, can see that he is mentally doing the maths as soon as the offer has been made. He inserts his final coin in the phone.

'Just think it through my lovely. We belong together. It's the only way. We could just make this happen. We don't need anyone else.'

Then his money runs out and he puts the phone down. He flashes me a look of sheer hatred and scurries down the corridor and out of sight. We are all but a walk on part in so many other people's stories.

I pick up the receiver, hear the soothing ringtone. I run my finger over the face on the card and feel a tingle of excitement as I dial in the number and wait for her to answer.

The ringing stops and someone says 'Yes?'

I make my voice a touch deeper than its natural tenor, to accentuate my manliness and my confidence.

'Is that you, err Roxy?' I say looking at her name on the card.

'Sorry, I didn't quite make that out. It sounds like you have a terrible cold or something? Say it again.'

I sigh and repeat the question. People can never keep up with me.

'I can be whoever you want me to be my lovely,' she says.

'Can you get here right away? I'll make it worth your while. I will require some discretion. I am quite famous you know.'

There is a slight hesitation on the line.

'Where are you love?' she asks.

It pains me that she does not ask for more details of my fame. Perhaps she has already recognised my voice and has no need to. I think of saying something but decide not to spoil the surprise, in case she has mixed me up with some lesser celebrity. It is not all that often a prostitute gets to hang out with a chess player of my standing.

I tell her where I am and ask how long she will take to get here.

She pauses again.

'Half an hour, but understand, it's £50 an hour and people will know where I am.'

'Okay,' I hear myself saying and she hangs up.

Perhaps that moment was the thrill. As good as it is going to get. As I stand by the phone booth, suddenly I feel sad. Almost ashamed even. Perhaps all men are ruled by testosterone and an emptiness that can never be quenched.

But it is not for me to make excuses or to seek to understand what others might do. It is hardly my fault that I am drawn to prostitutes. It is not as if I made a conscious decision to be this way.

I've always hated men who present one face to the world and another in places like this. Not obvious which facets of their personalities are more real, more authentic. Or why anyone would care.

Abusers all to a greater or lesser extent, although no one is ever wholly one thing or another. We all have our secrets and our needs. Our petty failures and darker sins. All of it temporary, over and done with long before the morning light. Leaving no trace.

18. The problem with the British

I go back to my room and lie on the bed to wait for her. Real champions only look forward, never back. I try to buck myself back up by re-remembering some of my incredible accomplishments. The last time I won the British was quite something.

Nine rounds in some God-forsaken seaside town. Torquay, Scarborough, Blackpool, Llandudno, Hull, places like that are all one and the same when you are focussed on your chess, thank goodness. I do not have a distinct memory which it was. I hate the idea of swimming in the sea. I do not do beaches. The thought of dozing in the sun when you could be working at your chess holds no appeal for me whatsoever.

I was the world number four and had just qualified for the World Championship Candidates tournament. The next highest ranked player in the British that year was Mottram, who was around the number twenty mark by that point. Still, I had always been criticised for not doing more for British chess. For having forgotten my roots. For not putting enough back. I was more than generous in the fee I agreed to take for participating.

They said it was the most they had ever paid anyone, but it was still below my normal rate for that time.

In the first round I played some local worthy, just around Master level, and things nearly went wrong. He played carefully, the position became dull and sterile and a normal player in my position who was expecting to win as a matter of routine might have panicked. Not me. I just waited. I could see him growing more excited as the game progressed, as he inched closer to managing a draw against the great Tennessee Greenbecker. The story he would dine out on for the rest of his career. Doubtless he was already composing the piece he would write for *Chess* magazine on his amazing achievement, barely even diminished by the fact that he had the white pieces.

They were all stood round the board as my chances of victory appeared to have withered away – Mottram, Page, Johnson, Shurrock, Pink and Lam, my main rivals for the British that year. I could see them sniggering and exchanging glances that I was clearly meant to see. Willing my opponent on. But they were wasting their time. All of it served to make me more determined.

We reached an ending of rook, same coloured bishop and four pawns each, and my path to victory opened. Forget the maxim that all rook and pawn endgames are drawn. That only applies if you don't know what you are doing. My opponent put his pieces on reasonable squares, made moves that from a general principles perspective appeared sensible, but if my knowledge and ability to calculate matched that of a mainframe computer, he had essentially come to the fight with an abacus.

Gradually, I got my king a stronger foothold, found a way to slightly minimise the range of his bishop, created a pawn island weakness in his position that had not been there before. I was winning, and when an hour or so later he resigned there were tears in his eyes.

I felt no joy. He had made me work harder than he should have done. His was hardly a scalp that would enhance my reputation. Still I had won and that was all that mattered. On reflection, I felt only contempt that he had not been able to hold such a position and disdain for my rivals who had stopped watching as soon as the tide turned. I remember telling him that I had never previously been made to struggle as much by a player as weak as him, but he did not seem to take the compliment.

After that it was easier. I got into a pattern of sleeping in my hotel room in the morning, which courtesy of the tournament sponsors, was in the same hotel as the event itself. I would be at my Board at precisely 2.30 in the afternoon for the start of each game, and when I was done, I would head to the hotel bar for the night. After the early rounds, there were throngs of players and officials wanting to accompany me, looking to bask in the reflected glory that comes from drinking with a superstar. More stories for their books and magazine articles, the online posts that define the mediocre. Those first few nights were fun, but nothing lasts forever.

Over time, things seemed to go a little bit wrong. I was more of a whisky drinker, in so far as I was a drinker at all in those days, and people seemed to come to resent buying me doubles. Then there was an argument with Mike Webb, allegedly the new great hope of British chess, since proved not to be so.

My game in round four had just finished with a win that

took me to 4/4 and Mike was playing on the next board. All youth and arrogant promise. The kind that is built on hope rather than concrete evidence. He had a stone-cold win and missed it, blundering to defeat. As he tried to suppress a tear, he looked every inch the failed prodigy. Standing there watching, I found it impossible to hide my contempt.

'You are a fucking idiot,' I am alleged to have exclaimed at the top of my voice.

This caused Mike to stand up and take a swing at me. It is fair to say that he punched like a chess player, completely missing and falling back on the table, scattering plastic rooks and other pieces all over the floor.

'You still box better than you play, you fucking prick.' I am alleged to have said by way of retort, although my memory is somewhat hazy on that point. I do remember Mike running from the hall in tears and lodging an official objection with the organisers as to my conduct.

A passer-by commented that Mike was not much more than a kid, but so what? If he wanted to be a top chess player, he needed to develop some backbone and to stop weeping and punching like a toddler.

For some reason the story of Kasparov in slightly different circumstances went through my head at that moment. Kasparov lost to a young prodigy in some big tournament and subsequently went ballistic when his opponent was awarded the brilliancy prize for the game in question. Kasparov thought it had been a fluke. A poor game, nothing more. He ranted and raved at the organisers, leading a journalist to write that the real tragedy was that having lost to a child Kasparov proceeded to behave like one.

My circumstances were of course entirely different. I had done nothing more than point out that the emperor had no clothes and he had tried to punch me in the face for my trouble. Quite why anyone thought I was even remotely in the wrong was beyond me, but I was called before the organisers and it became clear they thought there was some sort of problem. They seemed unconvinced by my assertion that I was the victim.

I highlighted that if they ever wanted me to play in the UK again, they needed to make all this go away. I could see from their expressions that there were one or two amongst them who at that precise moment would probably have liked it if I did take my talent elsewhere, but they knew which side their bread was buttered on. Let's face it, I have always been the main attraction. British chess has withered on the vine during my absence.

Ultimately the English Chess Federation officials wanted my Candidates knock out matches to take place in London and if I got that far, the World Championship final to be played in the UK. That would only happen with my acquiescence. I had a strong negotiating hand.

Besides the publicity was great. Armies of journalists showed up at the venue. Hand to hand combat at the British made the six o'clock news and all the papers. Even though no one *had* been hit. I even turned down a chance to appear in *The Sun* with a page three model and a chessboard. A decision I later regretted.

I refused to accept even an official reprimand and the ECF let that go, though my request that Mike Webb be banned for life was rejected. It did all leave something of a sour taste. People thought that Mike might have been psychologically damaged by the experience. I had an extremely awkward conversation with his mother. I am not entirely sure that Mike ever played again, but that was his choice of course.

Somehow the rest of the event was just not as much fun. For whatever reason I seemed to have fewer people wanting to hang out and drink with me, albeit most chess players are lightweights and the fact that they could not keep up was hardly a surprise.

The rest of the tournament was relatively uneventful. I was banned from the hotel bar after a minor incident in the early hours following round six. There were plenty of other places to drink. By then I was on 6/6 and cruising.

I invited myself out for a curry with Page, Cram and Donnelly. Despite not being able to stand them, the truth was that they were at least okay players and I had no tolerance for those who did not know their Lucena position from their Philidor. We ordered poppadoms and dips. Page and Cram both had a vegetable Balti and plain naans. Vegetarians both. Another reason to despise them. I had a chicken jalfrezi, as did Donnelly, but I seem to remember that I did not eat much of it, preferring to focus on having a quiet drink.

I think it was Page who asked if I was an alcoholic. I was shocked. I genuinely had no idea where that thought might have come from. Cram said that a lot of successful people were functioning alcoholics, but he always did have the sort of diplomatic air about him that those who are half asleep often do.

I saw the assertions for what they really were, attempts to make me doubt myself, to put me off chess. I told them all where to go and stormed out of the curry house. Found a little bar down by the waterfront and sat quietly drinking, watching a ferry in the fading light of a summer evening making her way who knows where. People who can't really drink are always jealous of those who can. My energy levels felt a little depleted after that and my final three opponents were only too happy to take the quick draws I needed to end on 7.5/9 in outright first place.

I may have made some comments after the event about provincial shitholes and the buffoons who ran British chess, which perhaps were better left unsaid, but that's where me and Bobby Fischer were the same. Authenticity. The same ability to speak truth to power. To hell with the consequences.

Describing my fellow competitors as essentially moronic and not remotely in my league was just a statement of fact any fair-minded observer would have been happy to agree with. I knew most secretly supported my observations on junior chess players, however outraged they pretended to be.

The talented are always destined to suffer at the hands of second-rate officials and the mediocre we have no choice but to mingle with. Let's face it, where is the English Chess Federation right now, when I need basic help with my comeback?

I talked to Bobby on the phone around that time. Even he thought I should rein it in a bit. He wasn't quite his normal self. More subdued perhaps. This wasn't one of those times when I would put the receiver to one side, waiting for his rants about Jews to come to an end so we could talk some chess.

'The thing is, Tennessee, the whole thing is rigged. The ECF are not your friends. They are just an extension of the State, don't ever forget that. I fear they are already grinding you down.'

I know he would have approved of me dialling up Roxy. He always went out of his way to encourage me to have a little fun. I feel myself growing more tense as I wait. I think about studying game 38 from Bobby's book, his 1962 duel in Curacao against Keres, but it is no good. I cannot concentrate. I put the volume down. Think what might soothe me. How to relax. The best way to pass the time until she gets here.

I look at the old newspapers in the wardrobe. The sink and my lighter. I already know from smoking earlier that the room, in common with all the best, lacks a fire alarm, so why not? Where's the harm? There is no mirror that might crack with the heat.

I take a single piece of *Daily Mail* and place it in the sink. Light a corner and watch it flare. A single streak of gold that dances down the paper and then consumes it all, Edward Heath's face burning to nothing. It does not surprise me that his character has now been called into question. You can't trust anyone, that is what I always say.

I light two more pieces of paper, then another. A little pool of grey charcoal builds in the basin. Three-day weeks and short-ages of oil loom in block capitals before burning to ash in the small bonfire I have started. I am enjoying the warmth. No country log fire could be more impressive.

The flames are yellow and orange, with hints of green and blue. The smoke is fresh and clean. I consider adding some cider, just to spice things up a little, but I am always wary about wasting good drink. Besides, I am only playing. Passing the time. There is nothing serious going on. I am the master of this as surely as I am the master of the chess board.

What was it someone once said? There were three things

they could watch forever. An ocean, a baby and a fire. There is something about fire. The way it draws you in. Is hypnotic, addictive almost. The most powerful of all the elements. The one both closest to life and to death. I am always mesmerised by its warmth, its energy. Its capacity to renew.

Still I do not want things to get out of hand, considering there is still important business left to do today. I reach for the tap, singeing my hand slightly, and twist it full on. The water momentarily seems to give the fire new energy, before it smoulders away to nothing.

I hear a thump at the door.

'What the fuck is going on in there, mate?' the wifebeater shouts. 'There's smoke coming into our room.'

I am quite impressed by my achievement, but I know this is a moment to be conciliatory.

'Nothing, nothing at all. A minor accident when making toast. Don't worry about it.' I shout back.

He grunts and is gone. I hear his room door shut behind him.

'Some twat with a toaster,' I hear him say.

There is a little more smoke than I had perhaps envisaged, so I fully open the window and try to wave it out with my pillow. Everything is soon all pretty much as good as new.

I am ready and waiting for Roxy. My night is not done yet.

19. The woman at the door

There are a few false alarms. A woman in the corridor, talking loudly on her mobile. I am convinced it must be her. I stand behind my door waiting expectantly for a knock as the sound of her voice draws closer and then fades again. Then I hear a fresh set of footsteps. I turn the television off and desperately use the blanket on my bed to wipe the sweat off my hands, so I am ready to let her in. Again, I am mistaken.

Finally, I hear the click of a woman's heels on the landing. A faint echo on the hard floor that steadily becomes louder. Then a tap of knuckles on my thin door. I can feel butterflies in my stomach. Perhaps a slight sensation in my groin. If anything, I feel sick.

I look around the room and see it as an outsider might. I fear the impression it creates is not altogether good. Mess just seems to run away with me, wherever I stay. I have no idea why this is. Four empty cans are scattered on the floor and a sickly-looking pool of cider has spilled onto the lino. Something of a waste to be sure, and one that has given the room a faint smell of rotten apples and carbon dioxide. Other parts of the lino are still damp from me drying off after the shower. Cigarette butts fill the provided plastic cup. A further trail of grey ash runs across the length of the floor. A result of combining smoking and chess player pacing, so automatic, that I hadn't even noticed the burnt tobacco until this moment.

I look up and for the first time notice a large patch of mould on a ceiling made from 1960s era meshed panelling, most likely untouched since installation. The sink has probably also looked better, I concede, the basin filled with a mound of burnt newspaper that still belches a thin trail of wet smoke. Somehow the wall above the sink has suffered minor fire damage, a few brown stain marks that blend in with the general wear and tear around the wash area. Nothing the lick of paint the place needs anyway would not fix.

I find it difficult to gauge if the room smells of smoke, but I can imagine that to one not used to it, such a thing is possible. I suspect there is also a faint tang of urine, but I am very sensitive to such things, so most likely it is not particularly obvious. There is a very high probability that the various smells will cancel each other out. I must be fair to myself. How is it my fault that this room feels small and seedy? That it has more in common with a jail cell than a place people might pay to stay? It is hardly in keeping with a man of my calibre, but so be it. Much better hotel rooms await me soon.

But I fail to wholly reassure myself. I can't imagine away the fact that someone is knocking on my hotel door and I need to do something about it.

I feel sweat pouring off me, a growing feeling of dizziness in my head. The knock has triggered something of a minor panic attack that has nothing to do with the state of the room. I can tell myself that there is nothing to fear, but that is not what my body feels. It is as if I have been thrown back inside myself and am drowning. This always happens to me. I was a fool to think that things could be different.

I might as well be a fish thrown to the ground, gulping desperately in the thin, thin air, all to no avail – destined to flap about in a bucket coughing up blood until death arrives. Wind rushes inside my head and I feel like a child who is holding a seashell to their ear. I am drifting, drifting away. Through a tunnel. Toward the light. If this truly is the end than I am ready!

It might as well be here and now as anywhere else, for all the difference it makes. All my dreams for the future are but dust, yet so is everything else. None of it matters really. A moment of clarity that is up there with my finest discoveries at the chessboard.

I must have passed out for a moment, but I am sure no more than that, a man of my fighting qualities is not floored by anything for long. Not even death. The room swims hazily back into focus and I find that I am curled up in a foetal position on the floor, rocking gently back and forth. Sweat stings my eyes and drips from my shirt. I can tell I have leaked a little bit, but not majorly. Could I have been like this for longer?

I hear the knock at the door again and deduce I most likely only drifted out of consciousness for an instant. I still feel a sense of agitation, but it is less acute than before. I mutter softly under my breath to calm down. Inhale and exhale. Slowly. Take time to make sure that my lungs still work. Cough out a few remnants of soot. I am now sure that my heart is still beating and that my arms and legs are working. Everything seems to be in order. I am in control. I have been here before. This is nothing I can't handle. All is not lost.

Still, even now I am in a more serene state, I am annoyed with myself. All of this was avoidable, and I fear that I never seem to learn. There should not be anyone knocking on my door right now. I have only myself to blame.

Any chess player can be forgiven for losing a game. What is unforgivable is failing to learn the lessons from defeat, and then going right on in the future to lose the same game again. This is what the mess I am in resembles. I have discovered nothing that I did not already know. A familiar deadly combination is being played out against me and I am just as powerless as I was on every previous occasion to see it off.

Encounters like this in no way reflect who I really am. I have kidded myself once again, that is all. Fool, fool, fool. Why do I do this to myself? Intimacy never works these days. I can't even pay for it. Usually, I do not answer the door. Wait for the knocking to subside. The woman to go. Occasionally a pimp comes and bangs too, but not often. It all becomes a variation contemplated but not actually played. An event that has no existence outside my mind. Something that might not be real at all. Ignoring the knocking feels like it should be my best option.

'Is everything all right in there?' I hear a woman shout through the door. Her voice impatient, but possibly tinged with a hint of anxiety. Perhaps she imagines I am one of those freaks who has chained himself up and is now in the process of beating themselves to death. It had not occurred to me that she might hear my mutterings, foolish considering that the door is most likely made of recycled paper.

I must get rid of her. She is a threat to all I hold dear. I cannot remember whether the ability to hold and believe two contradictory thoughts at the same time is considered a form of genius or madness, but it is where I am. Who is to say why she has chosen to knock at my door? It might have been my phone call, but it is possible that has nothing to do with that and she was planning on trying to see me along. It is not as if I know her, so I would not like to ascribe any motive to her actions with certainty.

I shout at her to fuck off. Then I shout it again.

'Fuck you, you time-wasting wanker,' she yells, and I hear her footsteps fade as she walks away. I have triumphed again.

Still, the moment does not have the feel of an outright victory. I have never pretended to understand women. Women have never liked me. What to do has never been obvious. What to say. How to be. They did not really interest me when I was younger. I never really had much of a childhood. Perhaps not much of an adulthood either.

I had needs of course, but it was always easier to take care of them myself. A mechanical exercise. As routine as brushing your teeth. Without the embarrassment of dialling women up and not being able to go through with it. A few brief minutes at the sink and then I could get back to what really mattered. To a chessboard, and a world I understood.

There was one exception of course, one that sort of proved the rule, but I don't feel like thinking about her right now. Perhaps later.

20. Sick of experts

I stand up and walk to the sink to piss in it. For a moment nothing happens. Nothing comes out. I cannot cope with more problems in that department, not after all I have been through today. I concentrate. Try to reconnect my body with the neural paths in my brain that are meant to make things like this work routinely and automatically. We all take so much for granted until we no longer can. I squeeze and will it and finally I piss, staining the sink with blood and finding myself laughing with relief.

I do not want to read too much into what happened when I was hospitalised. In hindsight I acted too hastily on that occasion. It is most likely not uncommon to go a day without being able to urinate. Had I waited; everything would have righted itself. I would have mastered the technique of making my bladder work without any help from others. It was also a mistake to call Gabriel. To let him in on it. To open myself up to the propaganda of others.

They certainly had me where they wanted me, fool that I was, lying on a hospital bed, a so-called doctor squirting antiseptic fluid up my dick. Pushing in a catheter. The slow feeling of relief as my bladder drained. The weight of the urine bag akin to having an anchor tethered to my private parts. I asked her what would happen if she did nothing, whether my bladder would explode. She thought not, rather it would just lose its shape.

It was all lies. There was nothing wrong with me really. I was just momentarily confused and embarrassed, that was all. The State will take any opportunity it gets to humiliate their enemies. That's why they brought a woman in. She was far more likely to have been an agent for the ECF than a medical person. I just wasn't thinking clearly enough to see this at the time.

The tests I let them do were another blunder. A gift which allowed them to make up whatever they wanted. Bloods and scans. Their continual attempts to contact me afterwards. The claims that they wanted to help. As if anyone would seek assistance from people who told them they had cancer! A bladder cancer that appears to have spread extensively, they had added by way of a final creative touch.

I am sure the English Chess Federation put the hospital up to it. Most would automatically spy their fingerprints all over this. What better way to hold me back than to flood my system with chemo and other drugs I do not need? At the time, I admired the cleverness of the play. I felt flattered that they had seen me as a serious enough opponent to warrant such attention. I liked that Gabriel appeared concerned. That he gave me money. Appeared to want to help. It is only now that I realise, he was most likely in on the act with the rest of them.

I don't know. It is just that as I lie here, there is a part of me that knows things are not right. It is not what they say it is. Nothing that bad. But still, the way I sometimes feel is not altogether as it should be. Their false narrative has triggered something that might push my body over the edge. If anything is actually wrong, it is entirely their fault. There are only so many nights left to me to fail at sex or to become the world chess champion. Only so many more sinks I might set fire to.

I look at my right hand and notice for the first time that it has a fresh burn on the palm. A dark brown spot, relatively minor, but my eye is drawn to the damage. As I stare it starts to throb and I feel the heat beneath my skin. I consider running water over the wound, but the sensation is not altogether unpleasant. The warmth makes me feel alive, connected, somehow heightened. In touch with my body as well as my brain. Fuck them all. I know my body better than any of them. What it is capable of. What I can become.

I see older marks too, forged in other moments where I have literally played with fire, been its master. Controlled elements much less predictable than those to be found on a chessboard. I am always careful not to let things get completely out of hand. What happened at the hostel and the Red Lion were just unfortunate miscalculations, nothing more – and let's be clear, neither were *that* bad.

I have an instinct for self-preservation. I know how to keep the more practical aspects of my interest in fire under the radar, even at the risk of my joining the long list of others who have not receive the recognition they deserve for their contribution to society.

I must rely on chess for my fame. Still, that doesn't mean I can't dream about letting a fire really spread in all its delicious oranges and reds and blues and greens. Watching a tiny spark grow and grow, out of all control. The sensation that comes from witnessing people running to the scene while others run from it. Knowing I *made* this, that everything is happening because of me. Besides, the truth is, while I have not received the same level of recognition as Guy Fawkes, my body of work far outweighs his.

More than once way back, I have been the one to phone the Fire Service, having stumbled on a potential disaster. That is the impression my tone admirably conveyed. Happy to lap up the praise for my quick thinking in the face of adversity. For being the hero who stopped things from becoming much worse. Thank goodness you happened to be here, a gormless official once told me.

I should not take risks like that now. It is a long time since I have made such a phone call. There is too much in the State's files about me. The odds of someone properly joining the dots have grown in this more inquisitive age. Then the authorities would have all the material they needed to prevent me from making a comeback.

The sheer hypocrisy of it all makes me sick. Who doesn't revel in fire's cleansing power? It is part of the human condition. Apart from chess what else is there? To burn, to drink, to fuck. It all goes back to the beginning of time and who we really are. Warmth, comfort, a sense of well-being. It is only a matter of time until London burns again, one way or another, so it is perverse that society does not properly value the arsonists on their noble quest to forge the next chapter in our capital's history. The pioneers who seize the day while others stand by.

I think to that Second Great Fire of London. The power of renewal the Luftwaffe gifted the city when 100,000 bombs fell over two nights. It really must have been quite something. A larger area of London ablaze than in 1666. The Square Mile flattened. Thirty-one guild halls and nineteen churches reduced to rubble. St Paul's rescued against the odds, which I give you is disappointing.

In my view something should only be classified as a genuine London fire if St Paul's is razed. I assume Churchill did not know this when he denied St Paul's her destiny. That man never really had much sense of history.

The Germans took out Paternoster Row, the publishing district and five million books were destroyed by the flames. Sadly, despite their best efforts, it was not enough to prevent my mother from finding a way into print all those years later. Fuck her money. If she had never been published, I would just have made more cash of my own at the chessboard and in the casino.

I appear to be wholly reliant on my considerable wits today after all, and I am more than equal to the challenge. Still, knowing how well her work burns, I wonder how much more of London might have been consumed by flame had she been a published writer in that era.

For a moment as I imagine a raging inferno, I feel as I did when I looked at Roxy's face on her card, but the sensation does not last. Nothing works. Everything serves to mock me. No one understands chess or fire the way I do.

Chess journalists are another obvious case in point. None of them can make a living from the game by playing it. Rather they live off their cheap smears and a basic misreading of every position. Cling to a world they do not belong in by writing about it, belittling and rubbishing those of real talent along the way. Parasites all.

That imbecile Chris Hamish has always been a particular source of my anger. Stick thin, bespectacled, the air of a university professor, all knowing silences and general superiority. A terrible player. Barely an International Master. No match for me, even if I were to play him blindfolded. I doubt he could drink more than a thimble-full without falling over. Hardly a man. The thought of a minute in his company most likely enough to make anyone reach for the bottle.

Who was he to write an expose, albeit one that put on full display his buffoon-like level of linguistic imagination, claiming I had been 'checkmated,' by drink? How dare he assert that I had become an embarrassment to the game, that my talent had drained away, leaving only the dregs at the bottom of the bottle? That it was pitiful to look at me now.

There were oblique references to other matters that had been heavily lawyered, but I knew well enough what he meant – like anyone cares what that moron thinks. I do not have the energy to waste on the low-level writers, hustlers and kibitzers who all seek to drain my creativity and make money off the back of me.

I breathe in and out again, deep breathes, thinking calming thoughts. It is always easier to advise others that whatever they are troubled by does not matter. Can be framed differently. Explained away. It is harder to follow your own advice. Albeit, the worries of others are as nothing compared to having to deal with a vicious and unprovoked attack from a semi-literate fool.

I feel my ribcage rattling a little, which perhaps is not good but is most likely just stress. Ultimately, I will have the last laugh and Chris Hamish and the rest of that motley crew will be forced to write about my triumphs in the end.

I see the headlines now. Return of the prodigal son. Champion at last. The world rejoices in chess's finest hour. Forget Fischer - Spassky 1972, Greenbecker - Carlsen will now stand as chess's most famous moment. Why not? All my life has been leading me to this. I am truly the only Greenbecker worth writing about.

I think to the speech I will give when, by unanimous acclaim, I am awarded the BBC Sports Personality of the Year. I imagine Magnus being beamed in on a big screen. Smiling broadly, freely admitting that he simply could not match my talent. The computers demonstrating that I am now officially the most accurate chess player in history, my play so deep it goes beyond the comprehension of the super mainframes.

I sigh with contentment. It is difficult to imagine events unfolding any other way.

21. The Greenbecker Gambit

I pick up the television remote controller. Heavy and basic. Grey plastic face, with a few white buttons. I press the on switch and a bead of red flashes from the base of the contraption and then the television on the wall springs to life. The news is just finishing. Another stabbing in London.

The victim aged twenty-two. On the screen is a photograph of him in a green vest and blue jeans, standing with his mother and sister, arms around each other's shoulders. Posing for the snap. He is tall, dark skinned, with the look of a college athlete. A bright white smile, eyes warm and engaging. He oozes youth and possibility. The news reader says the photo was taken three weeks before he died.

The talking heads are blaming it all on an influx of knife crime amongst the young. I know different. It is all a product of the State taking out its enemies. I should really take to wearing a stab proof vest, but I am unsure where to source one. I consider if it is a task for Gabriel, but he is so useless he would probably return with a knitwear cardigan. Perhaps it is the lateness of the hour, but I feel almost fatalistic. If they kill me, they kill me.

My mood brightens as I remember inventing the Greenbecker Gambit. That moment of unadulterated joy not wholly tarnished by Chris Hamish and all else that followed. I had been looking for ideas before my match with Dubrovnik. Ways in which I might surprise him. They said that the old gambits did not work anymore, but I knew differently.

Back in the nineteenth century, it was considered ungentlemanly if you did not offer up a pawn. An even greater faux pas by your opponent if he declined to take it. That was how imbalances worked in those days. The trade of material for time, space and a quick attack. Famous chess games of the period are filled with sacrifices, pieces crashing through and routing the larger but more immobile forces ranged against them. It was not that players of that era were unaware of other considerations. Structure, square control, subtler ways to play. It was just a different mind-set, that was all.

I had been looking at the King's Gambit in particular. Spassky briefly re-popularised the opening in the 1970s. Kasparov was always doubtful. He said that Spassky did well with it because he was such a strong player, not because the opening was any good. I had this argument with Garry many times over the years and we agreed to disagree.

The more I considered the matter, the more I realised that Spassky had been onto something, but he hadn't fully unlocked the potential, his games hinting at but not quite uncovering even more promising lines for white.

I studied some of the deeper variations and then one evening it came to me. White potentially had a way to sacrifice a second pawn, to build a net that would exert a vice-like grip on the position. It only took a series of perfectly natural looking moves and black would be in deep trouble. I figured Dubrovnik might not be accurate enough to secure even this, far from desirable outcome, in which case victory would surely be mine.

Chess players are like archaeologists, looking back through the fossils of the past to uncover the future. Not so different from picking through the ash of London's former fires. Seeking new interpretations, unravelling layers of complexity and meaning missed by those who have gone before. The judgements of the past are never wholly settled.

If you want to be the world champion, it is very simple really. Assimilate all that has gone before and throw in some fresh ideas of your own. See the forward path more clearly than your contemporaries. These kids today with their computers are all well and good. Any fool can put a position into a search engine and ask it to spew out concrete lines and a silicon evaluation. What I did took a far greater degree of natural vision.

In the weeks before the match, I developed the Gambit further. Worked through all the permutations and potential refutations until I was sure I had it watertight. A place in chess history as the creator of something original and beautiful was at stake. How many opening variations does Fischer have that are associated with his name? Precisely none. I was confident by the time the match came around that I was ready.

Dubrovnik was a melancholic soul. Prone to deep sighs and mournful stares. I had heard the stories of his uncle throwing himself onto a railway line. His father's jail sentence for crimes unspeakable, but it wasn't that. I always knew the true source of his unhappiness. He had come to hate chess. The very thing he had been addicted to since childhood. The game he still aspired to conquer.

He had battled against considerable odds into the world top ten and the Candidates final. One step away from a tilt against the world champion. Everything he had ever wanted. Yet I knew he felt as trapped by his life choices as every backstreet accountant, checkout assistant and drug addict who has ever walked. He had willed his life to be defined by chess and now he was chained within it as if in a prison cell. Dark, imposing and immovable, with rituals unyielding.

This did not mean he was unprepared or that he was not trying to win. No, it was simply that where once there had been endless possibility and excitement, he now saw only work. He had told me on several previous occasions winning gave him little joy.

His real passions were fishing and writing terrible poetry, but neither offered the same route to stardom, or to any place much beyond the cheap damp flat that he lived in alone. I heard Dubrovnik used to send his poetry into Finnish literary magazines under an assumed name, as he wanted his writing to be judged on its merits in the Land of the Thousand Lakes. When that did not work, apparently, he sent the poems in his own name, and they still would not publish them. He was stuck with chess and he knew it.

Julian Barnes imagined in a novel what heaven might be like. A place where you could have anything you wanted, be anyone you wanted to be. The punchline was that it was never quite enough. That the price of having all your wishes granted was to tire of them in the end.

Barnes wrote that there were two groups who took the longest to grow weary. Literary critics seemed happy to go on arguing over the merits of books almost ad infinitum. Something I could well believe if my mother's friends were anything to go by, after all, there is nothing that quite beats the feeling that comes from rubbishing the work of others. Then of course, there were the chess players. The lure of playing another game did not quite last into all eternity, but it got quite close.

For sure, Dubrovnik gave the impression the hold chess must once have had on him, was seriously waning and this was something I hated him for. What right did someone like that have to stand in my way? If he did not want it as much as I did, how could he be as deserving of victory as I was?

At the time, my hatred was a useful spur to get the competitive juices flowing. Today, my contempt is deeper and more bittersweet. He stole something from me that mattered deeply. Received far more than the chess gods should have given him. I can only assume their hands were tied.

After two draws, in the third game, when I pushed my king's pawn, he did likewise, and a King's Gambit appeared on the board for the first time. This cannot have been a complete surprise to him. I had played it before and had even read his boasts to *Chess* magazine that it was fundamentally unsound. That such setups had no place in topflight international chess.

The look of smugness on his face lasted about as long as a December day in Finland. I played my innovation and watched him freeze, a sudden hesitancy in his previously confident mannerisms. These were the days before soundproof screens separated the players from the audience, and I could hear a ripple of excitement in the hall. Speculation as to whether the move had ever been seen before, which of course I knew it hadn't.

Dubrovnik managed the position well, initially finding the

best moves. But he was consuming huge amounts of time. I could see that he was even less happy than usual. I knew his position, having taken the second pawn, was theoretically as good as it could be, but he was less sure. He clearly had not considered any of this in his pre-match work. How could he have done?

He was a good player. More than good. Ranked six in the world. Yet somehow, pugilist rather than visionary. A flat track bully in the eyes of some. Found wanting in previous world championship cycles when up against the very best. Not a fraud or a phony, but no artist either. Chess was something pure to me, while to him it was something dirty.

Now he was truly on his own. On move seventeen the clocks showed that I had spent ten minutes and he was nearing the hour-and-a-half mark. The final critical moment – Dubrovnik was faced with three options. One, he could simplify by exchanging a bishop for knight and follow by swapping pawns in a way that would wreck his structure. Not great. The result-ing endgame would be very difficult for him. I would expect to grind him down. Secondly, he could just exchange pawns, which would give me scope to further reinforce my grip on the centre, leaving him grovelling without prospects. Finally, he could try and turn the tables, advance his queen onto the same file as my king and turn aggressor.

They say that attack is the best form of defence. It is not always the case, but a strong player does not like being bossed. Psychologically, being proactive is generally the most tempting path to take. The human thing to do. The match is always more attractive than the hose. With only thirty minutes left on his clock for the twenty-three moves needed to make the time control, Dubrovnik lunged with his queen. Just as my analysis predicted, six moves later it was over. He held out his hand and I basked in the cheers of the crowd.

I was exhilarated. I have never felt more complete as either a man or a chess player. The moments after the game were of the purest ecstasy and joy I will most likely ever experience, my mother's death aside. I do not think that even beating Carlsen will be able to compete with that day. It is hard to believe it was more than fifteen years ago. The element of the chess press not under the control of the State was delirious in its praise. Forget Bryne - Fischer. This was truly the game of the century.

'A moment when chess's capacity to surprise washed over me once more and I felt like a child again,' one normally hard-bitten journalist wrote. Sentimental idiot that he was, it was still the best line I had ever seen him craft. 'A game of startling originality. A thing of beauty,' another wrote. Little did I know, this was as good as it was going to get, and multiple forces conspiring against me would soon come to the fore. That even my greatest innovation itself would soon be under attack.

All gambits contain a dilemma. A trade-off. You offer up something in return for something else. Yet there is no promise. It is never certain that what is proffered will yield a greater return. That the sacrifice will not just be pocketed and swallowed up. Not all attacks break through and win. We do not always get what we deserve. Even when we do win, it is never quite what we thought it would be.

Nothing is ever quite enough. A defeat inflicts more pain than a win can bring joy. Normally that is, but the revelation of my gambit was something else. A stunning victory in a game that will be replayed for as long as chess exists. An opening system named after me. Or at least that was what I thought at the time.

They say that the genius does not make sacrifices in life. That they are the ones who get to do exactly what it is that they want to do. The suggestion is that it is those around them who make the real sacrifices. It is not true of course. Mere mortals have nothing meaningful to lose. It is only for the genius that everything has the capacity to fall apart.

That was how it was for me, but I was hardly the first. The State played the central role in Fischer's demise, but it was not only the State, Fischer's very brilliance left him cornered.

It is a sick paradox that only a few of us get to discover. That to continually win is ultimately to lose. That victory is as much of a charade as defeat. That just as when a fire is born and grows in strength, no matter the power, eventually all will turn to ash; so, it is with talent. Both emerge almost from nothing and in the heat of the moment can appear unstoppable. Yet the source is finite. In the end all fires burn themselves out. Time turns everything we say we are to dust. Just as death can be anticipated well before it becomes a reality, so can a growing number of defeats at the chessboard. No one can stand at the summit for all that long.

That was why Fischer got out when he did. Turned his back on it all after beating Spassky. The only way not to lose was not to play. Kasparov was always criticised for saying that if Fischer had played Karpov in 1975 instead of going into exile, Fischer might have lost, or if not then, certainly by the time 1978 came around.

Partly it was the vagaries of Fischer ageing, but also

179

something else. Fischer had destroyed a generation. Spassky, Petrosian, Korchnoi, Tal, Geller, Gligorich, Larsen, Taimanov, Mottram, Wengrower, Page and the others. All scared by him. None believed they could win. Defeated from the moment they sat at the board. For the Soviets, severe repercussions if they did lose, most secretly delighted to let someone else have the dubious pleasure of going down to the brash New Yorker.

Karpov belonged to a new era. Had no baggage. Was not afraid. I cannot help but think that Kasparov was partly right, albeit I would never have been brave enough to say this to Bobby. It was not just Karpov's youth and undamaged mental state. It was Fischer's growing fear.

When you achieve perfection, it can ultimately only be followed by something less. You can keep tempting fate, making it happen, pulling off the same trick, but in the end the inevitable befalls us all. We lose and fall back to earth. In the moments after my famous victory such thoughts would not have occurred to me. Now I live with them all the time.

I had not had a drink for six months prior to playing Dubrovnik. I did not even really want one, which was precisely why I knew it would be fine to engage in some form of small-scale celebration. A meal in a local restaurant with my seconds and a few hangers-on. A bit of pasta. Half a cider before we ate. A couple of glasses of wine with the meal. A whisky chaser by way of nightcap. A couple of ciders in a club after that. No more. I went to bed a happy man. Slept like a baby as they say. Woke up fit and ready for game four. Raring to go.

People point to that night as the turning point. Some say that with those drinks my good intentions went out of the window. It was not that though. I could easily have gone for the rest of my life without the need for another drop. I had the will power, the focus. It was what happened the next day that ruined everything.

Chris Hamish ran a piece in one of the broadsheets suggesting the Greenbecker Gambit, even if he was too ignorant to call it that, was not sound after all. That even after his queen move, there was an unusual knight manoeuvre at Dubrovnik's disposal which would have left his position perfectly fine. Most likely left him a little bit better even. He wrote that while I had won, I had been lucky. It was all something of a fluke.

As I read his article the blood drained from my body and I prayed only for death. Simply too much to take. I went to the restaurant bar and ordered a double whisky. Rolled the ice in the glass, feeling its satisfying clink, before downing it in one and ordering another. Then another. Continually rereading Hamish's article convinced he must be right.

Then it gets a little hazy, but somehow, I missed game four altogether and was defaulted. The first player to suffer such a fate since Bobby Fischer, when he failed to turn up for the second game of the world final with Boris Spassky. He had made a conscious decision not to show. A protest over the presence of a camera, the seating arrangements in the auditorium, the levels of noise. For me it was not quite like that. Rather, I just woke up to be informed that I had missed the fucking thing.

The match is still level, my team told me. It is still all to play for. I vaguely remember Gabriel urging me to get some rest. To get sober. To come back fighting. That was sort of what I did. I knew the alcohol itself was not going to make any difference, so long as my team made proper arrangements to get me to the games on time.

I shrugged off the fact that my second, Shearsby, quit in protest at my alleged unprofessionalism. I would most likely have fired him anyway. There was no question that me missing game four was entirely on my team and they all knew it. Besides, I reasoned, if anything, a drink or two was likely to free me up creatively.

Most likely, this could all have worked out well if the fools in my hire had more of a clue as to what they were doing. Getting me ready for the games that followed should have been a simple task, but they were not up to it.

I did play games five, six and seven. I had chances in each of them. Yet the fact that I had essentially abandoned my hotel room for the bar appeared to have some effect. I was never properly drunk, but never properly sober either, existing in a world of whisky and cider and tobacco while Dubrovnik doubtless sat in his room with a chessboard, a plate of stinking herring and his shit poetry.

For some reason, the patterns I sketched out on beer mats while I drank, never quite translated into accurate variations on the board. With every victory, Dubrovnik looked sadder and sadder, as if he was being buried ever more deeply in a world he had wanted to escape.

After I lost again in game eight the match was over. Dubrovnik offered me his hand with the pensive look of an undertaker, who knows he is going to get paid, but is still wary of offending. Reluctant to intrude on private grief. I touched it briefly before sweeping the chess pieces off the table. The sound they made was louder than I had envisaged, and they scattered further than I thought they would.

A white knight bounced off the stage and hit a child in the second row on the head and she began to cry loudly. That was the final straw. I collapsed into a heap on top of the pieces that lay on the stage around me, the battle now over, and wept and wept.

Don't believe the nonsense that the steward who then intervened was there to help me. He was part of a State-wide conspiracy and it was only in that moment that everything became clear to me. I had been well and truly suckered, just as in the UK Masters all those years ago. I had clearly learned nothing and had only myself to blame. It was the robbery of the century and I had been stupid enough to fall for it.

It was only in the weeks after the match that I asked myself afresh, what did Chris Hamish know about chess? Just because he had said the Greenbecker Gambit was unsound did not necessarily make it so. There was a certain logic to the line he set out, but the more I considered it, the more I wondered if I been too hasty in succumbing to his verdict. Finally, it dawned on me that Hamish had overlooked a potential consequence of his suggested knight manoeuvre and I had thrown away my life's work for nothing at all.

It should have been obvious that Hamish's analysis was misleading. He, in common with the entire British chess establishment had been waiting years for an opportunity to ruin me. It was clever work to find an idea complex enough to throw me off the scent, and Hamish undoubtedly had significant help on this front. Sound or not, it was enough. His mission had been successful. The match was over. I was out.

Was Dubrovnik in on the scam himself? More than likely.

Even he could not have remained so calm at the board unless he knew others were helping him. Was it any wonder that even before I consciously figured it all out, as the steward tried to pick me up off the floor, I had chosen to punch Dubrovnik in the face?

Yes, I claimed afterwards that it had been an involuntary action. That I had simply been trying to regain my balance. I also offered by way of alternative explanation that I had no idea what was happening and feeling somebody's hands on me feared I was going to be murdered, just as any normal person would. It was merely self-defence. A natural reflex. I broke Dubrovnik's nose, or so they say. Assume nothing. The fact that this became the official line just shows who had control of the media at that time. Unfortunately, it was not me.

As he got back to his feet, a tiny amount of blood streaming from his face, Dubrovnik nodded in my direction. 'I would most probably have done the same,' he said, before exiting the stage. I have not seen him since.

22. Eva

I was given a two-year ban from future chess events and ordered by the ECF to attend both a drying out programme in Arizona and an anger management course in Milton Keynes, but I refused to go to either. There was no need. I have had a drink every day of my life since then, but what of it? I am clearly in control of myself and my alcohol consumption. Everything I do is entirely my choice. No one has grounds to say otherwise, so what help could I possibly need?

They said I was fortunate Dubrovnik elected not to press charges. I would have relished my day in court, I can tell you that. Of course, the State could not have allowed such a happening. A few minutes of me in the dock and the foundations of modern-day chess and society as we know it would have come crashing down.

I should have filed a lawsuit of my own. Espionage. Counter-terrorism. Crimes against chess-writing. I did think about this very carefully, but Bobby talked me out of it. 'You run with any of that and you are not going to live long enough to get near a court room,' he told me sadly. I knew he was right. It was a classic stalemate of sorts. It just made me wish that I had hit Dubrovnik harder.

I should have done more to track Chris Hamish down too. It is annoying he is still at liberty to press on with writing – if his prose qualifies for such a noun – but I notice he fears me too much to write about me these days.

I sigh. Push the grey remote button once more and watch the television flicker. Donald Trump, all fake hair and orange skin, is standing there. I always had high hopes for him. Just as the religious right did not mind that he was not a Christian, I was fine that he was not a practising chess player.

I thought he might be the shock the system needed. I was one of the many who assumed he would put the chess authorities back in their box. It was hard to imagine the presidents of FIDE and the ECF being much of a match for his Twitter account. I have been bewildered by Trump's focus on other targets, clearly the chess authorities are even more powerful than I thought if Trump feels constrained in some way.

He promised me he would do more to sort world chess out, back when he used to tap me up for advice on his presidential campaign. What is it with politicians? It seems they will glibly say just about anything to get elected.

I would tell him he had to hit Hillary hard, which he did. I thought I was making headway with my suggestion that First Amendment privileges should be extended to include reasonable expressions using fire. He got a bit prickly on the flag point, even if I suspected that he most likely does not know one end of Old Glory from the other, but I thought we were broadly in agreement.

Trump would tend to glaze over and start playing with his

phone when I tried to explain the differences between FIDE and the ECF to him. In hindsight, I hoped for too much. I know why people still like him. He somehow gets away with living outside the rules. Legitimises bad behaviour. Does not give a fuck. Others project their own wish for such licence onto him. The same with Bill Clinton. Standing outside the system was ever more attractive than being within it. I should know. I hit the button on the controller and the screen goes blank.

I turn off the light and get into the bed. Pull the thin brown blanket over me. I can feel the mattress springs. The lone pillow too soft, devoid of proper shape. The room is not quite dark. The curtains are cheap and flimsy. London light is difficult to snub out entirely.

I hear the rattle of a train in the distance, the rhythm of a city still moving. I try and get comfortable, but it is not easy. My bladder aches. I curse, get up and piss painfully in the sink, but all the ash and charcoal mean it does not drain properly. A pool of reddish urine forms. It is hardly my fault that the sink has been poorly designed, is unable to deal with a tiny bit of paper and charcoal. If I need to go again, I can always use the wardrobe. It is not realistic to expect me to be trudging up and down corridors at this time of night.

I get back into the bed. Shift myself into what should be the right position, but it does not work. I am placing too much weight on my front shoulder. As I wriggle, I find that I am cricking my neck. I try again, but inadvertently crush my arm, which starts to tingle with pins and needles. This is what happens when you don't always sleep in a bed. You forget how. It is not just that though. I have found sleep increasingly difficult in recent years. I don't need as much of it. But there is more going on here than the vagaries of an ageing body.

Time presses most when I try to rest. I hear an invisible clock ticking down. Sense the fragility of my heart, the shallowness of my breath. Fear all those automatic systems I rely on to pilot me through to morning. Suspect they are capable of letting me down. Something I simply would not allow if I was awake. We are at our most vulnerable when we sleep. Only half a notch from death.

Perhaps it is worse still than that. The dead are freed from everything. No longer haunted by their dreams. I see everything so much more clearly when I sleep. That is what scares me most. Chess pieces dance in curious shapes and patterns, a different game, not the one I know. But still I must play, continually betrayed by both my own forces and those ranged against me. I am trapped in every game I have ever lost, but without the relief of a checkmate, a handshake and the prospect of beginning again.

The mistakes I have made are like a permanent scar tissue on my brain. Over and over. I see other things gone by. Mum, Dad. They are alive when I dream, and I do not want them to be. I want them both to stay dead. Her for her successes, him for his failures. I am better off without them. As clear to me all these years later as on the days on which they died.

Despite the thinness of the sheet, the bed is wet with sweat. It is better not to try and force sleep. Just close my eyes. What will be will be. Gently resting. Most likely as beneficial to the system as actual sleep and without the side-effect of terrible dreams. Sometimes I do doze without realising it. My body knows how to take what is necessary. I must trust it. Perhaps sleep was never realistic.

I don't even care about Carlsen and Caruana as I lie here. I think about my folder. What I write in it is not just about them or my path back to glory. Rather, it is the closest thing I have to a story. It is what makes sense of my choices. I can but view the world through an assessment of chess players and chess ideas and without it, I am nothing, devoid of any spark.

My words will probably one day form a training manual for the aspiring young player, an inspirational guide for everyone else. I will be properly bracketed with Bobby. Our time in exile. Our routes back to the light.

I did ask Bobby on occasion why he thought I was not more famous already, but the question never really interested him. He could be a little self-obsessed could Bobby. Something his friends always readily forgave him for. 'You are you Tennessee,' he would say. 'Find a way to make your peace with that.' Then we would most likely be off again with another game of blitz.

Sometimes I would chat to him about the Gunpowder Plot while we played. Guy Fawkes, Robert Catesby, John and Christopher Wright and all the rest. I could never quite gauge his level of interest. I would tell him that those who had played their part in trying to burn London to the ground formed a similar lineage to the previous chess champions of the world. Men who would be remembered and honoured for all eternity. That I was in the unique position of having the potential to be inducted in both halls of fame, provided I got the timing right. I remember Bobby looking up from a complex position when I first shared this thought with him. 'You British,' he joked. 'You are all completely nuts.'

I chuckle as I remember the banter we used to share. Friendship is important, if you are lucky enough to find someone worth being friends with. Bobby had his limitations, but at least we understood each other.

There was someone else once, more than a friend. Eva. An International Master from America. Her parents were both Russians who had settled in New York when she was a child. We met at a tournament in London. I was playing in the Invitational. She was in the Open. Eva was younger than me, but not all that much. I was twenty-three, she was nineteen.

It was a long time ago. My future pathway was already clear. I was in the world top twenty, the England number one, an assault on the world title already looming in my future. For her, things were less obvious. She was not really any good, and of course that became a source of tension as time went on.

She had short, black hair. Dark brown eyes. She always wore formal suit jackets and tight jeans. Long leather boots in winter, sandals in summer. I first set eyes on her when she stood watching the end of one of my games, staring intently at the position, never looking at me. I was winning and found a clever trick to bring the game to a rapid end. For half-a-moment our eyes met, and she gave me a tiny almost imperceptible nod and then was gone. I felt a connection of sorts. That something had passed between us. As ever my intuition did not let me down.

Several days later, I was walking past the analysis room and I saw her sitting by herself, scoresheet in hand, going through one of her games. 'Can I look?' I said and she nodded so I sat down, and we went through it. It was the perfect way for us to get talking. For me to find a way to converse at any rate. All in all, it was not a bad game, but I could see more than either of the players had. I managed to find just the right tone.

Supportive and encouraging but also perceptive. I always was insightful company especially if my companion wanted to talk about chess.

We had a meal in an Italian the following day. I had pesto and pasta and she had a margarita pizza. We both drank white wine and shared some garlic bread, oozing with butter. Not very adventurous, but somehow it worked. The music, the noise of other customers, the sound of traffic on the street outside. None of it mattered. There was only us.

I was captivated by the way she looked so earnest when she was talking, often clasping her hands together for extra empha-sis. She told me things I had already half-heard about her, her father still barely able to speak English after all these years, a janitor at the school she attended. The sort of place I imagine had metal detectors at the gate where it was common for kids to fail to turn up one day and then never be spoken of again.

Her mother worked in a laundrette. Sweated to buy a few shares on the stock market every month to build a better future. Never stopped believing in the American dream. Most of Eva's chess was funded by a New York chess programme that had a wealthy benefactor. Eva was the youngest of three. Her older sisters, both already married, had long since fled.

Before we knew it, lunch had merged into dinner and we were still sat there talking – the purest personal connection I have ever felt. I would still be sat there with her now if such a thing were possible.

Chess was Eva's way out. Her school had a serious chess club. The New York scene the place to be. She might not have been strong enough to make it purely as player, but who knew? I could see she had not yet wholly discounted the possibility, just as clearly as I knew that one day she would have to do so.

There were other ways she said. Writing, teaching, working with stronger players as a second. It had never occurred to me that someone could, or would even want to make a life in chess if they could not be the best, but as she spoke, I understood that it might be a possibility. Feeling relief that my talent would never reduce me to such meagre prospects.

To begin with, everything was good. More than good. We were inseparable at tournaments, tweaked our schedules so that we were always in the same place. She introduced me to new things, gave me a different outlook. I got quite into Russian poets. Valery Bryusov, Boris Pasternak even, we would take it in turns to read their works to each other. 'The Guest' by Anna Akhmatova was our favourite.

I loved her I suppose. She humanised me. Introduced me to her friends. Occasionally we had outings in groups to restaurants and museums and parks. Activities not always founded on chess. I had never previously known the joy to be found in frittering away an afternoon with somebody that you loved. Just talking and laughing. Having sex if you wanted to. Creating a world within a world where everything that once seemed important came to matter less. It was a revelation. I felt altogether a happier and more rounded human being. Then of course it all went wrong.

There are several factors I could point to. I was always suspicious of her Russian origins. At least the possibility that she might be a spy. Any number of the Russian players might have put her up to getting close to me to try and steal my secrets. Not just my actual preparation ideas, but my psychological make-up. How I approached life in general, adversity, other such questions that might give a State-backed grandmaster the edge against me. There was also her jealousy. Not in relation to other women, that was never the problem. No, it was more her jealousy of my chess. The burning brightness of my talent in contrast to her more prosaic abilities.

There were also things she would say. That I was possessive and irrational. Prone to mood swings, particularly when I drank. Once she saw me messing about with some matches and a can of petrol in a quiet alley behind the hotel we were staying in and misunderstood what I was doing. Just the normal things that might impact any relationship.

The truth is that the happier I got, the more I started to lose. It was almost imperceptible to begin with. I would still win the events I entered, but I might make an uncharacteristic blunder in one of the games and lose from a position where I really should not have done. Then there was a phase where I would start to slip up slightly more and generally only come second or third in competitions I had won easily in previous years. Still reasonable results, but I was no longer standing out as the undisputed future of chess in quite the same way.

Things came to head in Berlin where I placed tenth out of twelve and did not win a single game. I saw then that if I stayed with her that I would never be the world champion. She made life too easy. Too soft. I needed to be single-minded and ruthless or I would wind up just another player.

The look she gave me when I told her. Somewhere between hatred and surprise. It winds me even now to remember it.

'I really did not think you would treat me this way,' she said. Playing with the almost regal-looking buttons on her blazer. We were stood in the centre of Berlin, winter snow falling softly around us. A moment of intensity when lovers part, where one believes that there is everything still to say, and the other knows that there is nothing left to talk about.

'You will regret this,' she said, before turning and leaving me alone not far from Hitler's bunker, with only the cold and my thoughts. I did not particularly feel anything. That would come later. Even now I know it was both a hard decision and the right one. Another gambit of sorts, perhaps the truest. I sacrificed her to become champion of the world. A crown that all these years later I am still to win.

Later I heard that, despite the age gap, she was in a relationship with Michael Wengrower. Still, my results improved almost immediately. I was back on track. Chess and fire, altogether more reliable and truer mistresses. Easier to control. A better pathway for the truly exceptional than ordinary love.

If in this moment I happen to think to her, to remember times gone by, it is the product of age and whimsy, nothing more. I know my increasing tendency toward sentimentality is a major weakness that I will need to root out if I am going to stand any chance against Magnus.

Still, do not underestimate how tough life has made me. Or my capacity to do what is necessary to achieve my goals. That is why despite his youth and his wealth I doubt any bookmaker would be brave enough to take any money on Magnus. That should tell you everything you need to know.

Finally, I sleep, and my mind twists the world to other possibilities, distorts reality into a myriad of smaller shapes, like a glass smashing and fragmenting into pieces on the floor. Slivers sharp and bright, no longer salvageable, incapable of being moulded back into a whole. My mind dreams the stories differently. Sometimes I am with Eva. She is here with me in this room. I can feel the softness of her breasts against my chest, the smell of her perfume. Hear the peacefulness in her breathing. Am surrounded by her warmth. Perhaps she has just popped out to brush her teeth. Is close at hand. This is the glow I bask in.

Sometimes what happened is twisted a little differently. There are more recriminations. Others are involved. Her brothers. People think it is me who will not leave her alone. That the decision to end it had not been mine. That we might not actually have been together in quite the way that I thought. Sometimes there is violence. Fear. Misunderstanding. Things my general mistrust might spring from.

Sometimes the confusion of the night is darker still and I am not a famous chess player. Something smaller, less successful, the things that I imagine have happened to me have not. These are the darkest dreams of all, and I wait for morning and reality to reassert itself. My demons are not real of course, but is there any wonder that I occasionally take a drink?

23. Four queens

I part dream, half re-remember. The past cloying to me like sweat. The lightest of sleeps, the bleakest of memories. The UK masters. Dubrovnik. Eva's brothers. This translucent time when night edges toward morning always leaves my defences at their weakest, the past permeating the surface of my conscience covering what once was pure with an indelible stain, one that clings like oil to the feathers of a doomed bird.

Here in this room, in the gloaming, reality could be anything. Anything at all. People and stories continually distort and reshape in my mind – and all that might have happened mixes with fire and chess pieces that dance a demonic waltz.

Perhaps I have come to fear sleep. It does not cleanse so much as confuse. It is more difficult to know who you really are when you are lying on your back. I well understand the trick of forcing your brain down one path, then another. Scrambling your thoughts to the point that you can no longer be sure of anything. There might not be any other way to survive.

That infernal poker game tugs at me again. I wish it was no more than a dream, a confusion, a distortion, but I would not be in this room now if that were the case. I see the final card being turned over for what feels like the millionth time. The moment when everything was lost. I feel the pain with the same intensity as always. Like a punch in the stomach that leaves me gasping for breath. Trying to right myself in a world that has turned out not to be quite the place I thought it was.

The gasps of the onlookers. A sense of horror as to the enormity of what I have done, as they rip my poker chips from me, basking in the audacity of their well-executed hit job. I sit bolt upright in the bed, jolted fully awake, adrenaline coursing through my body. I feel winded, smaller somehow than when I settled down to sleep. It takes me a minute or two to regulate my breathing. Just my respiratory system playing tricks on me. I am more than equal to all such nonsenses.

I light up a cigarette and my lungs immediately feel better, even if the rest of me does not. This shitty room. This shitty world that will not let me rest. It really is not fair. I steel myself. No one said a life of this magnitude was going to be easy.

My mouth has a metallic taste in it, but I spit on the floor and that seems to help. I try to buck myself up. I rub my face with my hands. The feel of my beard on my fingers is always comforting. My coping strategy is to think things through. To retell my stories. To put it all out there. That way I will at least get it out of my system for a while.

Those seven cards offered so much and delivered so little. Four queens should be unbeatable and undoubtedly would have been in any fair game. I should have seen it coming. Bobby told me that the casino would be my undoing. He always reckoned that armies of agents had most likely spent their whole careers in training on the off chance that they would one day be able to fleece chess players of our standing.

I will not make the same mistake again, even if I sometimes fear my moment has passed, that my quest for glory might already have faltered somewhere between the card table, the bar and the floor Dubrovnik fell on.

Chess and poker are very different games. Perhaps I did not always fully appreciate that in the way I do now. Cards require skill, but luck plays a much bigger part than in chess. Yes of course, a chess player might go wrong, fail to find the best line, mishandle the clock, but what induces any of those things? Talent, or lack thereof? Perhaps technical. Perhaps psychological. The weakling who cracks under time pressure is hardly a true warrior.

A chess player rarely has anyone else to blame. We exist in a world of perfect information. Nobody else chooses to place our pieces on any of the squares they stand on. Our opponent is never able to do anything that was not sitting there in plain sight. Very few chess players run into the kind of global conspiracies that I regularly did – an extremely lucky opponent, a mild dose of flu, mangling our opening preparation, these are all simply excuses that losers trot out because the truth is unbearable. Sometimes a chess player's ideas are simply proven not to be good enough. Yet they are all we have. To openly admit their defectiveness would be to leave ourselves naked.

Cards offer a very different proposition. You must assess the odds and the percentages and then trust entirely to the gods – assuming nobody is cheating. In chess who has the better of an imbalance depends on what follows, it is what the player makes of the situation that has arisen as much as anything.

Future events are there to be shaped by the work of the player's own fair hands. Poker is no one's mistress. I can know that I have four outs. That the odds of me winning the hand are say 75%, but there is nothing I can do to then influence the turn of the cards. I can but sit there and trust to real luck. Dumb luck. No luck.

Without question chess is the better game. I really shouldn't have tried to play something else. I suppose a part of me always needed another outlet for my more reckless side. Who wouldn't want to make easy money without breaking a sweat? If things had unfolded as they should have done I would by now have been extremely rich.

For a long time, I was only a social poker player. A few hundred here and there. A pleasant diversion from my real work at the board. An opportunity for a quiet drink as much as anything. I did not properly consider what I was getting myself into when I started to play more seriously. What the risks might be. When you are used to winning as often as I am, you can sometimes take your powers for granted. The vagaries of time and a different game can leave you short at the very moment when you least expect it.

I dabbled a little on the chess circuit. Far less than most chess players I know. I have colleagues, top grandmasters who could not scrape together £20k a year who found they could make that in a single night at the poker table. Some drifted away from chess altogether as a result.

Poker does not hold you in the same way, Page once told me, it is not beautiful like chess, but it is far more lucrative, and defeat does not really hurt. It is all somehow less personal. You do not blame yourself for any missteps, what happens is never down to your decisions alone. What will be will be. You can only lose money, whereas defeat at chess is akin to losing your soul.

It transpired Page was not entirely right to think Poker was somehow painless, but the basic thrust of his theory might be broadly accurate. At least I would always have confidently asserted all this, until I managed to lose a fuck of a lot of money.

While a single hand might be luck, over the long run an ability to calculate properly will ensure that chips flow your way across the poker table. If sensible, a half-decent chess player should be able to make a stack. No single game should ever be able to make or break you. My own wisdom and good sense on this point should have been enough to save me but proved insufficient when ranged against the combined forces of the State, who lured me to my doom. If anything, I am a victim of my own good choices, but there we have it.

After 'losing' to Dubrovnik, I had a two-year ban to contend with. This did not stop me from playing in invitational events, even if for reasons I could not fully fathom tournament organisers went very quiet on me. I assumed at first it was because my strength would make a mockery of their congresses. That other players would not want to play, knowing that they could not win. Then I realised that the State had blackballed me, leaving me in a position as perilous as that of Guy Fawkes when he mounted the scaffolding. I certainly knew there were many in the English Chess Federation who wanted to see me hung, drawn and quartered!

I pressed my case via the usual backchannels. The ECF's Director of Home Chess, a man long suspected of secretly being a dissident. There was even a rumour that he had once said that if Yorkshire wanted to have its own grading system that was fine by him!

Then there was the nice lady at FIDE who had been appointed as my point of contact. I could tell from the way she always sighed a lot and tried to get me off the phone whenever I called, that she found my plight too much to bear. I was always convinced that whenever she hung up, it was so she could go and weep. I certainly worried that if she showed me too much sympathy, they would wipe her out. I did tell her this once or twice. She's still around, so I am relieved that my advice managed to keep her alive.

The point I always made to both was that losing to Dubrovnik in such ridiculous circumstances more than proved I was the strongest player in the world. That if Dubrovnik and FIDE had not conspired to cheat me; I would have been preparing for a world final. The least that the authorities could do was to lay on a series of well-remunerated tournaments on my behalf. Really, they should just have proclaimed that I was the world champion. None of this seemed to cut much ice. Hard to believe I know, but I had become something of a pariah on the chess scene.

The powers that be did not understand how much I could have done for chess's image as its new official bad boy. The scuffle between me and Dubrovnik generated headlines around the world, even if the media seemed to think it had been my fault. Even more galling, that Dubrovnik had the better of it.

I sometimes think this was when the fake news was born. I am sure Donald Trump recently highlighted this incident as being when he first noticed the phenomenon, even if he did make the point obliquely, such that I am one of the few who really understood what he was driving at.

Look how fascinated you all were by Bobby, I would tell them. Now I've emerged as someone who stands outside the system, a player generating mainstream media coverage and still you cannot see the opportunity that is right in front of you. You are getting both controversy-generating headlines and my brilliance, without some of Bobby's idiosyncrasies. What more could you want; you total fucking idiots? Chess is never going to make it big while it is being run by short-sighted bureaucrats who do not know one end of a pawn from the other. Sadly, my charm offensive did not work.

Gabriel told me that I had become too hot to handle. That my approach was not the right one. That my best bet would have been to agree to check into the drying out clinic in Arizona and to endure the anger management training in Milton Keynes. To properly sober up. To build a better understanding of my triggers and my coping mechanisms, whatever the fuck that might mean. To come out and offer apologies all round. To say that I had something of a problem with drink and depression but following treatment I was now much better and truly grateful to all those who had helped me. To find a way of conveying that I was committed to never hitting anyone ever again. To cut my dick off in other words.

I told Gabriel it was never going to happen. That he was demonstrating the mindset of every middle manager and back-street accountant I had most likely never met. True greats would never behave in such a way. Never apologise, never compromise, never do what is expected. Donald Trump certainly has it right on that score! Therein lies the road to immortality. That is what separates people like me from people like you, I told Gabriel.

I know Bobby Fischer would have agreed with me. We talked about things like this frequently when he was alive. People would ask him why he was so sensitive to the noise in the playing hall, the presence of the cameras. Why he would continually seek larger and larger purses for his matches and then sometimes offer to play for nothing. It was not madness. He did not in my experience lack rationality. Those who disagree in the main did not really know him like I did. It is just what people like us do. We push at the boundaries and see where it takes us. He became the greatest world champion of all time, and one day soon I will follow. We are both destined to be remembered in a blaze of glory.

Inevitably I took out legal proceedings against FIDE at the International Court of Sporting Arbitration and lodged petitions with various national chess associations for restraint of trade, but it all took time. I suppose I started to gamble a little more, for something to do as much as anything.

I set off to the casino that terrible night with my spirits high and the world at my feet. I saw it like this: at some point my ban on playing would either be lifted or would expire. Either way, a comeback would be easy. I had learnt my lesson from the Dubrovnik debacle. I would simply avoid reading the press next time around. I had been crazy to let them mess with my head.

I was essentially the world champion in exile. The more I thought about it, the more this point seemed obvious to me and no doubt everybody else. While I waited for the right time to secure my inevitable destiny, well, why not have a little fun? A quiet drink and a game of cards was surely the least I deserved.

24. Keith

The Gentleman's Casino was not necessarily in the best part of London. I think back to the long walk through a multi-story carpark – all concrete and orange signage – to get to the entrance. It was prudent to watch your back on the way in and, if the table had happened to be kind, your pockets on the way out.

The reception area was flanked by two large, balding security men, in cheap grey suits, the Casio insignia on a red cloth background woven onto their lapels. You had to be a member in order to play, although it seemed that anyone who knew their date of birth was permitted to join. Yet nonetheless, somehow the cheap plastic membership card gave the whole thing a sense of exclusivity.

There was a flight of stairs up to the floor of the casino itself, a large room that smelt of hoovering and polish and the seepage of money. Huge television screens beamed football into every corner. There were no clocks on the walls. Free soft drinks were always available for the players, an innovation chess would have done well to copy, albeit perhaps with a stronger selection of beverages. A plethora of fruit machines piloted mainly by fat old ladies in tracksuits who studied the display screens with the same level of concentration that I would a game of chess. There was a roof terrace through the large glass doors in the far corner, with a few tables and chairs and cigarette bins, which it appeared to be good form to ignore in favour of stamping fag-ends into the deck.

The Casino reminded me of every chess tournament hall I had ever played in before I reached the elite level. It wasn't so much the decor. That was plusher than would be found at most chess events. No, rather it was the way it felt. A sense of excitement and anticipation heightened by the somewhat stale air. The opportunity to join with others in the immediacy of the moment, where life is reduced to and given meaning by the wait for a turn of a card or the move of a piece. A place where anything might be possible.

The roulette wheel is a mug's game. The odds stacked against the players, yet the sound of the white ball bouncing on the black disc, the way it dances from slot to slot before spinning and coming to rest on a number with a degree of pre-ordained certainty, is something to behold. All outcomes would appear possible, inevitable almost, if you thought about them for long enough. It had to be Red. Black. Even numbers. Odd numbers. A nice green zero. Number 12.

If I ever watched for a while, I could see the patterns as clearly as in a game of chess. I was generally wise enough to know the perception was a mirage. A false narrative. The wheel has no memory. The stories as to what might happen exist in the heads of the watchers and nowhere else. I did forget all this on occasion, but what to do?

Then there were the blackjack tables. In hindsight I should most probably have played this game. The dealer still has an edge, but it is not so great, and a skilful player has a reasonable chance of eking out a return. The truth is, I found it repetitive and boring. Stick. Take another card. Split. Wait for the turn. Nothing to do but watch. Poker is so reductionist compared to chess, but blackjack takes it to a whole other level.

So it was that I mainly played poker. I liked the feel of the chips in my hand. Not dissimilar in some ways to playing with chess pieces I had captured, feeling their smoothness, bumping them together, forces now wholly mine. The poker chips were of different colours and values. Blue, red, green, black, purple – the high denomination plaques I generally preferred to use once I had started winning.

There is always someone both richer and poorer than you in London. Even a serious player on the London gambling scene like myself would acknowledge that. I had built up a big stake over the proceeding weeks. More money than most will handle in a lifetime. The trouble is, there is always a game where the stakes are higher. I should have been more careful. Rather one day as a lion than one hundred as a sheep is all well and good, but not if you get eaten.

The previous few weeks had been terrific. As I picked off the patzers over the green baize, my confidence grew and grew. I felt like a master of the universe once more, my winning streak rivalling anything I had achieved at the chess board. It seemed entirely logical, given the brilliance of my play, that the amount I was prepared to gamble on a single night would continue to grow. £1000. £5000, £10,000. It was as if I had been touched by God. I simply could do no wrong. Before I knew it, I was sitting on a fortune.

I was mainly playing with doctors and lawyers. People who ran their own businesses. Men of mystery from the street who could not quite be placed but were respected for their card play and their worldliness, to say nothing of the money they could bring to the table, the origins of which were no one else's business.

The fact that you would not want to ask too many questions part of the allure, the feeling of being in a sub-culture where you truly belonged. This was a world where to draw up a seat and buy chips was to shut out the mundanities of everyday life. It was a form of coming home. I liked the easiness of it all. How it mirrored the enclosed world of the chess tournament. As I moved up the tables, increasingly my fellow players were famous pop singers, Russian oligarchs, people of serious wealth.

I should have realised that the Russians were inevitably going to be working together to thwart me. I am not even sure now whether any of them were oligarchs. Much more likely that they were spies pure and simple, who had happened in on an opportunity too good to miss.

It must have been obvious to everyone that if I was bankrupted, it would make my chess comeback much harder. I would lack the means to overturn my ban. Would not have the resources to put in place the team necessary to support my comeback. I would well and truly be in zugzwang.

Besides which, I am sure the Russians thought they could learn more about my psychological makeup as a chess player from my poker. I should have been wiser to it all. At the first hint of a Russian accent I should have left the casino and never gone back. The trap was so obvious that I failed to see it altogether.

There are not many people out there who can say that they have walked into a casino with £400k and walked out later that same evening with precisely nothing. Fewer still who have managed to lose £600k on a single hand – I was up before I was down you see. Everything was going my way.

In chess you pursue your winning positions to the very end. In poker you need to know when to quit, and it turns out I did not. Albeit, I doubt they would have let me leave when I was sitting on a stash, had I tried to. I cannot beat myself up for carrying on. It could and should all have been so different. Best to think of it as an investment decision that did not work out.

I will remember my fellow players on that final table for the rest of my life. Heck, I was related to one of them. My cousin Keith was playing with seemingly limitless chips. A much younger, extremely pretty woman in a white sequined cocktail dress and black high heels who was hanging off his shoulder that fateful night, most likely trying to catch my eye. Fellow punters nodding at Keith's every comment with extreme deference. Seeking autographs and selfies. Basking in the reflected glory of a supposedly successful man.

I had first spotted Keith in the casino a few evenings earlier but had not recognised him, faces never having been my strong point. Yet when we happened to both be washing our hands in the gents, I could feel him looking at me as if he knew me. For a moment I assumed he was one of my fans. Famous chess player recognised in London casino is hardly a story. The sort of thing that could have happened to me on a regular basis.

The way he hesitated before offering a greeting gave me pause. Triggered the thought that we might *actually* know each other. I stood stock-still, waited for him to break the silence. When in doubt, doing nothing and all that. After a pause he said 'hello Terr... Tennessee,' and I knew at that moment it was Keith.

He had the sort of fake politeness about him that the shifty often do. He knew how to pretend to be your mate. All that false London charm. He nodded at me, asked how I was keeping. To his credit he did enquire about my chess. Unbelievably, despite all the press, he had heard nothing about my match with Dubrovnik. This is what happens when people live in a bubble and lose track of what is really going on in the world.

We shared a few drinks that night. Reminisced about the old times we both pretended had been better than they were. He said how close he had always felt to my mother then told me a little more about his music, but I wasn't really listening as people never show themselves at their best when banging on about their ambitions and supposed accomplishments.

My mother could not write. Keith could not sing. Yet somehow the world was more accepting of the pair of them than it ever was of me. I will grudgingly acknowledge that despite my best efforts, I could not help but admit I had heard of a few of Keith's songs. I had hoped at the time that he might have been making it up. That it might have been a different Keith who had sung them, that he was just pretending to be someone he was not. He always had a capacity for fantasy about him.

Sadly, my later research proved beyond reasonable doubt that Keith was indeed Keith. I have phoned up a few music stations over the years to tell them that this is not a man who should be allowed on the airwaves. That with regards to what happened at the casino Keith was as culpable as any of them.

The Establishment is never interested. They will always protect their own. Whether he was a Russian agent or sent by FIDE or the ECF, I cannot be sure. I have no doubt that one way or another he was integral to the efforts to steer me onto the rocks. That is family for you.

It saddens me that I have no real conception of what a normal family life might be like. You might say that I protest too much. That all the elements most people associate with families were there for me. A mother. A father. A brother. A house. A school. An introduction and frequent lifts to and from chess. Yet this is only to see the surface.

A house without love is only a house. I always, right from the beginning, felt different, unwanted, somehow separate. If there are details I do not want to talk about, I trust you will accept that some things are best left unsaid. That the fashion today for everyone talking about everything is not my way.

The trouble is that while the chains of family may be invisible, they will continually pull you down like the heaviest of anchors. Keith was as bad as Gabriel who was as bad as my mother and my useless ineffectual father. To misquote Larkin, they fuck you up, the whole fucking lot of them. When it transpired that the chess world did not want me either, was it any wonder that I struck out on my own? That I chose a life on the streets instead?

Do you understand how freeing the streets feel compared to the chains I found myself in? There are no expectations on those who chose to stand outside society. Few rules that need to be followed. Charities dole out plenty of food. It does not take much to find a hostel or a cheap hotel if you are prepared to comply with the fire regulations.

I once spent Christmas Eve night in a pool hall with a washed-up drunk who dribbled and played badly. I can honestly say I was happy. Grateful to be so far removed from my family, my past, racking up points that meant something and nothing as we took it in turns to sink red and yellow coloured balls into the plastic pockets.

I remember the feel of chalking my queue, the smell of the green baize. It was all a form of heaven. The ambience not all that different from the casino. If I have no meaningful template for normality, I am lucky I was blessed with a talent that rendered that chink in my armour irrelevant. I always understood that whatever the game, the game is everything.

I seem to have become side-tracked again, one of the habitual dangers of genius. Anyway, Keith must have been watching me for a while. He doubtless knew he was too much of a non-entity for me to recognise him without an introduction. He might well have sold millions of records, but apart from those who bought them, I am sure no one else had ever heard of him.

Keith had plenty of time to set the whole thing up. How else would two Russian agents have happened to ingratiate themselves with me in that particular casino? I will grudgingly admit that the full machinations of the workings of State espionage remain beyond me.

Sergi was tall and thin, with a crooked nose and a hint of scouse in his Russian accent. He would nod at me with reserved politeness, but he never said much. He always wore an expensive tailored black suit and black tie, looking every inch the undertaker that in some ways he was.

His slim fingers were never still, always playing with his chips, such that if I ever won any of them, they would feel sweaty. When he walked, his movements were springy and over-coordinated in a way that reminded me of a cat. He smelt faintly of strong spirits but vodka most likely had the same effect on him as orange juice might on others. He probably had Putin's number in his mobile. He had doubtless been trying to rig chess matches for the Russians since the Karpov era of the 1970s at least.

Alexander, Sergi's somewhat younger colleague, was a man who did not appear to be in the best of health. Grossly over-weight he would periodically waddle to the roof terrace and lean against the barrier with a cigarette in each hand, shaking and sweating while singing the chorus of 'Mambo Number Five' over and over with a chuckle in his deep Russian accent.

It was rumoured that he ran a number of brothels, but he never mentioned this to me, so either it was not true, or he recognised that I would have no interest in such a thing. Alexander wore a bright Hawaiian shirt, heavily stained with sweat under each armpit. A huge gold medallion hung around his neck. He was always keen to engage in banter.

'Hey Mr Grandmaster,' he would say with a friendly chuckle, 'go easy on us please. We do not have your big brain! No violence either! We are not as tough as you!' Then he would slap his thighs hard and tears of laughter would stream down his face.

Even now, when I know it was all a con, I miss the camaraderie that seemed to exist between us. His humour was just a ploy to set me at my ease before ripping me off, but I cannot wholly hate him. The truth is he understood me. We understood each other. In some ways we were kindred spirits. Simple hustlers going about our business. It was just on one occasion he got the better of me. I am not always so philosophical, but I sensed a brother in Alexander, he was certainly more fun to be around than Gabriel ever was.

The final player on our table was a short black lady of indeterminate age. She might have been fifty, perhaps thirty. It was the way she was turned out, heavy makeup, dark sunglasses she never lifted, which made it difficult to tell. Everybody who plays poker is wearing a mask of some sort. Trying to at any rate. She was no different. However much she needed to play, wanted to play, she held her disdain for the whole thing a little closer to the surface than most.

This manifested itself in the reluctance with which she touched her poker chips and her general reticence to engage with the rest of us. She wore an expensive brown fur coat, diamond chandelier earrings, jewelled rings on every finger. There was always some sort of personal bodyguard looking on discretely. She sipped vodka and tonic and rested the glass on a silver matt.

We had been playing together on and off, with others, for the previous week or so. The stakes were high, but the money seemed to end up roughly back where it started. Keith had taken a stash from me the previous night with a better full house than mine, but I reclaimed it with a nice flush early in the evening.

The thing about Keith that annoyed me most was that it seemed to just be a game to him. He cared more for the free drink and food that was provided, the pretty girl on his arm, the questions from his fans, then he did the flow of the money around the table. I wanted to punch him on the nose, to shake him from an insouciance that rivalled Dubrovnik's, but he was fortunate that just my imagining this was enough for me to keep my entirely natural impulses in check.

I was also jealous of his fans to begin with, but I reminded myself that my own were simply more respectful and would never dream of putting on me in the way his did. I suppose all singers are actors too. That his studied indifference was doubtless part of their plan to lull me into a false sense of security. To trick me into not concentrating properly. Had I known this at the time, I would definitely have punched him.

25. The irony of the king

That terrible night everything was going my way. Nearly every hand had been a dream. Being dealt pocket aces in the very first round appeared an omen for what was to follow. Full houses, runs and straights, all too often I had the nuts – a hand that simply could not be beaten. Even when I had nothing, my bluff was often enough to take the pot.

Yes, of course I had some reverses, but they were irrelevant in the scheme of things. The stakes were getting exhilaratingly high, and I was winning and saw each upping of the ante as a gift. I was giddy in the moment. Enjoying the hit of the money, the rush of winning. I had most likely made more in the previous few hours than in the entirety of a chess career at the top of the game.

It was getting late. The warm bonhomie, such as it was, of my fellow players had long since cooled. I could see something akin to hatred in their eyes. Even Alexander was not cracking jokes anymore. What I did not realise was that the stakes we were playing for were not a lot of money for any of them. This was still just play, or a government mission. It certainly was not fundamental to their personal financial viability, whereas the mound of plaques on the green felt in front of me represented the entirety of my wealth.

Why I did not walk away when I was up, I will never know. I did mean to go home. To call it a night, but when you think your luck is in you want to make the most of it. You always want more. I should have been given credit afterwards for at least considering the option of acting more prudently – the hand where it all went wrong had been meant to be my last, which I suppose as point of fact it was.

It started so well. My first two cards gave me what is known as pocket queens and seated next to the dealer and betting first I thought that was worth £50k. Keith and the jewelled black lady were next to bet and both folded leaving just the Russians.

Sergi paused for a long time. Played with his poker chips. I was sure he was struggling. It transpires I misjudged his hesitation. More likely he had an earpiece through which he was receiving instructions and the reception was a touch crackly. Then he matched my bet. Alexander immediately followed suit, grinning broadly, '...a little bit on Monica all night long,' he sang to himself, his good mood now mysteriously restored.

Next came the flop. A queen, a king and a five. I now had three queens, and it had to be assumed, the nuts. I pushed hard and put a further £150k in the pot. Sergi, playing more quickly this time, raised me to £200k. Alexander folded, but with a suspiciously big smile for one who had just lost so much money.

'You are killing us, Grandmaster,' he said. 'Your brain is too big; your fists are too strong. We are not in your league. Thank God for woman and song, as I'm out of money now,' he laughed.

One way or another the two of them were working together. I was starting to grow suspicious even at the time, but what could I do? I did not want to write off £200k and I had a brilliant hand, but there were several scenarios I needed to consider carefully. First, Sergi could already have three kings. That was extremely unlikely though. Secondly, he might have a pair of kings or possibly even kings and fives. Thirdly he might be stone cold bluffing me.

I suspected that he had something, but not enough. That was the most likely alternative and the one that suited me best. I was ecstatic as I considered what it meant, and my initial suspicion melted like snow in springtime. A few minutes from now, I would be leaving the casino with a million pounds in my pocket.

Fool, fool, fool.

I made the only logical move and raised his £200 to £250k, so I was now in for £300k. Sergi followed my bet but made no effort to raise further. The pot was now huge, most likely the biggest ever seen in this part of London.

There were numerous spectators now. People who could only dream of playing for stakes like this. An Indian man picked at his teeth with a toothpick and stared on intently. A lot of the casino staff seemed to have found a reason to gather and look on. Then came the turn card and it was the happiest moment of my life since the death of my mother – it was a queen. I had four queens! An amazing hand, mathematically almost certain to be the best on the table.

My dilemma was that I did not want to put so much down that Sergi folded. I elected for a mere £100k. I have often wondered if this was the big mistake. Would a more significant sum have caused him to fold? Was what followed all my own fault?

Probably not. It had nothing to do with the bet or what was on the table. Whatever you do makes no difference if the whole thing is rigged. That is the only explanation for what followed. Sergi knew how the cards were going to fall. He looked at me. Stared at the two queens on the table. Pretended he was trying to assess what might be in my hand. Sized up my stack of chips, leaned forward and asked me how much I had left.

I half-shrugged, trying to contain my excitement, praying for a massive mistake on his part, one which seemed to follow when he leaned forward and said, 'All in,' pushing about £400k into the middle. I heard Keith say, 'Oh shit,' under his breath. Just his way of covering his own tracks. He was obviously as guilty as any of them.

'All in,' I said, trying to keep any hint of hysteria or exhilaration from my voice. It did not matter though. He had made his choice. There was no need to act now. It was what it was. Done. Victory was almost mine. My remaining chips now in the middle. The pot into seven figures. I saw that the casino manager was in attendance, a bear of a man who could have spent a lifetime working in a place like this for a fraction of what was on the table now.

A few more members of the security team also made their presence noticed. Expressionless. I still wonder how they train them to give so little away. Everyone was watching. No one moving a muscle. Doubtless the right people would step in if Sergi caused a scene when he lost.

A glamorous woman in a sparkly gold dress came and perched near the edge of the table. She smiled at me and winked conspiratorially. I felt a slight stirring in my groin but forced myself to remain completely focussed on the job in hand. It was not so different from some of the big chess games in my past. A hushed crowd of spectators keenly looking on. Me the centre of attention while others marvelled at my genius.

'On your backs,' the dealer said, and I proudly turned over my two queens, causing a gasp from the onlookers who could see that I had four of the fucking things. The Russian hesitated for a second before turning over two kings. A good hand. Three kings enough to win most of the time but not today. The victory was almost certainly mine. With one card to be dealt, providing it was not a king, I was going to be a millionaire.

The irony of the king. The chess piece I knew more about than any other. Hadn't my whole career been based on hunting down my opponent's king and defending my own? Who would have thought in a game of cards the king would prove to be my nemesis? The dealer turned the final card to reveal the king of spades in all its terrible blackness. A shovel less welcoming to me than the one that will eventually be used to dig my actual grave.

I do not know if the card was marked in some way or if it had been swapped for a king previously concealed up a sleeve or magicked up from a secret compartment. The mechanics of the fraud matter less than the consequences. It is just that in chess, when you lose, after the event you can always figure out why. It still bugs me that I cannot put my finger on quite what happened at that table.

I gasped at the sight of the king. Felt my knees go weak, instinctively reached into the middle to rescue my chips and was gently but firmly pulled away from the table by the security guards.

They took me into an office and gave me a cup of tea. I told them that I appreciated their kindness but would prefer it if they all fucked off. Which was more than justified when I later realised that it was the most expensive cup of tea I had ever drunk. It was not even a good cup of tea, too weak, with too much milk. Not that there is such a thing as a decent cup of tea really, it makes your teeth go brown and ruins your insides. You don't know where you are with it in the way that you do with a can of cider.

Keith came in for a bit, but his banalities and attempts to ease his conscience just annoyed me. Before he left, he had the decency of reassuring me that he would not tell the family. It was only at that moment that it occurred to me that that was precisely what he was going to do. Yet again something else I take no satisfaction in subsequently being proved right on.

Later I realised the Casino staff must have also been a part of the conspiracy. It simply was not possible for the cards to fall that way of their own accord. I had been swindled. I would not have been surprised to learn that the tea was lightly laced with bromide, just to ensure I did not kick up more of a fuss.

I spent the rest of that night walking the streets, trying to make sense of what had happened. I stood for a long time on the bank of the Thames looking across the water at Parliament and Big Ben. I would have been justified in trying to blow the whole fucking lot up – the State was causing me more problems than it ever did Guy Fawkes. Still, even at my lowest ebb, I still found it in myself to be magnanimous and continued my walk instead.

26. A Coventry postmark

Somewhere nearby a couple are having sex and I hear animal-istic grunting and high-pitched squealing. Then laughter. Then nothing. It makes me feel awkward. Embarrassed. As if I have intruded on something that was not meant for me, but I have done nothing other than sit here on my bed, minding my own business.

In another nearby room, music is playing loudly. An old, old song that I know well. 'All Tomorrow's Parties' by the Velvet Underground. I listen to the mournful beat, the lyrics I first heard at a time in my life when my connection was with the music itself rather than the story. I try not to overanalyse, to lose myself in the rhythm rather than the sentiment, to sit outside myself at least for a moment.

I cough, but when I light a cigarette I feel much better. I am sure when you have smoked as much as I have that tobacco is no longer harmful. My body can assimilate nicotine much as it does water. Not that I drink a lot of that. I have a Churchillian constitution. Just another one of my many blessings.

It is still quite early. Dark outside but the city is already moving. The road teems with traffic. I pull back the thin curtain, feel the draft, look at the trail of red and white car lights. London never really sleeps I suppose. It might burn from time to time, but it barely rests.

I am more awake now. I know I will need to be on the move again soon. The room is a mess, there is no doubt about it. Somehow in the early morning it all looks and smells worse than last night.

There is a reek of urine from the sink. I inspect the basin then wish I hadn't. The congealed mess of blood, piss and tissue paper is going to take some shifting, most likely by someone with specialist equipment and training. The fire damage is also worse than I thought. The wall is streaked with black. That whole area looks somewhat charred and worn out. It might take more than the coat of paint I originally envisaged to put right.

Still no matter, it was not a particularly good room anyway and it is hardly my fault that it is particularly susceptible to damage. I am prudent enough to know it is easiest all round if I leave before anyone connected with the hotel casts an eye over it. While housekeeping does not strike me as being particularly high on the list of activities that the hotel manager has an interest in, the state of this particular room might be a little difficult for him to ignore. To shrug off. He might want to ask questions. Might even seek to blame someone, however ridiculous that sounds.

I cannot face trekking to the bathroom, again, but given the state of the sink I really have no choice other than to piss in the wardrobe. It will scarcely be noticeable, I am sure. Just a case of putting into action the plan I had first considered the previous night. Perfectly logical and coherent. No cause for alarm. I open the wardrobe door and aim into the far corner. Then I shut the wardrobe and pull the packet of wet wipes and a can of cider out of my bag, as well as the two handwritten letters Gabriel gave me in the Red Lion.

I wipe myself down and pull on my suit, then I sit back on the bed to read my correspondence. The first has a Coventry postmark. I am immediately suspicious. Who did I give Gabriel's address to in Coventry? Have I been hunted down by a sleeper agent embedded in the city? Is it possible that the envelope is filled with some toxic nerve agent and that when I open it I will slip into a coma before dying horribly? All such possibilities are very real. It is as well to be careful.

Foolishly, I sniff the envelope for signs of anything suspicious or harmful. If it did contain a bioweapon I would most probably be dead by now, but seeing as I am not, I decide I might as well open it.

Chess Master!

We heard about the trouble you had at your place, what with the fire and everything. I went up there with some of the lads earlier today and the place is in a hell of a state. We can well see why you can't stay there. A house that is missing a roof can hardly be habitable!

We enjoyed spending some time with you in the Oak. I hope you found our advice on your comeback to be of help. Jezza says he hasn't laughed as much in ages. We are certainly not used to having a man of your distinction in our midst.

By the by, if you do fancy a drink in these parts again it might be best if we meet in the White Horse. The landlord at the Oak is not happy with you. He said you would know full well why that is. He's always been a grumpy sod at the best of times though, so you probably don't need to take that too seriously.

Well Tennessee, I'm not much one for writing but we did want to wish you all the best. I'm not sure if chess ever does make it onto the tele, but if you ever are, me and the lads will be watching and cheering you on.

Best!

Rich

I am trying to remember which one Rich was, but the effort is too much for me. My nights in the Coventry Oak are all a bit of a blur. I remember Jezza well enough though. He was always asking me stupid questions about chess and then falling about laughing. It was probably a mistake for me to give him my brother's address. I was never quite sure how serious he was about it all. The thought of me making a comeback did seem to induce a degree of hysterical excitement and merriment in him that will doubtless soon be mirrored up and down the country. I must remember that this is not just about me. So many others will get such joy from my return.

I look at the second letter. A London postmark on this one. I recognise the handwriting. One of my longer-standing fans.

Tennessee,

It has been a long time and I did just want to check that you were still alive? Please do let me know! I very much enjoyed our conversation outside the British Chess Championship building. I am so sorry that they would not let you in. Gabriel said if I wrote via him, he would pass any message along. Please do drop me a line and let me know how everything is going.

Paul

He never was the sharpest tool. It is not as if I could drop him a line to say, actually I am dead. Bit unfortunate all things considered, but I'm making the best of it, please do keep in touch!

I should not be too hard on him – normal people simply do not have the mental capacity that geniuses like me possess. Even so, when it comes to it, I will make sure Paul gets a ticket to my match against Magnus Carlsen. I take out my lighter and set fire to his letter, for something to do as much as anything. It takes easily and flares up in a burst of orange flame. I throw it to the floor and stamp the fire out.

I am restless now. There is no longer a reason for me to be sitting around in this God-forsaken room waiting for death. Fuck Gabriel. Fuck my lack of money. I refuse to let people who claim to be doctors mess with my head. They are all challenges that might crush a normal man, but I will overcome them. I have a top journalist lined up for the interview that will launch my comeback. I know where Magnus Carlsen is playing. Today will be my day. I have a very good feeling as to all the next few hours will bring.

27. The natural history of a family outing

Fire escapes have their uses. I have always had a semi-professional interest in ensuring I know where they are. I am glad to be free of my room. It is shocking that hotels rent out spaces like this, which deteriorate so quickly in the course of a night. I would once have written a letter of complaint, but I will most likely leave it on this occasion. Burning the place down would do everyone a favour, but I am not really in the mood, and they are all welcome to it.

I have resolved to be discrete. I do not want there to be any awkward questions. The fact that I found no evidence of bugging devices when I checked in does not mean there weren't any. Either way, they have now had a few hours to get to work, so the whole of the lobby is probably fully wired by now; another sensible reason to avoid it.

The only footsteps on the lino are my own as I walk toward the emergency exit. A large cracked window across the corridor drips with condensation. I notice it is missing its handle and hangs limply in a wooden frame that has long since started to rot.

My rucksack is heavy on my shoulders. The strap has cut into the skin on my back. I adjust the weight of the load, try and make everything more comfortable, which works to a point. My throat is dry, my bladder stings a little. I have the dull pain between my temples that only a can or two of cider is capable of shifting.

I pass a black man who is sitting by the fire exit smoking dope. I guess he has not been to bed. He wears a large green wax jacket, deep blue cords, a pair of purple Doc Martens. He has a brown rucksack by his side. What strikes me most is the look of complete serenity on his face. Utter contentment. It might not mean his every moment is like this, I know that, but in the here and now he has achieved a state of being that is beyond me. I tell myself that I will make more of this day than he will. That my drive and sense of purpose might not make me happy, but it is nevertheless what sets me apart from most of the people I meet. Perhaps I am trying too hard to convince myself that my choices have been the right ones. I don't know.

The fire exit door has a warning that an alarm will trigger if it is opened. This strikes me as unlikely. I push down on the metal bar and find myself standing in a concrete stairwell, just as the building does indeed begin to echo with a wail. It is hard to envisage what management were thinking of when they installed such an intrusive system. Still, if it gets everyone up and on with their day, I have most likely done them all a favour.

Electing not to hang around to receive everyone's thanks in person, I hastily make my way down the stairs, through the back door, and then I am outside on a cold London morning. Free. I enjoy the feel of natural light on my skin, the sense of space you always get when you leave any building for the city beyond.

My London. I like the smell of the air in the tube stations. Somehow heightened and rarefied, all of oil and possibility. The famous places you can claim and imagine are for you and you alone. There is a gap by a lion in Trafalgar Square, a step outside the National Gallery, a bench by the Science Museum that all belong to me. I am no tourist, far from it, I've just found a way to take ownership of spots that others walk by without even seeing.

Beyond that, I know where all the right sort of cafés and hotels are, the best places to follow chess on the internet, where to bed down in an emergency. I should really write a rough guide to London. I suppose one day I might.

I would like to think that other families might have happier days out in the capital than I did when I was a kid. I would certainly put in my guide that it has always struck me that the Natural History Museum is ripe for torching. Our family outing there long ago still makes me cringe with shame, even if I can no longer be sure exactly what happened. I can only tell you what I think I know.

My mother had not really wanted to come, I remember that all right. Gabriel and I were restless, and my father struggled to control our bickering as we jumped up and down on the ripped blue seats of the British Rail carriage, shouting excitedly, pulling on shreds of foam and playfully throwing them at each other. That's what children do isn't it? It's just normal behaviour, but it was too much for her to cope with.

She tried to ignore us to begin with, scribbling in a notebook with a bright red pencil, occasionally breaking off to sigh and to swear under her breath at the ongoing distraction we caused.

As the train made its way toward the capital, my mother's mood continued to worsen. The crunch came when I accidently threw an apple at Gabriel and it hit her in the face. She completely lost it, lashing out with her hands, landing blows on our legs and torsos. Digging her nails in.

She went for my eye at one point but seemed to think better of it at the last second, scratching at my cheek instead and punching me in the stomach, leaving me winded. She spat on the floor, oblivious to the stares from our fellow passengers. I suppose the apple had hit her quite hard. It was pale green, a Granny Smith if memory serves – I watched it roll along the aisle. Then Gabriel burst into tears. I remember him weeping and my mother yelling at him to shut the fuck up or she really would fucking kill him.

In some ways her words were worse than the physical aggression. Even a hack like her knew how to coin a phrase – 'I feel like Marley in a *Christmas Carol*, the pair of you shackled to me just as the cashboxes were to him,' she said. Then she laughed and told us we were fat and weighed her down literally, spiritually and metaphorically, far more than Marley ever had been by his cashboxes. She concluded her reflections by noting that whereas Marley was only cursed until the end of time, it was as if she had endured the pair of us for much longer than that already.

Anyone who had a literary talent like hers was always going to have to pay the gods back in some way she lamented, but mainly she blamed our father, who was doing his best to shrink into his seat. With his genes what chance did we have? It was highly unlikely any woman would ever want either me or Gabriel. Our general repulsiveness meant, as Jews, we were doing the Nazis work for them, as we were never going to breed.

Chess club was for children who had no friends, so entirely the right place for a turd like me. She could not give a fuck, whether I beat my fellow freaks. 'It's not really a surprise that the other kids bully you though is it? I'm always telling everyone, it has nothing to do with you being so, well odd. People must instinctively hate you for a reason. I feel for anyone who has ever tried to spend a day with you. I know exactly how awful that is. Never forget how fucking worthless you both are.'

My father appeared to be growing progressively more anxious while all of this was unfolding. I could hear him muttering under his breath, 'It's fine, it's fine. All fine,' taking care not to enunciate clearly enough for his words to constitute any form of challenge to my mother. In situations like this, he always seemed to shrink further into himself, but in a way that was vaguely meant to hint that deep down he was on our side. Say what you like about my mother, she was at least true to herself, which was more than could ever be said for him.

Finally, a lady intervened. Fifty something I would guess, with the air of a teacher or a magistrate. A faint trace of Scot in her accent. She came over and asked if everything was all right, a look of deep suspicion and wariness on her face. I could see other passengers looking on, all no doubt sure something was wrong but uncertain as to what could be done – finishing their journeys in peace and quiet most likely all they really cared about.

Everything is great, thank you, my mother said. In those days, saying that in the right accent and tone was usually enough to bring the conversation to a close, and so it proved. Somehow the carriage visibly relaxed after this and we sat in near silence for the rest of the haul into London, my mother returning to her notebook, Gabriel weeping softly in a way that was not especially audible if you focussed on blanking the sound out, my father wearing the faintly manic grin that I have come to most associate with him – we are having fun, this will be all right, we are just a normal family. I hate people who can't face the reality of their situation, and of course that was my father all over.

What else can I tell you? We queued for a long time in the rain. The museum was too hot and cloyingly claustrophobic, albeit I think that had more to do with the dynamics of our family unit than anything else. Nothing good was going to come of that day. My father's attempts to inject enthusiasm as to what we were looking at – oh wow, another stuffed bird – fell flat and we mainly limped around in a silence laced with recrimination.

'Why are we here? Can we go home now?'

'You are all so ungrateful. I don't know why we had you. I could have been doing something useful with this day. Just wait until I get the two of you home.'

My mother might have kept her hands to herself while we were in the museum, but the look of pure hatred on her face was in many ways more hurtful than being hit.

It was just a product of being young, of still having expectations, the hope that things might be different – that if I could find a way of being different, she would too. Back then I thought that everything that happened was my fault. In some ways I still do. It is hard to shift a feeling of guilt. Things tend to happen to people for a reason.

There must have been something about me and Gabriel that made her the way she was. Over time of course, I progressively got deeper into my chess, moved into a world that worked for me, that gave me some freedom, and of course she had no desire to follow.

When we were leaving the museum, I bought a plastic model of a woolly mammoth with money that I had saved up for the occasion. I removed it from the packaging and rested it on the escalator at South Kensington Underground Station. A tusk fell off between the cracks and was swallowed up by the moving steel stairs. My mother whacked me hard across the head with the back of her hand making my ear roar with the rush of blood. 'You are such a fucking idiot,' she snapped. Then she picked up my now single tusked toy and threw it in a bin. 'If you can't look after nice things you don't deserve to have them,' she said.

On the way home, I fantasised about burning the museum down. Piling all the remaining woolly mammoths from the museum shop into a bonfire, with her perched on the top like a Guy. It would take a lot of petrol to get the plastic to take of course, but I figured it would have been more than worth the effort.

28. Rejection

The supreme irony was that she wrote a piece for a glossy magazine about our day at the museum. I saw the thing on our kitchen table and could not help but read it. She had a good eye for detail, a nice turn of phrase. What was scary was that her account was anchored in certain aspects of the day that really had occurred. They were cleverly described, the feeling of the train wheels on the ancient track, the solemn grandness of the building, the sense of stepping into and being part of history. The four of us standing together as a family. It was just that all the bits about us bonding and having a great time were completely made up.

That is what writers all do I suppose. They create the worlds they want to be real. Either that or they do not know that they are liars. Never trust anyone who does not speak the truth, that is what I say. I remember reading her article and then heading to the bathroom to be sick. Later I torched the fucking thing in the garden. Making a small fire in the derelict greenhouse frame. When it had burnt through, I pissed on top of the smouldering ash.

I do not have to wonder who Judith Greenbecker really was. The gap between the dreadful mother I knew and the wise and all-seeing woman who wrote what she did. She was both things, that is the truth of it, however unsettling that might be. If it scares you, just think what it has done to me. That I am nobody's fool should be obvious by now.

As much as they disgust me personally, deep down, I can understand why others like her books. There is something about the rhythm and the pace that draws you in. Her tone is generally a confiding one. I can see why someone who did not actually know her would feel as if they were talking to a friend. She crafts thoughts that stay with you. The scary thing is that her work is recognisably her. I can hear her voice in every paragraph she writes. I know where the facts that underpin some of what she dresses up as fiction come from.

Take what you know and twist by half a degree, that was the secret she once told me – even if I know she twisted things so hard that they broke, like the wrist of a child being assaulted by an abusive parent. Writing, the way she did, is all about brilliant technique. It has nothing to do with the heart.

The voice of hope for a new generation, that was how my mother was badged. There was a time when lines from her books were plastered on the sides of buses, on the tunnels of Underground stations and on posters outside public libraries. Her face was everywhere. Finally. After years of obscurity when her writing served only as an excuse for not having to interact with her family other than to dish out abuse, there was tangible proof in the world that her words mattered. She had at last become someone.

I would say that her fame caused her to leave us behind, but she had done this long before a fucking word she had written was ever published. Her worldly success was nothing more than a further way for her to mock us.

When we were growing up, she lived in the kitchen but she rarely cooked. A small typewriter and reams of notebooks covered the table. Jars of ink in glass bottles. Blacks and blues and greens. They reminded me of ancient medicines. Fountain pens, heavy and substantial in the hand, with silver nibs that dribbled. Ink stains all over the table and on the floor. Like the debris from an operation that may or may not have been successful.

Our kitchen smelt of paper and hope and words trying to connect and somehow failing, as well as the tinned food and cheap bread we all lived on. Meals that could be made without messing up her precious workspace were all we were allowed.

I don't have any memories of her not writing. I can imagine her typing away while I suckled at her breast, though it strikes me as altogether more likely that my father bottle fed me. Him offering up one of his own nipples is a more plausible scenario than her doing so.

Writing was her world and hers alone. As soon as I was old enough, I started to build a world of my own with my chess. It was a matter of my authentic talent, my mother's false talent and Gabriel and my father being complete non-entities. That was just how it was.

In the early years' rejection letter followed rejection letter. They came in all shapes and sizes. Nice letters, form letters, silence. Not a good fit. Interesting but needs more work. Not for me though. You are a very gifted writer keep persevering and it will come (but please don't write to me again). You can't write for pickled eggs. Consider if there could be other things. Maybe… But no.

She would read the letters out loud, repeatedly. Pacing up and down as she did so. Completely oblivious to the rest of us looking on. It was as if she was trying to discern some hidden meaning. Some secret code that would help her on her way. Honestly, there was a time when I could have recited whole chunks of the fucking things.

None of the feedback seemed to make any difference. She had to do it. Had to write. For its own sake she said. One book rejected, then another, then another. My father earning the money and bringing us up, to the best of his very limited ability, while she toiled away.

She said she saw rejection as a badge of honour. Her view was that making it as a writer required the laying of a path based on rejection slips. That you needed the hide of a rhino to have any chance of succeeding. She had the hide of two such beasts, she always said with an even laugh, not remotely tinged with hysteria.

She would tell the story sometimes, of Evelyn Waugh's first book. Him showing it to a friend who hated it. Evelyn deciding that the only logical reaction to such criticism was to kill himself. Running out into the sea with the intention of drowning. Being bitten by a jellyfish and rushing back to the shore. A wise decision all things considered, but my mother was made of sterner stuff. Frankly, had a jellyfish ever got in her way, I am sure she would have shredded it with her bare hands.

Agents, publishers, journals and magazines. Everybody said no, if they bothered to say anything at all. She just kept at it. I think it made her tougher though – however much people protest, rejection must have an impact on all of us to a point, and the only way she could cope was to cut herself off emotionally.

If she'd had any empathy to begin with, it drained away from her a little further every time the postman walked down our drive. Perhaps I am fooling myself and she was an out-and-out psychopath all along. Might she have been just the same even if she had never written a single word?

It all started to change when we were still relatively young. An actual book published. A print run of five hundred. Sales unexceptional. Reviews, in so far as there were any, generally positive. I will never forget the look on my mother's face when she held her first book in her hands. The publisher had sent a few copies and she opened the brown cardboard package and pulled one out. Rubbed her fingers over the sheen of the cover. Smelt the paper. Smiled with a look of satisfaction no new mother could have bettered.

You might have thought it would have given her a sense of validation, but I'm not sure it made much difference to her for more than a few minutes. A day or two at most. Publishing can be a let-down; I remember her saying.

She just got on with the next book, and that inched her reputation forward a little further. The story of two brothers growing up on a council estate and the scrapes they got into. She robbed and twisted much of what had happened to us to write it. I was astonished to see how much she knew about me being bullied, something that she had never taken any steps to prevent. The way I was cast as unreasonable and difficult and frankly unlovable.

As the writer, it was only her word that counted for anything, her version of the truth somehow enshrined as gospel on the page. She made it sound like our family life was some form of haven, a refuge from a mad, bad world. What a joke that was. Her writing made her appear to be the perfect mother. You can do anything you want with words, but it does not make it necessarily true.

Gabriel felt that issues with my mother were entirely down to jealousy on my part. He would grant that she could be a little cold. Prone to fits of temper and violence, I suspect he would acknowledge all that, but he thinks I make too much of it. That I risk turning the past into something it is not.

Perhaps that is the easy way out. To kid yourself that everything was really all right. It certainly seems to have worked for him, and of course he could be onto something. Didn't Winston Churchill do something similar? Make his unhappy childhood happy by convincing himself that it was so? It might be the only way for some people to survive.

My mother did not love me when I was a child. She was mentally and physically abusive. A hundred years later, Gabriel might be able to kid himself that things were different, but I cannot. He might have surrendered the past and not be man enough to claim the future, but that is why he is who he is, and I am who I am.

I sometimes wonder whether my chess was just a way of trying to get her attention. To show that I had talent too, was worthy of interacting with her as a fellow artist. There was a time, briefly, when I thought that my mastery of the game impressed her, but it was never really like that. What writer wouldn't want a child whose hobby consisted of sitting in silence at a chess table hour after hour? Unlike chess players, writers are all phonies. The power of the pen and all that. Things have a way of looking definitive when set down in black and white.

The reader has no way of knowing that a writer is a fraud or a charlatan. That they have moulded their material like Play-Doh to suit a set of circumstances. That every sentence has been re-worked until it is just so, or not, depending on the skill of the author. Chess is far more noble. You only get to make each move once. There is no capacity for taking things back. A real live opponent is actively trying to thwart you at every moment. There is far more authenticity and honesty to the whole enterprise.

I don't know. I have got to this late stage in my life without resolving any of this and it does not do to dwell. The present is the only thing you can do anything about, and I know I must focus on that.

I do remember my mother being asked about why she wrote, and it was one of the few occasions when I agreed with what she said. Her take was that writers should only write if they saw the book that emerged at the end as reward. That for most authors, there would be no fame or glory. Likely not all that many sales. That if you wrote because you were looking for praise and validation you were probably writing for the wrong reasons.

She said even a successful and critically acclaimed book, of the sort she immodestly hinted she now wrote, would leave you cold if you had unrealistic expectations as to what might follow its publication. She never really let on about the expectations she had herself, which I know she harboured all along.

Chess can lead you into a similar trap. I see that now. The only reason for playing should be for the sake of the game, though for me this is now impossible. In some ways I am more my mother's son than I care to admit. I have always wanted the favour of the crowd, to be eulogised, to be fully recognised for my talents. Bobby can keep his darkened rooms, thank you very much. It was a point of contention between us. He cared mainly for chess itself, I always had an eye for what it could bring me.

We would sometimes play speed chess for three days straight, and every single game mattered to him as much as the last. Chess was the only thing he was interested in when he was playing, the rest of the world could go fuck itself. I remember toward the end of the second day he was still cursing a miscalculation he had made in a complex rook ending hours before. 'You've got to let it go Bobby,' I told him. 'I would always worry about doing that,' he said. 'What would I have left?'

If you want to know the truth, I think Bobby was somewhat spoilt as a person. Even as a kid he had behaved badly, by all accounts. It was just that he was such a superstar that, when the incumbent could take no more, another willing fool was always ready to jump in to become his new best friend.

It wasn't like that between the two of us of course. We were peers in a world where Bobby had no others. I still miss him, that is for sure. But if it falls to me to put the new generation of computer geeks in their place then so be it. I know Bobby will be rooting for me from wherever he is now.

I now understand what I must do. This will be my final attempt at a comeback. If I do not move quickly, I am destined to shuffle off my mortal coil with precisely nothing. On a chess clock as the final seconds tick down, you can be moments away from the game being over with you about to be declared the loser. Your hopes are at an end if the tiny red flag falls. There is a metaphor in there somewhere.

I can feel the flag beginning to teeter on my life. Yet a lot can be accomplished in the last few moments. Positions can be transformed. Losses turned into draws, draws into victories. Everything that has gone before rendered meaningless by the final fling, the last hurrah. Lucky or not, those last breathless moves can come to define everything. It is just a case of being patient and hanging in there. This is how I must try and see things – all is still possible.

Chess is my one true companion. Even if I am like many a married man who wakes up one morning and no longer wants his wife. Not in the same way as before, at any rate. Like many a husband, I still remember what it was I used to see when I looked at a chessboard.

The sensual pieces so perfectly formed and smooth to my touch. The smell of possibility on their perfectly shaped bodies. It is easy to fantasise about the perfect combination, the climax of checkmate. The feeling of contentment that follows the culmination of the act. Even if none of it means quite as much as it did before.

There was a famous tournament that used to be held in Bognor Regis back in the 1950s. Every year someone would break into the playing hall after dark and saw the heads off the knights. No one knew who was responsible for this act or why they did it year after year. The speculation was that it might have been a disgruntled player who had lost a critical game to a knight fork and had henceforth been determined to take it out on every wooden knight they could get their hands on.

I have seen old black and white film of one of the senior event organisers being interviewed. He said he had never seen anything like it. There would have been a period, and quite a long one, when I would happily have sawn heads off knights, dismembered bishops or smashed offending rooks to pieces if I felt they had wronged me, but I'm not sure if I would anymore. A little bit of my passion has gone for good now, and even if there is nothing I can do about it, that troubles me. Perhaps a real marriage is what remains when the passion is spent. I just hope that is something more than nothing at all.

29. The Weimer Republic

It was certainly not a night to spend on the streets, but inevitably I can see that many have. Ten or so just on this road. A lone woman who looks forty but might be twenty, sitting in a dirty sleeping bag in a shop doorway. She is wrapped in a large coat and has a pink knitted hat on her head. She smokes a cigarette through fingerless gloves. Wherever she has come from, she has not been around here for long and I do not think we have ever spoken.

Further along are a couple with their dog, sitting outside of their small orange tent. Daniel and Stacey. I know them both a little. He is ex-army. Traumatised by what he had seen. Abandoned by those he once protected. Everything fell apart, he spent time in jail and when he got out there was nowhere else for him to go, not anywhere he could cope with. Stacey, I am not sure about, but most people out here are running from something. Nothing to tell, she says when people ask her about herself.

They both have a major drug problem, but they've got each other. There are plenty of people with a roof over their heads who don't have the bond they share. They won't go anywhere that means they can't take their dog, a fat boxer who snarls at everyone else but dotes on the pair of them, so they are destined to live out the foreseeable in various doorways.

It might seem like a strange choice, an irrational one, but when life screws you up, you don't always see things as others do. I should know. As they have told me, you can rely on a dog in a way that you can't much else in this life. I suppose that is probably true.

There are a couple of clusters of men, one or two solitary figures who choose to go it wholly alone. I know that one is here because he lost his Disability Living Allowance. He is called Michael. With his health issues it should never have come to this, but he was asked to go for a reassessment and authority scares those whose experiences of it are less than benign. It certainly terrified him. He figured that the very act of walking in would see him signed off as fit for work, so he didn't show and now he has nothing. That was his judgement call.

I know there are those who have encouraged him to change his mind, to take the test, but I am not so sure. As I have said to him before, the State is going to do whatever it wants to do, we are all but pawns. His basic instinct to stay clear strikes me as a sound one.

I will let you into a little secret. What you think you see on the streets of London is not wholly the reality. It is possible to make a reasonable living begging, especially around Charing Cross and the Strand. So many people will give you sandwiches and pastries, money too. Fifty pounds an hour tax free is perfectly doable, if you know how to paint the right picture. There is plenty of free hot food laid on by various charities.

It is not so difficult to get social housing if you can be bothered. It's just that a roof is not always the priority if you are an addict. Half of those you see camped out on the pavement go back to their flats at night. Begging just a way of funding serious drug and alcohol problems. Society makes it too easy. No one wants to hear this, but I know it is true.

Some just drift into all this. It happens more often than you might think. I have heard many variations of the same story from people over the years. It usually starts with an extreme form of trauma. An addiction that can no longer be managed, a pain that can no longer be submerged. All control slips away and gradually everything unwinds.

You lose your job. You can no longer pay your bills. You get evicted. You crash on friends' sofas until they tire of you. It is only going to be one night. Then another and another. Then over time getting the drugs you need becomes everything. There is no longer space for the life you once knew.

The structures we build around ourselves are never as robust as they seem. Few have the foresight that I do to understand the role of the State in all of this. The manipulative lengths they will go to, to bring people down. The unseen sleight of hand behind many a personal disaster. There are dark forces at work in the world, of that there is no doubt.

Many people end up like this, even though they do not even play chess. Is it any wonder that the State goes to such lengths to attack a man of my talent? I might like a drink, but I don't do drugs. I am a world away from these people, even if I understand all too clearly the ties that bind us together.

It seems the November cold has pricked at my appetite. It surprises me that I might want to eat, especially so early in the morning. Magnus Carlsen most likely exists on a diet of genetically modified vitamins and organic vegetables, and I am going to need my fill of carbohydrates to compete.

Does his lifestyle and all that fresh Norwegian air mean that he will outthink me in the long endgame battles ahead? I hope not. I have come this far. I know how to beat incredible odds. How to truly make the most of who I am. Diet has nothing to do with talent. Besides, now that I am planning on eating a bacon roll or two there is no longer an issue.

There is a small café I know nearby, half-lodged under a railway bridge; not much more than a wooden hut, but it is convenient and more than enough for my needs. I will grab something to tide me over before heading across town to the internet café, where I can get down to studying the early games from the Carlsen - Caruana match.

A red and white sign above the entrance proclaims that this is, 'Jimmys Place.' I wonder if there is some sort of law that says shop and café owners are not allowed to use apostrophes, but I have long since accepted that there is nothing I can do about this. I order a bacon roll and a black coffee with three sugars. The coffee is only to keep my hands warm and because I like the smell.

I am served by a fat white man most likely in his fifties. Perhaps a little younger but not looking good on it. He wears a red and white striped apron. White, grease-stained trousers. A black shirt, open at the neck, that has seen better days. He takes my order with a grunt, pushing his hands through his greasy black hair as he turns and heads out to the kitchen through a beaded curtain. A few moments later I hear the hiss of the bacon in the fat. Smell the aroma of burning pig. Already suspect that this was a bad idea, but it is too late now. I am committed.

A transistor radio is playing, and when one of Keith's songs come on, I stick my fingers in my ears and start shouting until the proprietor returns and asks me to stop. I ask him if he knows that Keith is a Russian agent, but it turns out he doesn't. He tells me he couldn't give a fuck either way. When the masses are indifferent to the growing grip of totalitarianism, we really are in trouble. It is like the Weimar Republic all over again.

He hands me my coffee and a white bacon roll wrapped in tinfoil. He takes my money without a hint of thanks. He has no idea that I am a famous chess player, but for once I don't care.

It is almost easier just to be a man in a café unobtrusively ordering a bacon roll. Nothing more, nothing less. I had planned to take my food and go, to eat on the move, but I find I am still a little more tired than I thought. So, I take the weight off my feet and sit at one of the four plastic tables.

There is one other customer, a thick set man, who is sat at the table next to mine with a large bottle of cider in front of him. He stares at the tabletop, deep in thought and then his phone rings and he is almost immediately ranting and weeping. I try to filter him out, I hate people who make a public exhibition of themselves, but I can hear every word.

He is telling the caller that he is the only person he can talk to. That if it was not for him, he would have killed himself long ago. He highlights how honest he is about the drugs he has taken. He has done this. He has done that. Then the State (even if this is not the word he uses) goes and holds it against him. His baby is covered in bruises, but nobody has an explanation as to why this is. How can they expect him to manage supervised visits if he is in London and the kids are in Bristol? He says the new social worker, 'just ain't all that.'

'I know God has a plan for me. He must do, or I would be dead by now. The trouble is that I just can't work out what it is,' he says, before ending the call. He puts the phone down and stares into space. He looks almost stoical as he takes a swig of cider, doubtless plotting his next move.

I want to tell him that we both have challenges to face, a world that does not understand. That you can never let the State win. That it is important to seize the day and to avoid being defined by your adversaries. Yet a sixth sense tells me that it would be unwise to say any of these things. That my wisdom might be beyond his comprehension. He does not look the type to recognise a distinguished chess player and missing out on my advice is his loss.

I turn my attention to my food. The bacon roll has been smeared in mustard and ketchup, neither of which had I requested. Fat drips from the corners, blending with generous globs of margarine. I take a bite and feel the warmth within me. The bread, the meat. True staples of life. Then I take a second bite and feel sick. It is too rich. Is simply not what my stomach wants these days. I spit the mouthful out and manage to regain my composure without vomiting. Just dry retch once or twice and gently clear my throat.

The proprietor and the man who is still looking to understand God's plan for him both stare at me for a moment, as if assessing whether I am about to die. I see a momentary look pass between them. Even here, I am the outsider. I cannot imagine that seeing customers practically choke to death on the terrible food he serves is that rare an occurrence for the chef in a place like this. The arbiters of the Michelin guide are unlikely to be rushing through these doors anytime soon, that is for sure.

I push my plate away. Take a swig of the coffee that almost does for me, then move the still half-full cup away. No matter, I will have got some nutrients from all this. I have had more than enough for now. Magnus Carlsen has doubtless been playing on his computer while I have been building myself up. Ninety nine out of a hundred I would wager he is currently studying an opening line that I am never going to follow – and more fool him!

I use the toilet and then leave the café, pausing only to share with the proprietor a flash of insight that seems so obvious I wonder why it had not occurred to me sooner. The guy must be in the pay of the State. That's why he plays such propaganda on the radio and openly admits he does not care whether Keith is a Russian agent. Thank God I did not eat more of the Bacon roll. It is most likely laced with Novichok. The proprietor does not even deny my allegations, just resorts to a string of expletives that serve only to confirm his guilt.

30. Parliamentary sovereignty

I feel properly awake. All systems switched on. I am processing the threats I face with a degree of clarity that impresses me. I am mentally at the top of my game. I think to the day ahead, what it might hold. My plan is simple enough. Head to the internet café, then meet Jasmine for my set-piece interview. Lay further groundwork for my comeback.

Still, I cannot shake the feeling that I am progressing too slowly. My remaining money is not going to last forever. When I tried to urinate in the café not very much happened. I can tell myself that I did not need to go, but my bladder now feels uncomfortable.

The threats around me are certainly mounting. Hearing Keith's music once would be unfortunate, but to do so in two different establishments can hardly be a coincidence. If I turn up at the café and someone is reading one of my mother's books, that will be yet another sign that the net is closing in.

The State must be toying with me. The letters about the court cases. The medical nonsense. None of this is good. I have a growing realisation that I need to move quickly. Magnus is playing his match only a few Tube stops away after all. Can I really afford to wait much longer before issuing my challenge?

I contemplate the pros and cons. I am not fully ready. I have not finished my study of his games. There is more work that I had planned to do on my folder. I might be able to get by on talent alone, but why take the chance?

Besides, Carlsen is in the middle of a world championship match. Might people think that was a reasonable excuse for him to avoid dropping everything to take me on? It would certainly be a difficult dilemma for him. Carlsen has little to prove by beating Caruana. Notwithstanding the draws the two of them have played out to date, he is considerably the stronger. I would of course be an entirely different proposition. A big risk for Magnus to take.

That Magnus Carlsen is most likely not fully prepared for me might cause him to hesitate. Yet the more I think about it the more I see that since the rumours of my comeback first began to circulate, he must have started to put the hours in to study my game. Even so, he would not be expecting me to turn up without warning. Such a move could be an incredible surprise tactic. If truly being the best means anything to him, he will feel honour-bound to take me on immediately, even during the middle of a world championship.

My hunch is that he will prove man enough to want to play me. He dreams of being the best of all time and he would not be able to satisfy himself or anyone else if he tried to claim that mantle having swerved Tennessee Greenbecker.

What of the current challenger Caruana? Is it possible that he would just stand aside if I turned up in Holborn? He might usher me into his seat with a smile and good grace. Then again, he might not. It is possible he will cling to the delusion that he is more entitled to play Magnus than I am – the kids of today have no respect for their elders.

Then what? I have no doubt that there would be a huge clamour from the audience for me to play if Caruana dug his heels in and refused to budge. After all, it is likely that many of the fans present bought their seats with the dream that I might appear. There can be no other explanation for the exorbitant price of tickets on the black market.

Even if Caruana and Carlsen both play ball, and the more I think about it, the more likely it seems to me that they would, the chess authorities might be a different matter. Have they not done everything in their powers to snuff out my career? Would they really let me take my rightful place on the stage?

The president of FIDE would probably prefer to be in an early grave than to see me as world champion. I doubt the current chair of the ECF would be much more enthusiastic. Still, when has an official ever proved a match for any man whose moment has come?

I don't know exactly what the right thing to do is. I will let my intuition guide me. Like all analytical people, I often do not know exactly what I am going to do, until I have done it.

I have money in my pocket but am of course extremely wary about taking a taxi. It is practically akin to inviting the State to abduct me. Still, having seen how I made Gabriel test my cider in the Red Lion, the powers that be will not have predicted that I might let my guard down in such a way so soon afterwards. They won't be geared up to kidnap me.

Besides my foot hurts and if the worst comes to the worst,

I can always jump out of the cab's window. Tears of laughter stream down my face as I realise I have outwitted the State once again, they simply cannot keep up with the way my brain works.

I stick my arm out and almost immediately a white taxi pulls up and I get in. The driver is a grumpy bastard who does not acknowledge what I am saying as I tell him where I want to go. Rather he grunts, as if to suggest my choice of destination is dubious, but then it might be that I am reading too much into his indifference.

He is quite a young guy, in his twenties I would guess, and deeply engrossed in a radio discussion on Brexit. I repeat the name of the internet café. I tell him I want to go there to study my chess. I am rather good at it. You may well have heard of me I say, by way of easing him into a conversation with a man of my standing.

He peers at me in his mirror and asks if I have been crying. A touch of hay fever, I reassure him, nothing more. He asks if this is particularly common in November and I tell him that unbeknown to most, it is peak pollen season. He says he already knew that, and I double over with laughter but can see he has no idea that he is the source of my amusement, which makes this all the funnier.

'So, what do you think of Brexit then?' he asks me, no doubt realising that my views are likely to be more interesting than those of the people on the radio. I get a hold of myself and consider his question. The potential impact of leaving the European Union on the world's chess authorities is not something the mainstream media has properly covered. I was always in favour of exiting, as I thought it would weaken the grip of

FIDE and the ECF. Make things more fragmented. A little easier for stars the State has turned against to be free. Is it any wonder that so many chess officials are working secretly behind the scenes to stop Brexit from becoming a reality? Gabriel has told me that this view is utter nonsense, which is normally a pretty good indication that I am working along the right lines. Brexit is a form of political fire after all.

I think it is unlikely that a taxi driver who can't tell summer from winter would be able to assimilate ideas as profound as these, so I opt to share a more mainstream observation.

'The State wins whatever happens. That's what I think. Another reason why I would never vote, as well as not wanting to give them information on my thinking. I'm pretty sure Brexit was just an Establishment trick to distract attention from Operation Yew Tree.'

I can see him taking this in. It is clear I have struck a chord.

'You could well be right sir,' he says. 'I am sick to death of the whole thing. We voted to leave, so why are we still in? I honestly thought the day after the referendum, all these foreigners would fuck off and we would have our country back. There would still be others to kick out, but it would be a start. Now who knows? It's just another betrayal. I honestly don't know why people like me bother to vote. We would be better off protesting outside Parliament.'

'Or going one better and burning the fucking thing down altogether!' I shout enthusiastically, banging the seat hard with my hand for extra emphasis. 'I'm pretty sure Guy Fawkes had it right all along! Brexit proves his point.'

'I can't have shouting in my cab,' the driver yells, but then obviously realises he is wrong to try and silence me. He cannot resist asking for further clarification once I am sitting quietly and have complied with his request to put my cigarettes away.

'Everything burns in the end,' I explain. 'It is generally for the best. If either of us had any guts, we would head for Parliament right now and torch the arseholing place to hell! That would give the State a clear message that they needed to get on with things. That parliamentary sovereignty needs to be respected!'

He laughs a little nervously. I can tell he is tempted by the thought. I mean who wouldn't be? Guy Fawkes' name lives on for a reason. Many have dreamed, but few have dared to follow. The reality is the two of us are no different. If I delay, at least I have the excuse of having a world chess championship I need to win.

'Wait for Tommy Robinson and then everything will be sorted. He'll get all the Pakis out too,' he says, clearly lacking genuinely revolutionary fire.

I consider asking whether kicking all the foreigners out might be bad for business for a London taxi driver, but I can't sustain enough interest to make the point out loud. Instead I opt for a question that I think is likely to interest him more.

'Did I mention that I was a famous chess player?' I say casually.

'Well, we don't charge extra for that, sir,' he sniggers. 'It's a funny thing for you to mention though. I had a world champion in here a few weeks back. Some Russian bloke. Garry, what's his name? Kasparov – you heard of him then? I looked him up on the internet afterwards, and sure enough it was him. Seemed to have quite a high opinion of himself. I got the impression he thought he could drive a taxi much better than I ever could, if you get what I'm saying?'

I should have known Garry was in town. London is one of his most frequent haunts, since he based himself in New York after all the threats back home in Azerbaijan. I can imagine the driver banging his head on the steering wheel as Garry immodestly droned on about his many triumphs over Karpov in excruciating detail.

It must be a relief to have me, a man both more content to hide his light under a bushel and by far the greater natural talent, in the back of his cab. I am pretty sure Garry does not have any insights on Brexit that would rival my own.

I suppose Garry is something of a Jekyll and Hyde character. He can be the best of company. Charming, witty, oozing charisma. Or he can be a total jerk. I always think he was a little sheepish around me. It must have been obvious to him that if it had not been for the bottle and the chess authorities, I would have been world champion back then rather than him. He was an accidental world champion when you thought about it like that. I think that is why he could also be a bit moody in my company. I remember him even calling security once when I tried to cordially greet him outside the BBC studios, having gotten wind that he was there doing an interview. I am sure he was just having a bad day, nothing more.

The driver pulls up outside the café and I see the fare is £14.50, so I pull out a five and a ten and hand them over, telling him to keep the change. He does not look overly impressed.

I smile as a thought occurs to me. I will ask Garry to be one of my seconds when I make my comeback. I am sure he will be only too delighted by the offer. He might be a bit past being a principal these days but working as one of my helpers will be the next best thing for him.

As I prepare to get out of the taxi, I say to the driver, 'I'm Tennessee Greenbecker. The next chess champion of the world.'

'Never fucking heard of you mate,' he says, and before I can react the taxi has gone, and I am standing by myself on the street.

31. A bit of a balls up

I rummage in my bag for a can of cider. They are ridiculously strict about the consumption of alcohol in the internet café and won't let me stay if they catch me drinking. It does not seem to matter how many times I tell them that the cider that somehow got into a keyboard I once happened to be using was merely incidental to the fact that it immediately stopped working. If they will buy such cheap equipment it's hardly my fault if it doesn't last very long.

I try to recall if I am currently banned but have no idea, and anyway it makes no difference. I can but try and see what happens. I take out my lighter and have a cigarette. I try to avoid looking at the packet, but unfortunately get a glance of a pair of blackened lungs on the front. A moment to myself for a quiet smoke, who could begrudge me that? Is not every man entitled to such a thing before getting down to work?

London is fully moving now. The streets are filled with people on their way to offices. On the opposite side of the road, I see a film crew and for a moment am tempted to dive up an alleyway to hide, but before I can properly weigh up my options they are gone. A surveillance operation checking up on me. Did they lose their nerve when they saw I was looking back at them? That is the most likely scenario. I shout 'no,' very loudly and then 'fuck off'. I finish the cigarette and stamp it out on the pavement, drain the last of the cider and throw the can to the ground. I will not let the State divert me from my path.

I push through the door into the blinking half-light of the café. Four banks of computer screens, most of them empty at this time of the morning, the owner behind the counter trying to fix his mobile with a little yellow screwdriver that looks as if it might have come out of a Christmas cracker. I can tell that he remembers who I am, but he does not say anything. Without so much as a nod he takes my money for two hours of computer time, a cup of tea and a piece of fruitcake.

Why would he feel the need to talk? We have completed our business. I have known him to get angry if I choose not to buy food and drink. It is not as if any other aspects of my behaviour are in anyway anti-social, so I have never been able to think of anything else I might have done that would incur his wrath. I have certainly been canny enough to thwart him on the food front today. As he returns and hands my purchases to me, I avoid the temptation to laugh in his face.

The cake is wrapped in plastic cling film and he has placed it on a white paper plate of the sort that might be used at a budget wedding. I would not care to speculate as to how long it has been covered like this, waiting for my custom. Perhaps it is just as well that I have no intention of eating it.

He has put too much milk into my tea, but I don't really care, and he points wordlessly in the direction of the sugar pourer which is made of clear plastic with a metal lid that has white granules clinging to its outside. It would be hilarious if it transpired that the white stuff was cocaine rather than sugar, and I laugh loudly and bang my hands on the counter as I enjoy the thought, before being told that I must be quiet.

He tells me to be careful not to spill anything. I am tempted to tell him that everyone knows a can of cider has a lower centre of gravity and thus is inherently much more stable than a cup of tea and a saucer, but on his head be it if he wants to take the risk. However, I doubt that science is really his thing, so I choose not to waste my breath.

I imagine that someone has dipped the pourer into their beverage in the recent past, but that does not bother me. Better than sticking it up their nose I think, and laugh again, before being told that this is my final warning.

I remind myself that I am not here for the warmth of the welcome or the quality of the catering. I flick a crust of sugar from the top of the pourer then drain some of my tea into the saucer to create more space to give myself a reasonable helping of the white stuff.

This is what life is all about really. The day is working out as I hoped it would. I have made my way here without incident. My bladder appears to have settled down again. I am free to get on with my chess in relative peace. Perhaps I do not quite convince myself. I don't know, it is hard to explain.

The fact I sense that underneath my breezy exterior I am not entirely at ease has the effect of unsettling me a little further. It should not matter whether the café owner has chosen to greet me warmly or not at all and it disappoints me that I care, but I must admit that to some extent I do. I must learn not to see such things as somehow being a verdict on myself, to give such transitory moments a meaning and a value they do not deserve.

I remember chatting with the artist Sean Scully a while back. He always had the right idea on this front. He told me not to give into the critics. That Chris Hamish was a nobody. I am sure he would have hated the guy who runs the café every bit as much. In fact, I think he mentioned something about the terrible quality of the fruit cake here. It might have been the first thing he ever said to me, I can't remember.

Either way, he told me that whether it was art critics, chess writers, or café proprietors, the trick was not to care what anyone wrote, said or thought about you. It was essential to believe in yourself. Sean's pictures consist of stripes and simple squares and sell for around one million pounds each. I can imagine why that might make people bitter. I think he accepted that they could never have the same intrinsic value as my chess games, but he always tried to make the best of it. He knew how to put a brave face on things.

I told him that I would not have punched Dubrovnik on the nose if I had been lacking in self-belief. That I was just showing that I did not care about critics and rivals in my own way. He laughed, but I was never quite sure if he got the point.

I asked him if he had ever thought of making art out of fire. Perhaps mixing ash into the paint for his next series of works. If that was too much, I suggested he might just stick to black and white squares, like on a chess board. He got quite arsy at this. I think he knew how easily I would be able to knock out my own works, most likely for a couple of million a time if I wanted to. He did not seem very interested when I reassured him that I was too busy to embark on such a venture.

I haven't decided yet whether I want him to do my official portrait. I know he would leap at the chance, but I worry that his abstract techniques might not result in the best representation of someone with achievements as concrete as mine.

I stand for a moment at the counter. Plate in one hand, cup and saucer in the other. I try and cleanse my mind by thinking calming thoughts. I imagine an empty tower block, primed for demolition. All its stories now told. I have been hired to get rid of the thing. To erase the asbestos-ridden carcass of concrete and steel from the world. Forget wrecking balls and dynamite, the only thing needed for a job like this is a simple match and a bit of paraffin. Everyone understands. This is precisely what I have been hired to do.

I am the master of ceremonies. People look on expectantly. Watching me practice my craft. I strike a light and tell the crowds to stand a little further back. The spark grows and soon the empty building is lighting up the night sky in all its reds and golds and oranges. I bask in the cheers and the back slapping, the warmth of the blaze on my skin, the sense of an imaginary job well done. There, in that moment, I am free.

The thought of fire always soothes me. Restores my sense of balance. I feel a momentary pang of sadness that Guy Fawkes did not get to see his own work reach its culmination, but I feel much better now. It is time to study.

I make my way to one of the computer tables and place my cake and tea down on the table, spilling a little and scalding my fingers. A light brown film of liquid starts to spread but I wipe it all up easily enough with the back of my sleeve. Then I take my sleeve and twist it hard to squeeze what I have just mopped up onto the floor. I rub the drips into the dirty lino with the sole of my boot.

I take my rucksack off my shoulders, feeling relief as the pressure of its weight comes off my back. I feel myself creak a bit but do a couple of discrete stretching exercises and then feel fine. I place the rucksack at my feet and sit down on a black swivel office chair, readying myself to get started.

I am wary of computers. I do not always find it easy to get them to work and often need help logging on, but today I manage without incident. There is something unnerving about seeing a lump of plastic and silicon spring into action, a previously dead grey screen suddenly flickering into life.

Computers make me deeply suspicious that I am being monitored. What is it I hear about that God-awful Amazon device, Alexa? That there are literally millions of State agents listening in on the inane conversations of those who have been foolish enough to purchase this in-house bugging system. It makes me laugh to think the State was probably hoping that I would buy one. More fool them! I will never make it that easy.

Besides the snooping, I do also have a certain fear as to the radioactive x-rays these machines emit. Bobby was onto something with this, and I must admit in an ideal world I would not go near a computer without at the very least wearing a lead vest. I think Bobby also had his fillings removed because he was worried that they were being used by the State to transmit signals to him or to read his thoughts, I can't remember exactly which it was.

The thing with Bobby was he would talk at me a lot, especially toward the end. It could be a little hard to follow his precise train of thought. Most of my fillings had fallen out of their own accord by that point, so that at least was one less thing to worry about.

It is time to get down to business. I take a tentative sip of the sweet milky tea and google Carlsen – Caruana. I am shocked by the headlines that greet me. 'Carlsen and Caruana still deadlocked after YouTube 'leak' controversy,' reads one.

It appears that a clip from Caruana's training camp titled 'Today, In Chess: World Chess Championship Fabiano In Training,' was recently posted then removed very soon afterwards by the Saint Louis Chess Club, where Caruana trains. Inevitably, it had been copied and uploaded to multiple other sites by then and was impossible to remove from the public domain.

As well as showing Caruana working with Grandmasters Rustam Kasimdzhanov and Alejandro Ramirez, a laptop screen with a ChessBase file is clearly visible, as are several previous Carlsen games that Caruana has picked out for particularly intensive study. I find myself shaking as I look for further details, trying to stay calm as I marvel once more at the power of the State.

There is speculation as to whether this is a 'ghastly blunder,' by Caruana's chess club or part of a skilful campaign of misinformation on the part of the challenger. Carlsen is quoted as saying he will have a look at the video and make up his own mind. His manager Espen Agdestein has acknowledged it is more likely this is a big mistake by Caruana's team than something staged. Norwegian Grandmaster Jon Ludvig Hammer says he thinks that the information is authentic and could be a 'devastating blow.'

This is not good. Even knowing which grandmasters Caruana has been working with will give Carlsen a big advantage. That much is obvious. Carlsen will know Kasimdzhanov and Ramirez well and will have a fair idea of the sort of advice they are likely to dispense.

While this is a disaster for Caurana, the two theories being put forward are both likely to be wide of the mark. I cannot believe that such a thing was either a mistake or a clever trap to throw Carlsen off the scent. No, what has happened is that the State has chosen to flex its muscles. To show that when it comes to chess it is more than capable of stealing whatever information it wants and using it to any end. It is doubtless all intended as a warning to me as much as anything.

I have always been unsure as to what extent there is a Norwegian Secret Service, but I imagine there must be such a body. No doubt they would liaise with their Soviet counterparts to get Caruana's material into Magnus's hands. They are a pretty devious bunch of course. Skilled at this sort of counter-terrorism operation. I know Magnus will not have been involved personally. He is too much of a gentleman, but there are forces much bigger than him at play in all this. Once the material was published on the internet, who can blame him for reading it?

Nothing is private. Nothing is sacred. Here in the twenty-first century a grandmaster's preparation is weaponised data. Chess ideas are at the forefront of human thinking, so is it any wonder the State takes such an interest?

None of this is good for me. I feel sick as it sinks in that the same people who published the Caruana training video will undoubtedly be plotting to steal my own secrets. I cannot wholly discount that they might have found a way to take a photocopy of my folder without me even realising. This is the sort of happening you read about all the time.

I bang my head against the table as I contemplate this prospect. Once, then twice. I let out a light howl, to clear my throat. I stand and say firmly, 'I will not let them fucking win.' Then I assert this idea a little more sternly by banging my fists for extra emphasis. The proprietor is next to me before I know it. 'Please, please, don't do that,' he says. 'Perhaps you need some help?'

I see his game. He wants me to throw myself at his mercy, so he can report back to his State paymasters. It would take a lot more than an offer of help and a shit piece of fruit cake for me to fall for a trick like that. There is no way he is stealing my folder. I look down at my rucksack. I can see its bulk inside the canvas. I look back at him. He knows I know – that I have thwarted him this time.

I tell him, I am quite all right. He looks at me doubtfully for a moment. Says somewhat crossly that any more outbursts and I will have to leave. I can tell he does not mean it, is just trying to save a bit of face as much as anything. He may be working for the other side, but I know he is still flattered to be in the presence of greatness.

I sit back down on at my terminal. I need to get a better understanding of what is going on. What I might be up against. Frantically I try a few Google searches, cursing the online footprint this will leave my enemies, but it is a compulsion I cannot control:

Tennessee Greenbecker Opening Preparation
Tennessee Greenbecker Chess Secrets
Tennessee Greenbecker World Champion

They all come back blank, so I suppose that is something. I take a sip of tea and try to calm down. That there is nothing on the internet is a positive.

If they had anything and were cannier, publishing glimpses of my secrets in the same video as the Caruana material might have destroyed us both with a single blow. I am not altogether sure I could have recovered from that. I must be thankful they lacked both the data and the foresight.

Then again, it might be that they are simply toying with me, choosing to scare me now and waiting to publish what they have when my match with Carlsen is fully under way. Just because they have chosen not to move yet, does not mean they lack options.

What I have written so far in my folder is doubtless the chess equivalent of the complete works of Shakespeare. It could do untold damage to my chances if it got into the wrong hands. Society as we know it might not survive my latest thinking on the Queen's Gambit. Who would ever listen to a prime minister or a president ever again, if ideas as compelling as mine were public knowledge? It is highly likely that I would be more popular than Jesus, or at least The Beatles, and no State is ever going to tolerate that. I would be assassinated in an instant.

That said, I suppose I do have going for me that my ideas are quite subtle. Even Magnus himself might not make much sense of my folder, were he to read it without me on hand to explain the finer points. I must try and be positive. If the State suspects I am operating at a range above that of normal comprehension that might be enough to save me.

32. Dead poets

I still have plenty of time before my interview with Jasmine. I try and remember who she said she worked for. *The Sunday Times, The Washington Post, The New Yorker.* I think it was one of those. Their readers are going to be in for a treat! I imagine our interview will most likely make the front page. Be the front page even. It will double or quadruple their regular sales. Every household will want to buy at least one copy. I make a note that I will need to charge a significant fee for this conversation, considering how much money it is going to make Jasmine's paper.

Perhaps Jasmine will want to make this a regular thing. While my diehard fans will clamour for a daily interview, I am not quite so fanatical. I would prefer to maintain an air of mystery. Perhaps weekly might be a decent compromise. It is possible it would work best if a new Tennessee Greenbecker supplement was created. Failing that, perhaps *The Sunday Times* magazine could run a one-off edition dedicated to me. Even if Jasmine works for a different paper, I am sure she could arrange something like this easily enough.

I try to remember which my best side is, but they are both pretty good, and the cameraman will doubtless know how to take the perfect shot. I consider my pitch. Do I lay down the gauntlet by putting an explicit challenge out there to Magnus, or do I just announce that I am back and wait for him to come to me?

They are both great options. I can finesse all this nearer the time. Jasmine will advise on what would play best with her readers. I know they will be delighted and supportive of whatever path I chose to take.

Now all of this is settled, I am ready to study some chess. I play with the keyboard and a blue and white chess board appears on the screen in front of me, pieces all lined up, waiting for me to start scrolling through the moves. I could simply look at the algebraic notation and play through the games in my head. Many chess players who are far weaker than I am can do likewise. The truth is though, I am a little tired and I always like the sensation of watching chess pieces do their work. I have paid my money to be here so why shouldn't I enjoy the full experience that such technology can provide?

I take a bite of the fruitcake and then wish I hadn't. It is dry and surprisingly bitter, and it makes me cough and feel a little sick. I gulp down a mouthful of tea, but that only makes things worse. The liquid is scalding and burns my insides, leaving me winded. I gasp and double over, relieved there are only a couple of other customers and that the proprietor is in the kitchen so does not see.

I try and regain my composure. I would have a very good case for suing on health and safety grounds, but the State is never going to let me win a court case and the matter is probably best left. I could really use another cigarette, but I know that is impossible here and I must get on.

I quickly look over game four which, after Carlsen played the English Opening is an extremely boring draw. It would suit me to face this flexible system, as it would allow my superior positional sense to come to the fore. A little less contemporary theory is needed with this opening than certain other setups, which will also help me.

Judging by the game, it is hardly as if Carlsen is playing the English in a way that is to be feared. I smile to myself as I imagine facing this in the first game of our match. I am sure I could get far more out of the black pieces than Caruana manages. I am as good as one nil up already!

Then I turn my attention to the first three games and my mood further improves. All also draws. There is really nothing for me to worry. The opening game is a one-hundred-and-fif-teen move, seven-hour whopper. Woody Harrelson, who apparently is some sort of actor, was hired to make the first move on behalf of Caruana, but he could not even get this right. He pushed Caruana's queen's pawn forward two squares, but Fabiano had to ask for it to be changed as he had wanted to play his king's pawn. Harrelson apologised and said he had misheard Caruana's initial request. This is what happens when people get involved in chess who do not know anything about it. What an embarrassment! All for the sake of adding the 'glitz,' that comes with a celebrity I for one have never heard of.

Had they asked me to make the ceremonial first move, there would not have been any problems. Albeit, my presence would have totally overshadowed the two protagonists. I have to say, had I played the queen's pawn, I would not have been as philosophical as this Woody was, had Caruana tried to change it. Sometimes top chess players simply do not know what is good for them.

The obvious conclusion from game one is that Magnus played poorly. His great strength has always been his ability to grind players down from positions where he has only a miniscule advantage or even none at all. Yet here he cannot do it. More likely his mind is not fully on the job. He knows I am lurking in the wings. It could be that it is agony for him to put these moves out there in the public domain, knowing I am watching and waiting. Studying. Sizing him up. I would have the beating of him, whether I had seen these games or not. I think he must know this, which probably makes him feel even worse.

Some might wonder whether the State has got to him. Compromised him in some way, but only an amateur would think like that. They more than have their hands full in keeping me down, without going after Magnus as well. I think the explanation might be more prosaic. Magnus has peaked.

It can certainly be a sign that a player is past their prime when they fail to convert positions you would once have expected them to. That was certainly poor Bobby's fate in his rematch with Spassky. I confess I fear my own ability to close positions out is a little diminished, but I have no doubt in Magnus's seat I would have won this one easily.

Magnus's post-game quote gives me even more reason for optimism. 'It's a bit early to draw conclusions... my head was working well but obviously the conclusion of the games shows that I still have things to work on. Overall, it's encouraging. Better than I've played recently.' For him to be so positive about such a failure gives me incredible hope.

What also makes me chuckle is that Magnus has said that with the game finishing after ten in the evening, it had not been easy to find anything to eat in London. If only I had known this, there were plenty of places I could have taken him. We could have sat together in an all-night café. He could have eaten, I would have drunk. We could have talked chess.

For a moment I have an image of us sat together, hunched over my pocket chess set, playing through one of Bobby's 60 Memorable Games. Two fellow practitioners. More than that. Two peers. Discussing our fellow world champion. Seeing just that little bit more than Bobby ever could.

He would most likely have told me that I was the only one he could really talk to about these games, just as Kasparov had once said the same to Karpov. I am sure Magnus would have been grateful for some of my insights on Fischer's endgame play, certain facets of which are likely to be beyond the understanding of a player of Magnus's generation. Likewise, I would have happily pretended to be interested when Magnus showed me some opening improvements that he had discovered while playing with his computer.

No one else in the café would have had any idea that the two finest minds on the planet were in their presence. To an outsider we might simply have been shuffling tiny figures on a wooden board. They would have no way of knowing that we were searching for the key to everything.

I wonder what else we might have talked about. The pressures of fame. Thoughts on our rivals. As a bunch they would certainly have given us plenty to bitch about. Perhaps we would go beyond chess. Talk about what any of it really meant. Where it would take us. The meaning of life.

Perhaps it would ultimately transpire that we were not the masters of chess, but its fellow prisoners, destined to act out the same circus tricks over and over for the benefit of an audience that did not really understand what we were doing. That while I might have seen Magnus as my enemy, blocking my way to the title that was rightfully mine, there was more that bound us together than set us apart. I must remember not to let this insight stop me from destroying him.

I look at the final position in game one and it has a certain half-symmetry to it. Six of the seven remaining pieces are on white queenside squares. The one surviving white pawn is on a black square. Black has the extra pawn, but it is going nowhere. The position is exhausted, the silicon figures somehow conveying the sense that they have gone the full twelve rounds and all to no avail. The battle is over and all that remains is a story of missed chances and what might have been.

An Asian man in a black leather jacket, leather trousers and big brown boots has entered the café. His face somehow glistens in the light and then I notice that he has a metal spike piercing underneath his lip and an array of other earrings and spikes in his ears and nose. A tattoo in Chinese lettering on the side of his neck. He orders herbal tea and despite the place being quiet comes and sits down at the table next to mine. I half-turn so that we do not have to engage in conversation, but he says hello and I find myself saying hello back, even though I do not want to.

He has broken every London communal space convention there ever was and that is reason enough to be suspicious. I hate people who do not respect the personal space of others.

He could easily be a spy. This is exactly the kind of get-up the State dresses their agents in these days, so they do not arouse the suspicion of targets like me. Another underestimation on their part.

Now he has fired up his computer and I glance at his screen and see that he has brought up the poem 'London' by William Blake.

I wander thro' each charter'd street,
Near where the charter'd Thames does flow,
And mark in every face I meet,
Marks of weakness, marks of woe.

In every cry of every Man,
In every Infant's cry of fear
In every voice, in every ban,
The mind-forg'd manacles I hear.

How the Chimney-sweeper's cry
Every black'ning Church appals;
And the hapless Soldier's sigh
Runs in blood down Palace walls.

But most, thro' midnight streets I hear
How the youthful Harlot's curse
Blasts the newborn Infant's tear,
And blights with plagues the Marriage hearse.

'Dissertation,' he says with a shrug. He asks me what I am doing, and I find myself telling him that I am looking at some chess.

'Do you play?' I ask him.

'A little,' he says. 'A little. I'm just not quite good enough to make a living out of it.'

I contemplate telling him there is most likely no money in dead poets either, but I bite my tongue. The fact that he is admitting to being a chess player, of sorts, should make me more suspicious, but you must look at the evidence. His appearance is not really that of a chess player. I know the days when we all wore suits and ties in our tournaments are long gone, but even so...

I think what is more likely is that he is some form of pseudo-intellectual and that he became embarrassed when he saw that I was working at my chess while he was struggling to make sense of some musty old poem. I nod at him politely, but just to be on the safe side I tilt my screen so that he can no longer see it.

How many people think they can play but have no clue? I suppose that would be almost everyone. I know of many grandmasters who do not really understand the first principles of the game. Wengrower and Mottram in particular are useless blaggers and nothing more.

Chess is a good way of pretending to be clever and it does not take much to buff the image up further. Grandmaster Green always used to quote obscure historical facts and test people with bizarre logic puzzles. I knew his secret. He had bought a textbook containing such trivia and made himself a series of cue cards. We were stood in the car park in Daventry before a

4NCL game once when the wind caught his coat and a whole series of such cards scattered in the breeze. He ran about frantically trying to scoop them up, his neat handwriting jazzed up by bright underlinings in pink and yellow marker pen. 'Albert Einstein could have been the first president of Israel, but he declined.'

I have used that once or twice myself since then, but that is hardly the point. I really could use a cigarette, but I need to press on. Game two gives me even more confidence that Magnus is there for the taking. Caruana outplays him with the black pieces and takes an extra pawn into a rook ending, but then cannot make further progress and another draw follows. I'm pretty sure from a technical perspective that I would have converted in a position like that.

Still, that Magnus got into such a difficult situation shows that he is hardly playing like a world champion. Perhaps he knows as much himself. Is he even considering jacking the whole thing in? Abdicating his crown and advising the chess authorities to appoint me instead? It is possible, but it might be that he fears the adverse reaction of his Norwegian fan base if he adopts such a course.

I know that whatever happens from here on in, I am never going to be able to accept any invitations to play in the land of the midnight sun. His fans would most likely stone me to death the minute I stepped off the plane.

33. Only a draw

It feels like I've had enough actual chess for now, so I decide to turn my attention to securing Garry Kasparov as a second. I google his website. The white entwined letters GK appear on a black header. There are links labelled HOME, ABOUT GARRY, LECTURES AND EVENTS, FOUNDATION, HUMAN RIGHTS, DEEP THINKING, WINTER IS COMING, BOOKS, CONTACT.

There is a photograph of Garry wearing a suit but no tie, holding a white king in his left hand, staring straight towards the camera. A caption to the side of the picture reads MASTER CLASS in block red lettering. Underneath it says 'He may be the best chess player the world has ever seen. Now he teaches you how to improve your chess game.'

I consider whether this statement is libellous. My first instinct is that it must be. Yet, he surely ran it through his legal team. It is not immediately obvious why they were so relaxed about Garry opening himself up to being sued. Finally, I see. If I challenged him in a courthouse, Garry and his team would doubtless try and rely on the use of the word *may*. It is still a little embarrassing that he should be trying to oversell his accomplishments in this way, but that's what the insecure are prone to do. I am blessed that my own temperament is so different.

I click on the link to his books, which include what some idiots consider to be his seminal work – a multi-volume epic titled *My Great Predecessors*. It is Garry's assessment (with the help of computers) of every single previous world champion and a number of those who came close to taking the crown but just missed out. I was incandescent at the time to find that I had not warranted a mention. Beyond furious. There is professional rivalry and then there is blatant disrespect for your betters.

I click through to the contact page. There is an option of a form to fill in or an email address for his office. I elect to write him an email.

Dear Garry,

I am sorry the critics have not been kind to Your Great Predecessors. *I expect you have realised by now that your failure to include a chapter on me doomed your work to oblivion from the outset. I would still be open to you righting this wrong in any future reprint, for the sake of the fans as much as anything.*

Equally, if you think a single chapter could not do me justice (which was the most charitable motive that I could ascribe to you for my omission) I am open to any proposals you might have to write a whole book about my chess. Perhaps it could be called The Greenbecker Gambit. *Clearly, we will need to discuss my share of the royalties. I would imagine a 90% cut for me would be reasonable. I will leave that one with you to reflect on. Clearly,*

I will be happy to help if there are any elements of my play you struggle to get to grips with.

All of this can keep Garry. Frankly, I am a little annoyed we have started at something of a tangent. Please do try and be more focussed in the future. What I am really writing to you about is my forthcoming match with Magnus Carlsen. In an ideal world Gabriel would have approached you long ago, but knowing his level of competence as I do, I am assuming that is too much to hope for.

Having been alerted by a mutual friend to the fact that you might be available, I would like to offer you the opportunity to join my team. After all I have done for you over the years, often for very little thanks, I do feel that this is payback time. I think we both know that it is in the interests of the chess world for me to finally fulfil my destiny. In some ways Garry, this could well be your crowning achievement.

I need to be very clear Garry. I will be doing most of the media work myself. I really want your insight on the Sicilian and other such setups. Judging by your match with Kramnik, I will look elsewhere for tips on how to manage The Berlin Defence! LOL!

Given this is a unique opportunity to be a part of history I am proposing that you work for me for free. However, you can come back to me on this point if you wish.

Yours faithfully
Tennessee

I click send and watch my message disappear into the ether. I am sure it will not be long until I hear back from him. In fact, it would not wholly be a surprise if the same taxi driver ends up whisking him to me later this evening, and I imagine

Garry rushing into the internet café, sweat pouring off his brow, eager to get cracking. Grateful when I warn him off the fruitcake. These are exciting times indeed. Another good job done. Another wheel set in motion. As ever in life, if you want to get something sorted, do it yourself.

With Kasparov now in the bag, I open Bobby's book and look at game thirty-seven, which is titled 'Only a Draw.' I remember the last time that I saw Bobby. I made the trip to Iceland not all that long before he died. More than ten years ago now. Gabriel had not wanted me to go. He never thought that Bobby was a particularly good influence on me, for reasons that escape me now. In some ways I regretted going myself, not that I would ever tell Gabriel that. Bobby was a mess. Lots of shouting and swearing. Practically incapable of finishing a sentence on any subject without cursing the Jews. He looked terrible. His fear of doctors meant he rejected treatment that could have saved his life.

Many urged him to get help, but he always refused. I was generally more circumspect, which I know he appreciated. He was right not to trust doctors, or those in authority. Who is to say they would not just have killed him more quickly if given the opportunity? My own situation today helps me see this with piercing clarity – albeit, I will admit not trusting doctors did not help Bobby overly much either. Whatever choices you make, the State will ensure you end up dead in the end. Is it any wonder then, that humans have an inherent desire to burn everything down?

Bobby could still be quite lucid on occasion. I think he did have some regrets. In hindsight the reasons why he had walked away seemed less obvious to him than once they had been.

'Do not make the same mistakes as I have made, Tennessee,' he said to me. 'You've already been out of the game for far too long, it's time to get back playing, if the Jews will let you.'

I had long since reached the point where I knew that it was pointless to mention that the both of us were Jewish. I still appreciated the sentiment about me playing again. Bobby's encouragement always meant a lot to me. In his own way, he was telling me it was now on my shoulders to take forward his legacy. I was the only one capable of putting the kids of today back in their place.

We had an unbreakable bond. A shared clarity of purpose. People might have seen the wilderness years we had both spent away from the board as a waste. What did they know? The two of us achieved far more than anyone else. We just did it our own way, that was all. We gave as much as we could give. We were never afraid of our choices.

Time is pressing. I know I must head to The Breadline shortly. I read through the notes of 'Only a Draw.' I laugh at the double mistake on move fifty-six. Even Bobby would admit to me that he was never sure entirely what he had been thinking on that one! I still have it, of that there is no doubt. I am determined that after these years of exile my time is drawing close. If I fully believe in myself then nothing can possibly go wrong.

34. What your book is about

I step out of the internet café. The air feels different. There are dark clouds in the sky. Rain might be on its way. The scourge of every traveller. All those like me who venture forward in this world, reliant on our own resources. I tell myself that it matters not. Let it pour if it wants to. I am more than equal to the challenge. Nothing from the State on down is going to dampen my dreams or put my fire out.

Perhaps studying takes more out of me than it once did. In my mind the contours of the games I have just been looking at are already blurred. When I try and play them back in my head, I get confused between games two and four. Not a good sign. A lot is riding on my interview with Jasmine. Is it any wonder I feel distracted?

I worry that for all her credentials, she might be overwhelmed by a man of standing. Suppose she decides that she cannot do my story justice and does not print it? Suppose she gets the tone wrong? What if she fails to properly connect me with her readers?

I must put my faith in her professionalism. Jasmine will get down what I need. Not the story of me living on the streets that she initially pretended to latch onto. Not the cards. Not even my knowledge of fire. No, chess is my life. It is how I make sense of things. It is the version of me I most want to own. It is what serves to give everything else a point. It brings meaning to the lives of many others. Any reader could tell her this.

Interviews in general are something I have a lot of previous experience of, so perhaps I am worrying too much. Back in the day, those on the chess circuit were not too bad. Journalists wanted to understand my technical thoughts on the game I had just played. It was a language that I understood. If I was asked for views on my opponents, I was quite good at sticking to banalities. The libel actions I defended were entirely a product of idiotic editors. All recordings implicating me were manipulated so that my words were taken out of context, things I said rearranged to mean something quite different to what I had intended.

Was it credible that I might have stated that the president of the English Chess Federation deserved to be burnt at the stake? Fortunately, it was obvious to most that this was just a typically predictable attempt on the part of the State to smear me via a doctored cassette tape. If others sympathised with what I was alleged to have said, well that's also understandable.

My mother often mentioned that there was a question she hated to be asked in interviews. Namely, 'What is your book about?' Ultimately her book was about every word between the two hard or soft covers. If it had been possible to reduce the essence further, that would have been the book instead. Journalists did not seem to have the courage to tell her that two covers with nothing in between might have been the better way to go, that it would be a fairer representation of the emptiness of her heart. Instead they always seemed to make the mistake of asking her about what she had written.

I can imagine periodicals she appeared in often went bankrupt soon after features on her appeared, their readers deserting in droves. It is some consolation that at least these outfits generally printed on paper that burnt quite well. If I ever found anything she had featured in left around the house, I would take the publication into the garden and destroy it – always taking care to read the interview first to give my hatred a clearer shape.

As the pages turned to fire and then to ash, I would mimic some of her meaningless banalities. She would say that her story was about a journey. A tale of discovery. The ambiguity that runs through everyone. I care not for prizes and recognition she would lie. She was an arch-manipulator, that was all. Her hypocrisy and ability to hide who she really was continues to make me sick. Still, with my professional hat on, I can see how a few points along similar lines, with chess rather than literary references might really excite Jasmine and her readers. I will do what I must do.

It would be much harder for me to try and explain the true nature of my talent. I do not know why I see what I see when I look at a chessboard. I have no way of explaining that what appears as clear blue sky to me is but fog to others. Certain things are just the way they are.

If I sometimes feel that you might as well praise a dog for barking or a cat for sleeping as me for my skill at the board, that is just how it is. Although of course I play much better than most cats ever sleep. Genius by its very nature is enigmatic.

Most people who are bright enough to read Jasmine's piece doubtless already understand this.

I suppose there is a tiny part of me that still worries that Jasmine might be a secret agent. That this could all be part of a brilliant ploy to steal my folder, and to pump further information out of me. I don't know. I do not think she would have been able to fake being a successful journalist quite so effectively if she wasn't one, but I take nothing for granted. I will have to play it all by ear. Improvise if necessary. A story like mine needs to be told.

I take the Underground to Charing Cross. I worry about the rate I am going through money after already forking out on that taxi, but it is too far to walk. The State would not let me get away with taking another cab, that's for sure. I imagine heads have already rolled over me riding in broad daylight to the internet café. I laugh out loud at that thought and find that I am gasping for breath.

I savour a moment to appreciate my bravery and my brilliance, excited by all that is in front of me. Ultimately, this interview is my pathway to untold riches, so a Tube ticket is a mere trifle from an investment perspective. I buy a day pass and stick it in my back pocket.

The trains on this line always make me think to childhood holidays on the Isle of Wight. The retired London Underground stock that works its way up and down those few miles of wind-swept island track. We would rent a room in a cheap boarding house in Fishbourne with a view across the Solent.

In the day my mother would usually stay in the room and write, and my father would take me and Gabriel out and about

– to the long sandy beach at Appley, or to Brock or St Helen's. I liked looking out at the boats making their way across the shimmering blue water and imagining that I too was free. Sometimes we would go to Blackgang Chine. The theme park that was slowly falling into the sea. Nothing lasts forever, I would tell myself. Except perhaps for me.

I always had my pocket chess set of course. I would get up early in the morning, before any of the family stirred, to do some study, confident I was engaged in the most meaningful intellectual work that was happening on the Island that day. My mother would have been deluded if she tried to make the same claim, but either way she would generally be in a better mood in the evening, for having been left in peace to write during the day. Not that that was saying much. Even when she was being pleasant, I could never look at her without the fear of how she could be.

Back when Gabriel and I would still talk about things like this, he would often point to the holidays on the Isle of Wight as proof that everything had been normal all along. I suppose in a way he was correct. All that happened was normal to us. I just don't think much of it was right.

It is late morning now. The commuters are all in their air-conditioned prisons. The Tube is quiet. There are a few people in the carriage, but I find it easy enough to get a bank of four upholstered seats to myself. I put my rucksack on the floor in front of me, my feet up on the seats opposite.

It is not as if my life has been a complete disaster. Numerous chess players have got into far worse scrapes than I ever have. I remember some of the stories I used to read in *The Complete*

Chess Addict, along with the one about Alekhine, Capablanca and the peasant. Harold Davidson and the headlines he generated such as 'Rector's midnight call on waitress,' his attempts to save Soho girls from sin. Unfortunately, the photographic evidence at his clerical trial led to the conclusion that he was saving the girls for himself and he was ultimately defrocked. However much I beat myself up, there are merits in never opening your hotel door.

Then there was Norman Tweed Whitaker, International Master turned conman in the 1920s. Most famously, he got Lindberg's parents to pay him $100,000 for the return of their kidnapped child. Unfortunately, it transpired he knew neither the child or the kidnappers and was unable to extend any practical help. His efforts earned him a five-year stretch. Ridiculous I know. I say more fool the parents for believing him in the first place. If they were happy enough to hand over the money, why should there have been any comeback? He had offered them hope and who can ever do more than that? I mean really. Still, he did not let the experience crush him and went on to have a lucrative career clocking the mileage on car odometers.

Chess has had its fair share of rogues and chancers. Then there are the darker stories. Simon Webb, author of the beautiful *Chess for Tigers,* stabbed to death in 2005 by his own drug-addicted son. Brian Eley, who had a game that featured in Simon's book. British champion in 1972. On the run since the early 1990s. In the early days he could apparently be seen regularly playing in Amsterdam chess cafés. I would guess not so much now. The only British champion to also appear on *Crime Watch.* The English authorities had been warned all about him, or so it is said.

We played a few times of course. Brian always struck me as a deeply unpleasant man. Cold. Superior somehow. At tournaments a huge gaggle of children would follow him everywhere. Something else that would have been looked on with more suspicion in today's less naive times.

I do not know if these are stories about chess or about life. The world is certainly capable of being a very dark place. A lot can go wrong. In the long run chess is no form of protection against anything. Not only does it not necessarily make people happy, neither does it make them safe.

What to do? Perhaps the secret is to play as many games as possible. The feeling might be an illusion, as with so many other drugs, but at least while the game is in progress the things that can't be changed comes to matter less.

Finally, I make my way from the tube to the escalator, wheezing a little. As I stand on the moving metal steps, I think of my woolly mammoth and its lost tusk. The child I once was, pinned on a similar staircase at the end of a disastrous day. I am not that person anymore. This is a different time. I will reap the rewards for all the pain I have suffered. I have left my past behind.

35. A question of identity

I approach the exit gate and reach in my back pocket, but my ticket isn't there. Plenty of dirty tissues and a bit of change but that is it. Perhaps I have been mistaken. Could I have put the wretched thing somewhere else?

I try my front pockets, my coat. Nothing. I sit down outside the Perspex-fronted Underground office and start pulling everything out of my bag. My books, my toiletries. Clothes. The packet of Zip firelighters. My pocket chess set. I start to pile everything up and find myself shouting and banging the floor in frustration.

Two members of staff approach almost immediately. An Indian looking woman and a younger red-haired fat man.

'Is everything all right, sir?' she says. Softly. Politely. In a way that makes me think she might care, even though I know that's not how the State works. The young guy is eyeing me suspiciously, eyes bulging, almost as much as his belly. I notice that he has shaved poorly, missing a chunk of stubble underneath the chinbone of his otherwise smooth skin. I know that one false move and he will most likely beat me to death.

Perhaps this was the plan along. To steal my ticket and to use that as a pretext to murder me in Charing Cross Underground Station. I was so fixated on the Caruana video that I had not properly considered this more banal possibility.

Stop. I am getting ahead of myself. Yet again not thinking straight. Surely there are too many people about for them to kill me here. The trick will be to avoid being taken to some private room, where they can torture and do away with me out of sight. I must keep my head. Be polite and rational and hope for the best.

'It appears that my ticket has been stolen,' I say. 'But you probably know that already,' I add knowingly.

'How do you mean sir?' he says quizzically.

'I purchased a perfectly valid ticket, as you have doubtless already verified from the CCTV cameras, and now it is gone. I don't know how you managed to pull that off, but I take my hat off to the pair of you.'

I see them looking at each other. Weighing up my words.

'What precisely are you suggesting, sir?' she says, and I notice a faint smell of mint on her breath.

I try and stay calm. If others think I am shouting it is only that Underground stations tend to echo.

'I bought a fucking ticket, I now don't have a ticket, so you and your State colleagues must have stolen it. It is as simple as that. Now that I have rumbled you, I suggest that you let me on your way, and we will say no more about it.'

She sighs and I see that they had not anticipated me seeing all this quite so quickly. They have clearly underestimated my tactical capabilities.

'Just fuck off,' I scream accidently, but I think it was probably as well for me to assert myself. To show I will not be cowed. Their cheap blue uniforms and walkie-talkies mean nothing to me.

'Sir, it is an offence to travel on the London Underground without a valid ticket. It is an eighty pound fine I am afraid.'

'Eighty pounds! Eighty pounds! Outrageous! I have never seen such a sum of money in my life.'

'Well if you do not want to pay sir, you can always give us your name and address and the matter can be explored further in court.'

In different circumstances I might have pointed out that I did not technically have an address, but I worry this might give them grounds to detain me. It is tempting just to pay and be done with it. Cash leaves no trace. Still, having bought a ticket, paying again would, from a moral perspective, be the wrong thing to do. There is nothing else for it. I reach into my wallet and bring out my fake ID.

'The name is Wengrower, I say. Michael Wengrower.' They inspect the driving licence. It is a good fake. My photo and his details. It had been Bobby's idea that I should get something like this. I try not to overuse it, but it does come in handy from time to time.

Ultimately of course, this is another test. If my hunch is right and I have been deliberately targeted, they will know I am not Michael, but what choice do I have? The two of them look at the piece of plastic and take down the details. I know I shouldn't, but I can't resist. I say, 'Can I tell you my views on black people?'

'I really wouldn't Michael, I really wouldn't,' the gingernut replies. 'You are in more than enough trouble already. It is possible that TFL will also recommend charging you with a public order offence as well as the fare dodging. It will be for the big bosses to decide, but let's not push it any further.'

'I suppose it wouldn't help if I tried to bribe you?'

'That really is quite enough Michael,' the Indian lady tells me. Watching as I bundle my possessions back into my bag before escorting me from the station.

'Please do try and stay out of further trouble, Mr Wengrower,' she says to me as we stand at the exit.

At this point, I feel that Michael does not have much to lose.

'Go fuck yourself,' I shout on his behalf, by way of a parting shot.

What a fantastic triumph. The inability of the State to do anything right is quite shocking. I am sure Michael will make a terrible job of defending the case. Certain petty details are likely to cloud his rationality and result in him not being looked on favourably by the judge. Still, there is not much I can do about any of that. It should take care of him for a few years at any rate.

36. The interview

I head out of the Trafalgar Square exit. It is raining steadily now, but that does not bother me. Trafalgar Square is full of tourists happily filming each other. I can see Nelson's Column. I once heard a story that the architect who designed it later killed himself. I don't know if that is true, but it's a precedent that might usefully inspire others in his profession.

I do wonder why no one told him that Great Britain is an island. His Nelson just needed to look a little further, that was all. That's the difference between the truly great, like Nelson and me, and the ordinary people who shape inanimate objects and do other regular things. We always know how to visualise what really matters to us. To see further than the rest.

I walk past the South African embassy, with its simple photograph of Nelson Mandela in the window. Past the Co-op and the Pizza Express that is all of metal and glass. There is a man outside sitting on a piece of cardboard. He calls my name, but I ignore him. Then I turn the corner onto Duncannon Street, and I am at the Breadline Café. Simple glass windows. A red and white sign. A few metal tables and slated chairs outside the window.

Inside there is a glass counter at right angles, displaying cakes and rolls, soft drinks and biscuits. An extensive menu on the wall behind. There are tables for two along the window, tables for four everywhere else. Legs moulded into the floor. I hesitate, trying to work out whether Jasmine is one of the patrons, and a simple process of elimination suggests there is only one person here who might possibly be her. Drinking tea from a large white builders' mug that is resting on a saucer. Sitting next to her is a woman with Asian features and I can't immediately tell if they are together or not.

She sees me and gives that half-wave of hers. I wave back and approach the counter to order a tea, but Jasmine has got up and comes over.

'I'll get this Tennessee. My treat.'

I don't like to be patronised, but when I think about it, I am doing her a big favour by agreeing to be interviewed. Newspapers on the scale of hers have huge expense budgets, so given that, it is more than reasonable that she should buy the tea.

I would imagine that the lady next to her is most likely the photographer, even if I cannot see any obvious kit. Perhaps they do all this on phones now. Then again, she might be a senior executive from the paper, here to sign me up to a long-term deal. I will charge them a lot more than Boris Johnson for a regular column, that's for sure.

Outside of the chess fraternity, there have been one or two occasions when I have been interviewed by more famous presenters over the years, people who would put even Jasmine in the shade. I determine to remember this and ensure I put her at her ease.

Terry Wogan was my most mainstream foil. It wasn't the easiest. He seemed somewhat wary. Apparently, we sat down not long after his notorious interview with a drunk George Best and he had fears that I might turn out to be a similar character.

Well, I suppose I have the same sort of looks and charisma, so that was understandable really. I seem to recall that Terry did not understand chess all that well. I have a feeling that the BBC failed to show the interview in the end. I can't entirely remember why, but I presume the hand of the State was in there somewhere. I may or may not mention this to Jasmine. We will see how it goes.

Now that she is stood at the counter, I notice a certain hesitancy in her. It is to be expected. This is a big gig for her, despite her prominence. She smiles at me with her mouth but not with her eyes.

There is a newspaper on the side, and I glance at the headline as we wait for our drinks. It appears there has been a fire at the Red Lion, the damage more extensive than I thought. I still have a bit of the old magic in me. I suppose that is something. These things capture the public imagination for a reason. It might have been an accident, but I am pleased that my work has got people talking. A good omen for the interview.

'You came then,' she says. 'I wasn't sure if you would.' Her voice is a little more clipped than I remember. Her tone somehow more reserved.

'I am a man of my word. I did not want to disappoint your readers. I know everyone has been waiting for this day for much too long. Did you know that Einstein was offered the opportunity to be the first president of Israel, but he refused?'

She looks a touch surprised but does not say anything. She pays for our drinks. I am half-tempted by the cellophane-wrapped fruitcake – it looks infinitely moister than that on offer in the internet café. The numerous flavours of wafer biscuits look good too, but I don't say anything. I reach into my pocket and pull out my hip flask. Add a nip of something stronger to my tea, just to keep the cold out you understand. Jasmine is polite enough to pretend not to notice.

We sit back down, and she introduces me to the lady who is sitting next to her.

'This is Caroline,' she says. Caroline nods at me suspiciously and puts her hand on Jasmine's arm. Jasmine gently prises it off and they look at each other uncomfortably for a moment. Caroline is wearing tight fitting stonewashed jeans and a bright red blouse. On her feet are white pumps of the sort people used to don for P.E. lessons, which she wears without socks. She has placed her heavy winter coat, which is a pale blue with a darker grey fluffy lining, on the seat behind her.

'Hi Caroline,' I say. 'I'm…'

'Yes, I know who you are,' she says. 'We know who you are,' and she places her hand on Jasmine's arm again. This time Jasmine does not push it off and I notice that their feet are entwined underneath the table.

I am immediately uneasy. Could they be agents of the State? After all, they are clearly working together. If Caroline is an agent and Jasmine has brought her along, then surely Jasmine would have to be an agent as well. I try to tell myself that this is unlikely. Jasmine would not be the successful journalist that she is today if she went around setting the State onto her subjects. Besides, even a major paper such as hers can't afford to risk alienating an interviewee as valuable to them as I am.

Perhaps Caroline is indeed a more senior representative from the paper, someone who could not pass up the opportunity to meet me, but also wants to make sure the commercial aspects of the deal are right. She most likely does not realise how in demand I am. I hold all the cards here.

Still, her unwelcoming demeanour is a poor show really. I will bring this up with the editor and the owners of the paper when I meet them in due course. It could be that Caroline is just a bit jealous of both my talent and my obvious rapport with Jasmine.

'Where shall we start?' I say. It clearly falls to me as the possessor of the superior social skills to get things moving. 'I could tell you a little bit about my journey perhaps. My life has been a journey of discovery. I am a work in progress I suppose, but I know I am now standing on the cusp of immortality. I care not for the prizes and external recognition of course.'

I fear that Jasmine sniggers at this, but it is an involuntary reaction that she is quick to conceal by putting her hand over her mouth and breathing deeply. Caroline rolls her eyes. I should perhaps have gone into the interview more gradually; I can see I have left them somewhat overawed. I blame my mother. I sit still, unsure how to proceed.

'You weren't really what I was expecting to find,' says Jasmine, having now taken a moment to fully compose herself. 'Which is not necessarily a bad thing,' she hastily adds.

I can understand this. To happen across a man of my talents outside a Tube Station is not an everyday occurrence. The rest of Fleet Street will be kicking themselves when they realise the scoop that was sitting under their noses all along. Credit to Jasmine. I suppose it's her instincts for finding a story that have made her so successful.

Caroline seems to be inadvertently choking on her coffee. It must have gone done the wrong way and we pause to establish she is all right, before Jasmine continues.

'Originally this project was about interviewing people who were living their lives in the margins of the city. Those who were scrapping for survival. You certainly have something to tell us on that front, but what makes things different is that you have a famous mother and... a kind of unique backstory of your own.'

Unique. Thank goodness, she does understand after all. Even Bobby Fischer would not have pretended to be quite like me. I find myself admiring Jasmine's instincts more and more. Now is clearly the moment for me to move in for the kill.

'So, I thought I could tell you a bit about my chess career and my life in exile and why now is the time for me to come back and take on Magnus Carlsen. I think for £100,000 I would be happy to do that. Clearly, if you want to run more regular features on me, we will have to negotiate a different scale of fees.

'I would be happy to consider writing a daily chess column. I've got some fresh ideas on some of Bobby Fischer's *60 Memorable Games* that I know your readers would enjoy. I've always quite fancied the idea of writing a column on the history of London fires. What happened when, mixed with a few handy hints on how to start a great bonfire. How to enjoy the perfect 5th November. That kind of thing.'

Jasmine and Caroline are looking at me intently. I can see I have them in raptures, so I continue.

'How many of your readers understand why Guy Fawkes failed? Writing about the plot in letters was a bit of a mistake, obviously. Things have a tendency of falling into the wrong hands. The State reading it and Magnus Carlsen getting to see Caruana's opening preparation are one and the same really. If Fabiano knew his history, the disaster that has recently befallen him might have been avoided!'

'I'm sorry. I have no idea what you are talking about,' says Jasmine.

I see instantly that I am really going to have to dumb everything down for her readers.

'The State has always been useless,' I explain. 'Guy Fawkes was discovered when the undercroft beneath Parliament was searched. He managed to convince the soldiers that he was simply looking after some bundles of firewood. He was obviously very gifted, but even so, the soldiers were hardly of the highest intellectual calibre. I'm pretty sure Guy Fawkes could simply have offered up some fake ID and been on his way. Fuck! It makes me want to kick myself that he didn't try this when the guards returned later that night.'

'Um,' says Jasmine, but I am determined to finish the story. I know I've essentially given her a whole column's worth of insight already, but someone who has been as blessed as I am, can afford to be generous.

'I'll grant you his co-conspirators did not do a great job. It was unfortunate that Catesby's gunpowder got wet. Trying to dry it out next to the fire has understandably come in for some criticism over the years. It wasn't stupidity, historians who argue that do not know what they are talking about. No, I think it was just too tempting for him to be sat with all that gunpowder. The urge to use it must have been overwhelming. Waiting for exactly the right moment proved too much. I think most people in his position would have done the same. It's just human nature.'

Caroline turns to Jasmine. For some reason she says,

'I told you that this was a really bad idea.'

Jasmine ignores her. Perhaps she had told Caroline that this was a one-off interview and it is now obvious to both that I have enough to say to last most readers a lifetime.

'What was it like growing up with your mother?' Jasmine asks me.

'How long have you been together?' I say. I want to save them from the mistake of writing about my mother and then seeing their newspaper immediately go bankrupt.

'I don't think I know any other lesbians,' I say, just by way of making polite conversation. Strangely the observation seems to annoy Caroline.

'We're just people. We're not defined by our sexuality. Only a man would say something like that. You are in no position...'

I had not really clocked that Jasmine was that way inclined. If anything, I had assumed she was somewhat attracted to me, as anyone would be of course. I will admit this is generally what I assume, even though it is not always right. I must admit that has been made clear to me somewhat forcefully on occasion. Still, if this is what Jasmine feels deep down, that could likely explain Caroline's hostility.

'We've been together a long time,' says Caroline.

'Not long,' says Jasmine, simultaneously. They look at each other awkwardly and I can tell that this exchange is something they are going to come back to later. Still, there is nothing I can do about it. It has nothing to do with me. Just another thing from which I am excluded.

'I'm not exactly out yet,' says Jasmine. 'Growing up it was never really how I wanted to be. I suppose you get to a point when you can no longer pretend to be somebody you are not.'

'Some of us reach that point, at any rate,' Caroline says.

'Okay, okay,' Jasmine interjects. 'Let's just get on with doing what we need to do.'

'I did warn you,' Caroline says to Jasmine, but I haven't got the faintest idea what she is talking about.

'How many of your readers know what caused the Crystal Palace fire in 1936?' I ask, and I can tell from the look of surprise this is a question their editorial board has yet to properly consider. Before they can speak, I continue.

'That's right, none! Nobody knows – and does the fact that it was made of iron and glass not strike you as a little odd? How would something like that burn? You have surely wondered why there was never an official enquiry? That was never going to happen. It was all a State job. How many people have made the connection between that and the fact that the world's strongest ever chess tournament was taking place in Nottingham that same year? The whole country must have been crawling with agents of various States. It wouldn't surprise me to learn that they were all falling over each other in their attempts to burn something down. Surely this is worth exploring further. Your readers will be fascinated!'

'I think that's perhaps enough about fire for today,' says Jasmine. 'So… What was it like to grow up with your mother?' she asks. 'I hear she could sometimes be a difficult character, is that true? What about the story that she deliberately ran over Jim Crace's cat? What was that all about?'

I do vaguely remember some sort of incident with a cat, but I can't be sure if it was Jim Crace's. I think my mother had been drinking. There was certainly an argument at a literary garden party. Not that that was anything out of the ordinary. In my experience, writers leave whatever perceptiveness they have behind when they get up from their desks. What followed might well have been an accident. It was all a long time ago. I can no longer be sure. I shrug. Say nothing. I can think of no comment on the cat. I seem to recall my offer to incinerate the body was churlishly refused.

'What was she like as a parent?' Jasmine persists.

I hesitate. Stare into my tea. A difficult endgame position I had years ago in a match against Karpov comes into my head. The intuitive move was for Karpov to push his king pawn forward. That is what most club players would have done. Instead, Karpov pulled his king back a square, leaving me completely lost. Then he sat there preening and picking his teeth. All I could do was stare across the table at him in hatred, watching the grease drip from hair he considered unlucky to wash during a tournament. He had me cornered, just as I am right now. I see no way forward other than to talk about my mother.

'On your head be it,' I say. 'If you chose to write about this and your paper goes into administration as a result, don't say I didn't warn you. I doubt this is what your readers really want to hear about from me, but if you insist, I will tell you. It was difficult. She was distant. Cold. She lived with her books and in her head most of the time. I used to wish that she was more present but, ultimately, I ended up hoping for something else entirely. You do know she was violent and manipulative, don't you? Very handy with her fists. She made me drink out of the toilet bowl once. I was scared to death of her. Me and my brother, Gabriel, both were.

'Gabriel blots it all out now, says it was all fine. He is just kidding himself. I find that much harder to do. I suppose that is why I got so serious about chess at such a young age. I thought I was trying to prove myself to her. To win her love. Now I see that I was just trying to escape. It is a dilemma. I might not have become the world champion I am today had it not been for her, but I sometimes wish it could all have been different.

'People can wear many faces. Do you remember that book she wrote about a man who tracked down the prison guard who had tortured him? Finally, he finds him, but when he gets to his tormentor's house, he sees his torturer playing ever so gently with his blind son. He is thrown. This can't be the same person. But it can be. It is. The capacity both for evil and for good resides in all of us. I would like to tell you that when it comes to my mother, I am every bit as confused as the man was when he looked at the guard with his son. But that would not be true. I am not confused at all.'

'I can tell that I have their full attention. Every chess player knows there are times when just sitting and waiting for a moment is the best way to put your opponent on edge. Perhaps I overdo this for effect, as I hear Jasmine asking what I mean by this.

'Let's look at the evidence,' I say. 'The woman was a bitch. Anyone who knew her like I do, would hate her. On the one hand you have the books. They have been hard for me to read, but I understand why people like them. What does that really mean though? It is far too soon for any of us to really know if they are any good or not. The reckonings of history are a long way off. I certainly don't think her literary legacy is a given.

'There are too many others who were once considered an enduring part of the canon who no one reads now. I knew Beverly Nichols slightly through my mother. He always had a very high opinion of himself. It did not surprise me that when he wrote about his own legacy, he considered that two hundred years from now he would be spoken off in the same breath as Jane Austen and Beatrix Potter. I suppose it could still happen, but the odds-on *Cats ABC* or *Down the Garden Path* remerging are somewhat on the long side.

'Angus Wilson could not have been more decorated when alive. A Knight of the realm and President of the Royal Society of Literature, but his complete works ended up in the remainder bin. So, it goes on, *American Tragedy* was the world's greatest book in 1925 and hardly anyone today has heard of it. Dreiser is forgotten! Paul Scott anyone? Judith Greenbecker the novelist still might not ultimately amount to a thing. Judith Greenbecker the person is much easier to be definitive about. I can certainly do that. She was a terrible human being and if I believed in hell then I would want her to burn there.'

Caroline is staring at me intently.

'Do you not think you risk damaging your mother's reputation for no good reason at all? That in this day and age you might want to be a bit more careful about what ideas you give voice to? I don't think what you are saying is credible. You are a jealous fantasist. That's the truth isn't it?'

37. Before the net closes in

I trail off. I am not used to people doubting me, various other lesser, weak-minded individuals aside. It is not as if I really care what they choose to write about my mother. For once in my life this was meant to be about me.

I take a deep breath and realise I recognise the man at the counter – in the silence which has fallen I hear him ordering a mushroom omelette with chips and beans and a black tea. He wears a grey suit without a tie. He has a copy of the *Daily Telegraph* under one arm. He has put on weight in recent years. It would be a stretch to say he looks better for it.

Steff Holmes. A chess hack I can't stand. He tends to write wistful colour pieces bordering on the sentimental. I know he has written a book. I know he still works at a utility company as the writing does not pay. If he saw me, he would want an interview. Even if he is nowhere near the league that Jasmine operates in, part of me is tempted to go over and say hello.

I am not aware of Steff rubbishing my openings or writing about my alcoholism. While that is something, I am not actually cognisant of him ever having written about me at all. That is where my anger stems from.

He gives too much space to Bobby Fischer and Magnus Carlsen. His own days out at major chess events. Chess books that moved him when he was a child. Like anyone cares about any of that! He could certainly burnish his chess credentials by writing about me. He has missed an obvious trick on that front. His own chess is too useless for him to be trying to protect his own legacy by not giving me my dues. It is highly likely that he is in the employ of the State and they are bribing him not to write about me.

He stands at the counter, picking the tea bag out of his steaming mug with the wrong end of a spoon. He scans the restaurant looking for a seat. For a moment our eyes lock, but he pretends not to recognise me and takes a seat at the other end near the door.

Perhaps I have not given him enough credit. He would doubtless interview me in a heartbeat if he thought I would agree. However, he knows to respect the boundaries of the famous. He would not want to intrude, particularly as he will probably assume I am with a couple of groupies. That our next stop is likely to be The Charing Cross Hotel for a threesome. Just the middle of a typical day for a star like me. He might be a terrible chess player, but unlike Chris Hamish, at least he would appear to have some manners and the ability to accurately appraise a social situation.

Jasmine is trying to get my attention. I must have been lost in these thoughts for longer than I realised. She doubtless understands that her lover's career at the newspaper is now over, whatever she says by way of trying to make amends. At least now, we will be able to talk about chess. It is easier for me to say something myself than it is to try and pick up the thread of what she is saying to me, so this is what I do.

'Tell me again about your writing?' I ask. Trying to steer us back into calmer waters, to retake control before we get on to the stuff that is important, which obviously is talking about me. My diplomatic skills are often underappreciated. 'How did you get to be a famous journalist at a top newspaper?'

Jasmine looks surprised. Uncomfortable even.

'Who told you that?' she asks.

'Well you did,' I say. 'It's okay, I'm quite modest too, but it's fine to take credit for your achievements.'

'I'm not exactly famous,' she says.

Everything is relative of course, but I tell Jasmine that she should not let my own accomplishments detract from her own.

'Look,' she says. 'I have my own blog. Mainly about my life in London, places I've been, things I've seen. It is not a touristy thing. More about the London of the everyday. The city that somehow gets forgotten in plain sight. The people I meet who might not otherwise be able to tell their own stories. I write a bit about books and some more personal reflections too. I have a few hundred followers in theory, but I would guess about fifty people who read me regularly. It is not much, but it is still something.'

'It is very good indeed,' says Caroline, staring at me defiantly. 'How many people can say they are being read by anyone? You just need the right person to start following you and that will make a huge difference. Lisa Lynch had a tiny following before Stephen Fry discovered her and then everything changed.'

A blog. Fifty readers. Fuck. I have been brought here entirely on false pretences. Jasmine is not who I thought she was. I hate those who misrepresent themselves. No wonder she did not properly appreciate my suggestions about London's fires. She isn't of the necessary calibre to get it.

Damn. No wonder Caroline was so dismissive when I told her the truth about my mother. I am dealing with complete amateurs. This is all a total waste of my time and time is one thing I feel like I no longer have.

I feel my anger rising. Magnus is doubtless giving interviews to the world media at this very moment, while here I am, stuck in a café with a nice lesbian who writes a tiny blog. It is all Gabriel's fault. He is meant to properly vet my media opportunities, but again has been completely negligent in his task. I am going to let Garry Kasparov handle this side of things for me going forward. Being family only counts for so much.

'Un-fucking-believable,' I say. 'This is a complete joke! You knew you would never get to interview such a prominent chess player based on your own credentials, so you blatantly lied to get me here. How dare you? Have you any idea the damage you have done? The advantage Carlsen will steal on me now?'

I bang my head hard against the table and then bang it again.

'For God's sake, don't do that,' Jasmine says, and I bang my head again just to spite her.

'All this time I've been waiting to make my comeback, and thanks to you everything is going wrong. Are you working with him, is that it? Is this all part of a plot to distract me? You are all the same. For Christ sake, what have I done to deserve such a cruel and unforgiving world?'

'Please stop banging your head,' Jasmine says, and this time I do. Not because she has asked me, but because I feel I am developing something of a headache.

'The reason I want to do interviews like this is so that I can finally write my book,' Jasmine says, perhaps sobbing a little. She speaks softly but with intensity. 'I've provisionally titled it *Conversations in the City*. I will feel like I have done something important – I will have helped to tell your story and those of others like you. We can still get your interview back along the right lines if you would like to?'

'It would probably make more sense for me to talk to each of your followers one to one. I could do that. I have a good twenty minutes to spare after all. Fuck, that would give me time to talk to some of them twice. You will appreciate that this is a long way from my interview with Terry Wogan, which would have been seen by millions, had the BBC shown it. No offence, but it's very difficult for a man of my standing to reduce himself to being interviewed by a total failure like you.'

'Fuck off,' snaps Caroline. 'How dare you speak to her like that. It's fucking outrageous. I told you,' she says turning first to look at Jasmine and then back at me, 'you are just a pathetic fantasist, aren't you – Terrence?'

She spits out the word Terrence as if it is a swear word. The name the bullies used all those years ago. The name I have long since renounced. Why is it that people always try and hurt me? What do I ever do to them?

Jasmine looks aghast. 'We said we wouldn't do it like this!' she shouts at Caroline.

'I have no idea who you are talking about,' I say with all the dignity I can muster. 'Terrence belongs to a different age. A different time. I have no idea who he is anymore. If you were proper journalists, you would know that. I am Tennessee, not Terrence.'

'It doesn't really work like that does it, Terrence?' says Caroline. 'We don't wholly get to define who we are. She leans in close across the table. 'When you said that your mother was Judith Greenbecker, we googled you. We didn't expect what you told us to be true, but of course we discovered that some of it was. Judith Greenbecker had two children. Terrence and Gabriel. There's a surprising amount about you in your mother's Wikipedia entry. Do you want me to tell you what it says?'

I see it all now. Caroline sees me as a love rival. With my sexual charisma she realises she has no choice but to destroy me. I am shaking too much to speak. Have been rendered mute by this onslaught. It had not occurred to me that the State might hack my mother's Wikipedia page. That they would give old lies the ring of truth and put them online for all the world to see.

'You claim to be a top chess player, but whatever promise you might have once shown was a very long time ago. You are a loser with psychological issues, a drink problem and a suspected interest in pyromania.'

I had no idea. The State is even more powerful than I gave it credit for. I am so much more than 'interested.' An entirely false narrative has been constructed about me and people believe it! This cannot be allowed to stand. It might just be Caroline. A more rounded person who researched my life would not take long to draw on a wider variety of sources. I will not be defined by a fake Wikipedia reference! I know these things can be edited by anyone.

The explanation might be simpler than the State at work. It might have been Wengrower. Perhaps a Carlsen fan trying to make me a less attractive proposition to the sponsors. Perhaps

Caroline herself. I know these are all highly likely explanations and I cannot stop my anger rising.

'You, most likely, wrote all that yourself. You fucking, witch,' I yell at her. 'Let's face it, Jasmine probably does not write well enough to have done it.'

'Oh, fuck you,' says Caroline. 'It's not just Wikipedia though is it?' she says. 'What about all the other stuff?'

I stick my fingers in my ears and start to sing very loudly so I cannot hear her unhinged diatribe.

I am done for. Destroyed. The State is writing terrible lies about me. I have a sinking feeling in my stomach, akin to the occasions when I ended up wrestling Dubrovnik to the floor and I lost all that money at the card table. Our raised voices have drawn the attention of other customers. People are looking our way. The proprietor has come over. He has an accent I cannot quite place. Perhaps Italian. Perhaps Albanian. He has a neatly trimmed beard. His blue and white apron is new and fresh, his white chef outfit of an older vintage. He is usually polite, but never warm. I can see that today he is annoyed.

'What the fuck is going on?' he says, waving his arms in the air. 'Please either be quiet or fuck off.'

It hardly constitutes great customer service, but what can you do? My head might be spinning from banging it against the table, but the truth is I have never seen things more clearly my whole life. It has taken this false denunciation for everything to fall into place.

I fully recognise, perhaps for the first time, the magnitude of the forces that are set against me. The State has launched an all-out online attack against me. My secrets are doubtless being dissected in some government chess lab at this very moment. I also sense that if I act quickly, I can ensure that none of what has transpired will divert me from my goal. It must be now or never.

I have no choice but to issue my challenge to Magnus immediately. This very day. Before the net closes in.

38. Let's play

I stand up and struggle to pull my rucksack out from under the plastic table, but somehow, I manage. I reach into my coat pocket for my hip flask, down the remaining vodka in a single large gulp. Feel the warmth burn inside my throat. Caroline is staring at me angrily. Jasmine is crying. I hate them both. I love them too.

Without all they have said and done, I might not have seen the world so clearly. They have alerted me to the precarious nature of my situation. The need for me now to move quickly. To fully embrace the course of action I should have embarked on long ago.

Forget the nonsense about needing to prepare further. The practical difficulties that could flow from the Carlsen - Caruana championship being in progress. The administrative challenges FIDE might yet put my way. They all count for nothing. They are the worries of a man made from clay and I will not be that man any longer. I am made of steel. I have the strength to go where others fear to tread. To take decisions that others might balk at. This is what real champions do. I have failed to be true to myself for far too long, but all that is going to change now.

Jasmine asks if we can talk about it all, but I tell her there is nothing left to say. I tell her that she might not be much of a journalist, but she has helped a great man see his destiny more clearly, and history will thank her for it.

Caroline is yelling that I should be ashamed of myself. That I should be in jail. That people are looking for me. She says that my clothes stink of smoke. That she would not be surprised if I happened to have stayed in a hostel that has been in the news recently. She would also wager that I might have visited the Red Lion, given that the description of the guy they are looking for is remarkably like my own. For some reason the word arson is being liberally, and in my view misguidedly, bandied about.

Thank God Gabriel paid the bill. That is something to be thankful for. Didn't they ask him to stay put and he chose not to? Whatever I personally believe, I understand why others might think he has a case to answer. If only he was a more loyal brother, I could be free of this nagging doubt that he might somehow drag me into all this when they ultimately catch up with him. Another reason for haste, no doubt. I mean, who ever heard of a world chess champion being convicted of arson? Once the title is mine, I know I will be safe.

Adversity brings out the best in me. I need no more confirmation that everything I am doing is entirely along the right lines. It is time to be brave. Where others wilt, I grow stronger. It is time to take what is mine and to hell with the rest of them.

Quite reasonably, I yell at Caroline to fuck off and die and then I march out of the café, ignoring the rude stares of some of the customers. The shouts from the proprietor not to come back. Steff Holmes looking up from his paper. I figure that

315

if he doesn't choose to put me in one of his columns now, he probably never will.

I take out my lighter, hands shaking as I fumble for a smoke. I drag extra hard on a cigarette as I make my way to Charing Cross tube station. It is raining heavily. A cold winter's day. I care not for the elements. Miraculously, when I fumble in my back pocket, I find my Tube ticket. The State must have replaced it when they knew I was onto them. I hope this isn't going to let Michael Wengrower off the hook.

I light another fag as I head down the escalator. A TFL person appears to consider challenging me, but wisely thinks better of it. Word has most likely got around that I am not to be messed with.

I stamp my cigarette out on the platform and proudly shout, 'Now is my fucking time!' Delighted that no one on the platform challenges me. They all know! What I am professing is obvious! I yell that I will return to sign autographs later, and I can tell that this is appreciated. I am not surprised that a deferential gap opens up between me and the other commuters.

While it will disappoint my fans, I realise this could be the last time I ever take the Tube. It's pretty much going to be chauffer driven limos from here on in. I take the line to Leicester Square, change trains and soon I have reached Holborn.

I know where the London College venue is. It is not far to walk. Just as well as the rain is heavy now. I pass a grand old building, all red brick and white trimmings. More modern office blocks of concrete and glass. The 1960s-style Unite the Union headquarters, the Royal College of Anaesthetists. A white and yellow sign says 'Warning to Busses' and contains a red and white triangle with an exclamation mark below it, reading 'Low Trees.' Another notice highlights the presence of traffic enforcement cameras and a ringed sign says that this is a 20mph zone. There is scaffolding on several buildings. Repairing, renewing, burning and rebuilding; nothing ever stays the same.

Outside the venue are black and white banners, proclaiming 'FIDE World Chess Championship Match - London 9-28 November 2018'. One has a silhouette of Caruana. A few white flecks in his hair. Glasses. Nose slightly pointed. Carlsen's silhouette is a touch rounder and squatter. There are a smaller number of longer white wavy lines within his hair. His nose is less pronounced, but the chin is rounder. I doubt that either of them would much like this artwork, but they doubtless have other things on their mind. I am a little disappointed that there is not also a picture of me, but I suppose the State would never have allowed it.

There are further images. A black and white chessboard with three hands growing out of it, each of which hold a chess king. Around the corner a white banner that says 'Let's Play' in black lettering. I can see that I am going to need to think very carefully about my image rights. I will certainly need to sign off on photographs that get used. I think Magnus and Fabiano have been somewhat amateurish on this front. I suppose they are both just kids, it is unrealistic to imagine either one could be as savvy as I am.

I remind myself what I am here to do. It is disappointing that I have been distracted by the artwork. I despise my lack of focus sometimes, but there is a lot to take in. It has been a while since I have been this close to a world championship match.

I was too young to be with Bobby in Reykjavik, although

I know he found the notes I sent him invaluable. I was in Moscow and Leningrad for some of the Kasparov and Karpov matches. London for Kasparov – Short was an easy hop, even if it disappointed me that Nigel and his sidekick Dominic Lawson refused to have anything to do with me. It was almost as if they were not aware of my existence. I would have been in New York for Kasparov – Anand, but I had one or two difficulties getting into the US that I won't go into now.

I was never wholly comfortable at any of matches I did make it to. Yes, it was nice to be lauded as an expert commentator. To sign autographs and be eulogised by the fans. Many would ask for my opinion on the game in play then listen to my observations with an intensity generally reserved for a doctor's verdict on how much time the patient has left. Yet this is so much more exciting. This time I am here to play!

If only I had realised sooner, that all it would take was for me to demand that the challenger gave up his seat. Yield to me and my better claim on the stage. Everything could have been so simple. There was no need to have wasted so many years. This is all so obvious that it makes me want to cry, but what would that achieve? Any tears should be of joy now I have finally, finally seen the light.

The need to move before the State can close in on me has pushed me forward. It is amazing how quickly all can change. Even the most powerful of fires turns to ash in the end. I had not even fully realised this morning. There will not be another chance like this. I owe it to my fans. I owe it to myself. I owe it to Bobby. Today is the day when I will become everything I ever wanted to be. At long last it really is my turn.

Bobby said to me when I saw him in Iceland for the last time that he had taken things as far as he could. That his moment had passed, and it was going to fall on me to carry forward his torch. To show the world what real chess looked like. That it was possible to return from the street and to still be the very best there was. Chess players as real men, a world away from the plastic kids of the modern generation.

He did add a few further thoughts about the Jews and the like, which were not worthy, but I always knew Bobby did not mean them. A lifetime at war with the State took its toll toward the end, that is all. I have always known that I am mentally stronger than he was. I cannot believe that conversation was more than a decade ago, but one way or another today was always going to come.

It is getting on for four o'clock. Game five has been in progress for nearly an hour now. The first one Caruana has had to face with the fear that Carlsen's team knows all his secrets. I feel for him, I really do. By taking over the match, I will be doing the American a favour. It is a kindness. I am better placed mentally to cope with the machinations of the State than he is. I am always delighted when I can be of help to others. Caruana will most probably shake my hand and look on me with relief. This is what fellow chess players are for.

It is strange to think that the players are so close. I would imagine only tens of metres from where I stand on the sodden pavement. Still a world away in some senses, but not for much longer. They will all be in there. The chess journalists in the media room, live streaming their thoughts around the globe while munching on digestive biscuits. There will be a certain amount of bitterness and envy. Who wouldn't rather be strong enough to play in a match like this rather than simply commentate on it? They all know that no one on the planet beyond those two and me are worthy of such an honour. Still, that does not stop people from having irrational thoughts as to where their talent might take them.

There are no queues. I suppose those who were planning to attend are already inside by now. I see a lone camera crew filming an interview, gamely trying to ignore the rain that is soaking their kit, but the discussion is most likely in Norwegian and I do not recognise either of the bearded participants. I suppose this would count for a positively tropical day by Norwegian standards, which is why they are happy to talk outside. If only the BBC had shown me the same level of support Norway TV has Magnus, there is no knowing how much more I might have achieved.

I hesitate for a moment, just to firm up my next step, shivering in the cold. I look at the sign saying that the match is sold out today. I suspect people must have guessed I was coming!

Rain is now seeping through my coat and suit. Despite their undoubted quality the fact that my garments are old is starting to show. What does it matter? What does any of it matter? Such worldly considerations are beneath me. When I am world champion, I will buy a thousand new suits and burn them all. The things of this world do not count for much. Still, I intend to seize them now or go out in a blaze of glory.

If it transpires I face a binary choice between becoming world champion and dying trying, then so be it. How does that line go from that stupid film Gabriel loved so much? 'Do or do not, there is no try.' There would be a nobility that goes with perishing in such circumstances.

The choice has a point to it. World's greatest ever chess player dies on street outside Carlsen – Caruana has a certain ring. I would be remembered. Nothing scares me now. Having given all this a proper go, I would be equally happy in heaven or hell. Hell might be the better option. They certainly know how to make a decent fire.

39. Possibly back from the dead

There are two entrances. A VIP doorway that you would think should have my name written above it and another for those who are happy to watch the same spectacle without paying to eat over-priced caviar and drink supermarket standard champagne. Even in chess, we have alas sold out to the prawn sandwich brigade. Another thing I am going to have to fix. So frustrating that everything seems to fall onto my shoulders.

There are security men outside both entrance doors, which is something I did not anticipate. Tall, thickset guys who clearly do a lot of gym work. They both wear dark suits and waistcoats. Earpieces with wires leading to boxes on their waists. Black shoes as polished as the finest chess pieces you will ever see. State muscle. Despite my inner reserves of strength, I am not altogether certain that I could overpower both of them. Brute force might not be the best answer.

I know that the officials are also likely to stand in my way. That I must make an appeal direct to Fabiano and Magnus. Finding a way to get in could prove tricky if there really are no tickets available today. If I do not get this right, I could find myself back out on the pavement or with a crowbar through my head before I have even shaken hands with Magnus.

I still remember that wretched British Championship when they denied me access, knowing that my presence in the building would render their poxy tournament meaningless. That no one else could honestly look me in the eye and claim to be the British champion. I understand now that me being there would have made a mockery of the whole event.

What happened at the British was more about pride on their part than anything else. Possibly not helped by some of the things I said about the wife of a senior English Chess Federation official. An insight that crystallised after I had one or two drinks. Everybody already knew. Well, everybody apart from him, which I suppose was the problem. Most would have considered I had done him a favour – goodness knows, his wife had done others more than enough.

What to do, what to do? I consider the options. I could tell them who I am, plain and simple, and dare them to do their worst. If they murder me so be it! No one could then deny that I had given everything for my art. It sounds like a ridiculous idea, but I have learnt that a real chess player should consider the most unlikely of options. The risk reward trade-off is not wholly unattractive. It would certainly get their attention. They would never have anticipated such a brazen gambit.

I contemplate what other tricks I might be able to try. I could pretend to be someone else and claim that my ticket has been lost or stolen. I have the aura of a man who belongs at a match like this, an energy around me that should be apparent to the lowliest of officials. I think this might have worked once, back in the 1980s say, but it is not necessarily a given today. Security guards do not have the same room for manoeuvre as once they did.

'I'm terribly sorry sir, but if you do not have a ticket, we can't let you in. If it has been stolen, you should report that to the police. I have to say, sir, your knowledge of chess is quite remarkable. If it was left to me, not only would I let you in, but I would ensure that you got to play the match instead of Caruana. You sort of remind me of that brilliant guy. What was his name? Tennessee, I think? Seems only fair to me, but it is somewhat above my paygrade, sir.'

That would ideally be how the conversation would go. Still, I wonder if a variation on this approach might work. I cannot think of anything else and I am not brilliant for nothing. Sometimes all that is left is to hit and hope. I see now what I am going to do.

I approach the security guard at the plebs entrance.

'Hello.'

'Hello,' he says. With a neutrality that just about shades into politeness, but only just.

He is relatively young. Perhaps in his thirties. He has light brown skin and has that look about him of a boxer at his pre-fight press conference. Rippling muscles. An expression of glazed indifference that is really a form of focus.

'I wondered if you might let me in?' I say. 'I have important business inside.'

'I'd be happy to sir. Just show me your ticket and you will be good to go.'

I can see he has not made up his mind about me. Is unsure whether I have a ticket or not. Am I just another of the mild eccentrics who goes to events like this, for whom practicalities such as producing purchased tickets is always a stretch, or am I something else entirely? Even with so much at stake, I take pleasure in the fact that he does not quite know. Is not able to read me. I wonder if I might ever be able to get him involved in a game of cards.

If I had been organising an event like this, I would have made it mandatory for the security team to be able to identify the world top 100 and other chess luminaries by sight, but this is something else FIDE has clearly overlooked. I suppose I am also a little surprised that they haven't got a photograph of me on the front desk. The good thing about bureaucratic organisations from my perspective is that they are always so inefficient.

'The thing is, I don't have a ticket, but you still need to let me in.'

He sighs. Moves his head from side to side. Shrugs his shoulders.

'I'm terribly sorry sir, but I am not allowed to do that. We are sold out today, but there are tickets available for some of the later games. You would be most welcome to attend one of those. I could escort you to the desk, so you can make a booking if you like. I have strict instructions not to let anyone in unaccompanied who does not already have a ticket.'

I am desperate to scream at him that I do not want a ticket to a later game. I certainly do not want to *watch*. I tell him to fuck off and die but am very clever and do this without moving my lips or making a sound. He is too stupid to get the message. I follow up by saying out loud, 'Thank you, sir, that is very kind. Where do I need to head?'

I am hoping that he will take the hint and just point me where I am supposed to go, but he doesn't. Instead we go through the main entrance, walk together up a flight of marble steps and stand at a crowded desk.

There is something of a commotion. Spectators are complaining about their tickets. Apparently, they are only valid for time slots of half-an-hour each in the main theatre. I get the sense that this was not something that had been previously advertised. Imagine going to a football game and being told that you can only watch the action for thirty minutes at a time, I hear someone saying.

There are two ladies at the desk, and I can see that they are harassed. It is stifling. The security guard standing with me is getting restless. The queue is longer than he envisaged. I hear a blare of static on his transistor. He whispers something into his microphone. I see that he is torn. He wants to be at the entrance not standing in this queue with me but is wary of letting me go. It is time for some reverse psychology.

'I do so appreciate you waiting with me, sir,' I say.

'It's quite all right, just doing my job, sir,' he says back.

I am on the verge of apologising for swearing at him earlier, but I'm reasonably sure he will not remember my silent outburst.

'Really very kind of you. I'm not convinced I would have been able to master something like this on my own. Do you think when we've got my ticket, we might be able to have a cup of tea together?'

'Er, I appreciate the thought sir, but I am rather busy. Lots to do. I wouldn't want to hold up a man who is doubtless also as busy as you are,' he says.

'Oh, that's no bother at all. It would be good to get to know one another better. While I think about it, would you mind giving me your address? I am free for the rest of the week, so I might be able to pop over for a night or two if you like? I've got a couple of dogs I will need to bring with me, but they are nearly house-trained.'

'Er, I'm not sure that would be entirely convenient sir, besides I've always been allergic to dogs.'

'Settled! I'll leave the fuckers behind. They can easily fend for themselves for a week or so. I've got a very good folder as you probably know. My thoughts on chess and deep State conspiracies. I reckon if we give ourselves a month or two, we should be able to do them justice.'

I can see a look of growing alarm on his face. I wait to see if he will take the bait.

'I'm very sorry sir, but there is a matter at the main entrance that needs my urgent attention. Just wait here to buy a ticket and then go. I will be checking that you have left the building,' he says with as much menace as he can muster while seeming to remain polite.

'Indeed, I will,' I say. 'I'll make sure I find you to swap details before I leave, seeing as you are so insistent that I should come around.'

He grimaces and is gone.

I know how to do this now. I wait at the desk for a few more moments in case he is watching, then I peel away and make my way toward the parts of the building that you do not need a ticket for. There is a tiny cafétéria with a screen showing the game. At a glance I can see it looks 'drawish' already. I can see how Magnus might have made more of it, but of course that is why I am me and he isn't. The atmosphere is about as compelling as the overpriced cakes and coffees on sale. I perch at one of the raised, circular metal tables, wondering how long it will take before somebody recognises me.

A balding man comes and sits on the seat next to mine. He wears a green corduroy jacket and brown corduroy trousers. Opened-toed sandals on his feet. He reaches into a plastic Tesco's bag and pulls out a foil-wrapped cheese and cucumber roll and a copy of *Silman's Complete Endgame Course*. He barely acknowledges me and turns to a page on rook and two connected passed pawns v rook and pawn. As he reads and eats, crumbs from his roll fall onto the pages.

He has offered no form of greeting beyond his initial half-nod. In the chess world I would still rate his social skills as a touch above average. Occasionally he looks up from his book to take in the latest Carlsen – Caruana position on the monitor. Finally, the inevitable happens and our eyes meet. I wait for a flash of recognition. The moment when he will realise that he is in the presence of a true great.

I can more or less forgive a taxi driver or café owner for not immediately recognising me, but it would be unforgivable for someone who has purchased a ticket to the world championship match and happens to find himself sitting in such close proximity to a living legend such as myself, to make the same mistake.

Nothing. He says nothing. I try to put him gently at his ease.

'I'm Tennessee,' I say. 'Tennessee Greenbecker. My guess is that you knew that but did not want to say anything.'

He looks uncomfortable. Mind racing overtime. There are

many chess players who can remember every detail of the games they have played, but none of their opponents' faces. Perhaps he is one of them. I can see him trying to formulate a response. I sense he would rather be studying his endgame, although after a lifetime at the board, if he does not understand that one by now then he really is in trouble.

Eventually, it comes.

'Tennessee. Er, didn't you used to play for Nuneaton?'

Idiot. The man knows nothing. Society has dumbed down to an even greater extent than I thought. What has the world come to when a man can be admitted to a world championship match despite being unable to recognise a true chess great or to play a simple rook endgame? Nuneaton! I ask you. If the best chess teams in the world were queuing up for my services, why on earth would I have considered them?

My anger is rising. Everything is being stolen from me. Not just my title, but somehow my whole identity. It is time to take what is mine.

I try to make my way into the auditorium, but I find myself in a small shop that sells T-shirts and mugs, but no books. I have a quick look to see if my image is on any of the merchandise, but it appears not. At least that saves me the bother of a court case to seek my share of the royalties. I make a mental note that I really must fire Gabriel as soon as he starts acting as my agent again. That we have missed a money-making opportunity such as this must constitute criminal negligence.

Then I do see someone that recognises me. An ageing chess official I have sparred with many times over the years. I thought he was dead, but it appears unfortunately not. I guess there must be a lot of people who have clung to life solely in the hope of being around to witness this day.

He is looking at a white mug that has a photograph of Magnus Carlsen with one hand on his forehead, looking down at his position on a chessboard. He wears a suit and open necked shirt, the sleeve of which has ridden up, so that you can see the cuff is of the button variety. On the back of the mug it says in black lettering and questionable English. 'You need to have that, confidence, you need to have that absolute belief that you're absolutely the best and win everytime.'

The official's eyes narrow as he looks at me. My guess is that he was intending to steal the mug but has now thought better of it. The glance he gives is not obviously welcoming, but I know he has always been jealous of my talent. He holds the Magnus Carlsen mug in his sweaty hands, musters all his dignity. The shop is so tiny, that I have him completely cornered and he knows it. Unless he is willing to blank me altogether, he is going to have to talk to me.

'Hello Tennessee,' he says. His tone not altogether unfriendly. 'We haven't seen you in a long time. How are you keeping?'

I can hear the Geordie in his accent. A degree of warmth I had not been expecting. I must not lose sight of the number of people out there for whom I remain the messiah. The many who have been waiting for this moment with bated breath. Perhaps I have confused him with a different enemy. It can be hard to keep track.

I know most ordinary people will be relieved that finally we are about to do away with the pretence that Magnus Carlsen is the world champion. Many will be delighted that I have appeared, ready to bring the title home to England for the first time since Staunton. It's coming home, it's coming home. Chess is coming home! I happily sing in my head. Delighted that I have reconnected with a fan.

I congratulate him on not being dead, but he appears somewhat confused by this.

'It has been a long time,' I say. 'I think I am ready now.'

'I heard you had one or two… er… difficulties,' he says, ignoring my song and congratulations on his continuing longevity. 'Are they all resolved? Everything good?'

'You understand what the State is,' I say. 'They were never going to make it easy for me. Don't believe all you hear,' I add emphatically.

'I would not do that. No, no, no,' he says. 'So, what brings you to London?' he asks, but I can see that he realises as soon as the words are out that it is a stupid question. Why else would I be here? No one has more reason to be in this building than I do. Perhaps it is because he recognises this that he continues hastily, 'Quite a match, don't you think? It reminds me of some of yours from years ago.'

At last, a degree of vindication. I am about to ask him what his favourite match of mine was, but I do not get the chance. He smiles and turns from me to pay for his Magnus Carlsen mug. I hear him talking to the lady behind the counter.

'They are both such fine players, aren't they? We are in for a real treat.'

I hear the lady asking him who I am. She mentions that she has not seen me before.

'Who is Tennessee? It is hard to say really,' he says with a chuckle.

331

40. You knew this day was coming

I have heard enough. I will show all of them who I really am. I leave the shop and find myself in the commentary area, where Judit Polgar and Anna Rudolf are in full flow. A small hot room, a large camera on a tripod. A warning sign that if the camera is touched it will swivel both quickly and danger-ously. Anna and Judit sit at a table at the front. A few rows of blue chairs, all spilling over with chess fans. Most lean forward in their seats, as if trying to absorb some of the game's secrets through osmosis. I stand at the back for a moment, half-lis-tening, but I know I will be recognised if I stay for too long.

I wonder if I would like Judit and Anna to invite me to join them on the stage. They would be able to double the entrance price if people knew that I had joined the commentary team. I would need to be careful not to give too much away as to my actual thinking, given that Magnus and Fabiano's seconds would be noting down and dissecting my every word. Still, I am skilful enough to ensure that would not really be an issue.

It would be funny to see how the State reacted to me being on the stage. They could hardly murder me live on air, and there might well be too many questions were I to die of natural causes in the immediate aftermath.

As tactics go, it is not a bad one. It would do away with my element of surprise though. I also think it would be a form of copping out. I am built for the chessboard not the commentary room! To be diverted from my goals at the very last minute would be crazy. Perhaps there is a part of me that is scared. I wonder if I am secretly looking for diversionary tactics to put off the moment.

I don't know why that would be. They say it is better to travel than to arrive, but I don't think that is quite right. I have been desperate to seize the chance that is before me for so long I do not know why I am still messing about in the gift shop and the commentary room. No matter that so many fans are obviously keen to talk to me.

Perhaps I fear that this might all be harder than I thought. Not the mechanics. I am sure I will find a way to get my match with Carlsen started this very afternoon. It is more his youth and his confidence that is starting to worry me. I fear all the cider I have drunk over the years might have deprived me of some brain function that would have been quite useful now. I must stay strong. No kid with a computer can ever be a match for me, no matter how much mineral water he has forced through his system.

I make my way out of the commentary room. Past one or two further small rooms with a few chess sets, mainly being used by children who are engrossed in their battles. In the far corner is a musical chess set and Grandmaster Danny King is playing a game with some random guy on it. I can see he is a rabbit and in a simple endgame Danny marches a pawn up the board to queen with ease. He graciously accepts his opponent's resignation. Ever the gentleman.

Danny looks up. Notices me looking at him. I can see him thinking. Trying to clock if he knows me or not. Might well be about to say something, but I turn on my heel and head for the main playing hall. There is a part of me that has always wanted to be as smooth and polished as Danny King, but it is never going to happen. I take comfort in my superior talent.

I make my way into the theatre, which is at the end of a corridor. There is a lady at the entrance, waiting to inspect the time-stamped ticket I do not have. I am so close to being where I need to be that I can practically smell Magnus Carlsen now. I have not come this far to be thwarted.

'I am very sorry,' I say. I seem to be feeling a little faint. 'I think I just need to sit down.'

I can see that her first thought is to divert me away from the playing hall, back up to the atrium, but I do not give her the opportunity. I point my finger toward the door and keep walking. I fear she might be thinking about stopping me, so I start to sway.

'My heart isn't what it was,' I say. 'Just give me a moment. I know exactly what to do to ensure I don't die. Please don't interfere with me.'

I look across the auditorium. The place where I will become world champion. Guy Fawkes must have had a similar sense of anticipation when he entered the Houses of Parliament that fateful night, even if the sight that greeted him was more impressive than this. It is hard to imagine that even FIDE would have been incompetent enough to host my comeback in such a terrible venue. I wonder if it has been chosen to spite me.

The theatre itself is tiny. Rows of benches to sit on, all crowded. Dark curtains reminiscent of a 1970s school hall. A black backboard behind the players plastered with white sponsorship logos. A large chunk of glass sealing Carlsen and Caruana off from the audience. Something else I had not properly considered how to overcome on my way here.

I suspect the glass will be soundproof. This is an era when men are no longer men. In my day we would not have been remotely bothered by a bit of noise from the audience. Well all right, Bobby would have been, but none of the rest of us would have insisted on something like this. It just goes to show how far-removed modern-day chess has become from the ordinary fan. The person in the street who pays the bills. The minor league player who turns out for a local club, much as I once did as a child.

It is a bit like snooker. The fans love a character. Somebody with obvious flaws that they can relate to. I have always revelled in being a little different. In having an interesting story to share. I combine the popularity of a Jimmy White with the cold steel of a Stephen Hendry. Forget the clichés about chess players being mad. The game is more likely a way of keeping some who might otherwise have gone off the rails relatively sane.

From what I can see the typical chess player today has the mindset of an accountant. It is all study, study, study. Too many now have respectable day jobs. Luke McShane and David Norwood are both bankers, for fucks' sake. I guess whatever else happens from here on in, no one is ever going to offer me employment at San-tan-fucking-der.

My presence in the theatre has not gone unnoticed. I can hear a murmur of conversation, a ripple of anticipation. Finally, I must have been recognised. I am here, amongst my people, ready to take what is mine. I drop my rucksack to the floor. Rummage around inside for a can. A few of my firelighters spill out and I pick them up and put them in my pocket. I open the cider, the hiss as I lever the ring pull is louder than I had anticipated. I drink deeply, belch slightly. Throw the can onto the floor to the sound of a gasp from the crowd. I was ever the showman.

Two security guards have made their way into the hall, though not the one who was good enough to let me in earlier. He has most probably dashed home to tidy up his house in anticipation of my visit.

This pair seem quite keen to talk to me. Someone a few benches in says,

'What are you doing? This is the world championship, not a brewery. There are children present. Do you have no respect?'

The man must be a Carlsen supporter. Or an ignoramus. He will be mortified when he realises who I am. People start laughing at him. They are streets ahead. I have been recognised. I try and get some sort of chant going to build the atmosphere.

'Tennessee! Tennessee!' I cry, rhythmically clapping my hands and turning my head from side to side, beaming at my followers.

No one joins in. They are too excited to give vent to their joy. I wonder if it was the same for Jesus when he came back from the dead. Perhaps it was harder for him, without the internet to foreshadow his comeback. I doubt he had my charisma either. I feel exhilarated. My audience is spellbound. Waiting for me to make my move. To put right all that has gone wrong before.

I make my way down the side of the hall to the front. I am staring in on Carlsen and Caruana as if they are goldfish in a bowl. Carlsen is a little stockier than I imagined. In a dark suit and white open-necked tie. Caruana is leaner. They both have an air of seriousness and focus about them. It is almost as if they did not expect to be disturbed. I bang on the glass, but get no reaction, so I shout,

'You knew this day was coming! I am here now! Magnus, I issue the challenge! Let's get this on! I am ready! I am ready! What do you have to lose if you really are as good as you say you are?'

Nothing happens. They do not react. Just sit there, continuing to stare at the chess pieces between them.

'The glass is unidirectional! They can't see, or hear you, you fucking idiot!' someone shouts from the audience.

'We're trying to watch the game, you tosser!' somebody else shouts, perhaps the cheese roll guy who did not know one end of a rook from the other.

No one seems to understand. If I could get five minutes with Magnus and Fabiano, everything would be sorted. Their current game could be abandoned, sparing Fabiano's blushes. He is clearly on the verge of collapsing anyway, given his opening secrets are public knowledge. I will tell him that he should have stuck to pen and paper. A trusty folder. He will acknowledge the good sense of what I say, and I will pat him affectionately on the back. Perhaps offer him a role on my team, if he promises to be more careful with my data. I am sure he will be delighted with this offer, far beyond anything he could have contemplated when he woke this morning.

'I am Tennessee Greenbecker! The true champion of the world, I demand that Magnus plays me immediately!' I bellow at the top of my voice. I start to pound my fists on the glass, hurting my wrists. Feeling a rising sense of despair. I bang my head against the screen, but it quickly becomes apparent that is not going to do the trick either. I had never envisaged that the State would put such an impenetrable barrier in my way. There is no question that they knew I was coming. They have seen further ahead all along. This whole construction is here entirely to thwart me. I must quickly find another way.

The security guards are halfway down the auditorium. They had hesitated for a moment. Doubtless torn between the orders the State has given them and what they know to be right. Perhaps they feel like the soldiers who were ordered to turn on the students in Tiananmen Square. Except this is of a different magnitude altogether. Then I see that they were just waiting for reinforcements. There are four of them now. Moving very quickly. It will not take them long to reach me.

'I am the true champion of the world! The new messiah! Forgive them, for they know not what they do!' I cry, which I follow up by yelling, 'Why don't you all just fuck off?'

I thump the glass again, but it makes no difference. It is as solid as a block of concrete. A few years ago, I would have had the strength to shatter it into a million pieces with my bare hands, but perhaps not now. What else? What can I do? Then it occurs to me that there might be another way to create a hole. Just enough for me to yell through to the guys that I am here. If I can't break the fucking thing, it could well be that I can melt it.

The Security Guards are closing in. I have just seconds to make my play, but I know exactly what to do. I take out a few firelighters. Pile them on top of each other into a small tower. Take a moment to sniff the smell of paraffin on my hands. Enjoy the way the scent makes me tingle. I reach for my lighter. Everything is ready. Everything is good. This is going to work. I have never been closer to greatness than I am right now.

'You are out of your fucking mind!' somebody shouts, and I am distracted for just a moment. The next thing I know, my head has hit the floor and it appears that several people are lying on top of me. I can see the stars in the sky and planets dancing all around. I feel very big and very small. Both pawn and king. In my dazed state it is as if I am swimming within every game of chess I have ever played, and the sensation is far from unpleasant.

The State has got me. I can see that. Perhaps deep down I always knew that they would. I will never see daylight again. I gasp under the weight of the security guards. Then I am pulled to my feet, dragged from the hall and hurried out of the building.

41. London's burning

Perhaps this is the ultimate insult. They don't even call the police to arrest me. It is not worth the paperwork, one of them says. I am not invited to give a statement of demands. I am told that meeting Magnus Carlsen is out of the question. They show no interest in confiscating my folder, no matter how much I insist that they can't have it.

I am treated like a complete non-entity. The hours of psychological profiling they must have undertaken to hone-in on the extent to which their indifference would hurt me is unnerving.

The street is cold. It has stopped raining, but it is night again. Without fire, darkness always triumphs over light. My bladder aches. I have no choice but to try and urinate on a sign that declares this is the 2018 world championship, but nothing comes out. I squeeze harder, and still nothing happens. Even with extreme concentration and focus, I can't make it work. I stand over the sign, with my trousers around my ankles while passers-by pretend not to notice me, other than a Japanese couple who pause and get a camera out. I tell them to fuck off and they do.

Seeing as I can't piss, I spit on the sign instead, just to show my lack of respect for the FIDE regime. I half-wonder if my act of provocation will force them to engage, to confront me, to get this show back on the road, but nothing happens. I shout that everyone can go fuck themselves but get no response. One or two more commuters walk past, heads down, doubtless under instruction from the State not to engage. For the first time, I understand that I might be alone.

My inability to urinate is doubtless entirely down to my brutal treatment at the hands of the security guards. Didn't Bobby Fischer once go through something similar? I remember the pamphlet he self-published after he was wrongfully incarcerated by the State that first time – *I Was Tortured in the Pasadena Jailhouse!* He said he was stripped naked and denied food, water and telephone calls. Terrible, but at least they took the trouble to notice him.

I give up on trying to piss. Sort my clothing, start to walk away from the venue. I will not give the organisers any longer to dash out and make their apologies. They are going to have to live with the colossal mistake they have made for the rest of their lives. Magnus will be mortified when he learns I was here, and that the glass barrier failed to burn.

I'm pretty sure if anyone asks him who the best player of all time is again, modesty will compel him to give a different answer. By denying Magnus this opportunity they have stolen more from him than me. How many others at my level have gone to such lengths for the sake of their art? Few have given so much and received so little. I doubt that any of the rest of the world top ten know one end of a firelighter from the other.

Perhaps I have not been seeing things clearly. Perhaps my mistake has been to focus on something that is already mine. They know, of course they know that I am the rightful chess champion of the world. If nothing else, today has demonstrated that beyond all reasonable doubt. My chess legacy is so remarkable it needs no further burnishing. This might be more obvious to everyone than I thought. Why else would they have thrown me out? They must have realised I had nothing left to prove.

I have been chasing something too small all along. The truth is, I outgrew the chess world long ago. I am a man meant for a bigger stage altogether. The stories the world will tell about me even now are yet to be written. It is never too late. I would far rather die in a blaze of glory than lying on a hospital bed, weighed down by a catheter. I realise at last that I don't need to actually beat Magnus, just because I easily could. Everything that must follow is finally clear.

At first, I wonder if I should focus on St Paul's or London Bridge or Crystal Palace football club, but I realise that again I am aiming too low. It is true that people really are their own worst enemies. We create barriers and self-fulfilling prophecies of failure, when there really is no need. What separates winners from the rest is an ability to see through it all and to aim higher.

The Houses of Parliament always was my destiny. I need to finish what Guy Fawkes started. To follow in his proud tradition. What better way to get back at a State that is determined to destroy me? To do some lasting good in the world. To be remembered.

From Boudica, through to the Great Fires of London, the

Gun Powder Plot and the Blitz, this has always been human-ity's real calling. Burning and rebuilding. That is all there is. Everything starts and ends with fire. This is the true story of London. Visionaries like me are the heroes who help things along the way. I have my firelighters. A skill for making a spark take. A talent for imagining possibilities that others do not.

It will not be long until I squat down at the corner of the Houses of Parliament and put my lighter to a corner of a white cube of possibility and potential. For the first time in years, I wish I had a couple of my mothers' first editions to hand. They would certainly have got things going nicely, but it does not matter. I might use my notes on the more technical aspects of Magnus's play instead. I have no other need for them now. I am sure they will burn brightly.

It will not take me long to get there. Twenty minutes perhaps. Most of the security people will be watching Carlsen – Caruana on the internet, so providing they did not turn off in disgust at my ejection and resume their posts, Parliament will be a sitting duck. The place is falling down anyway. I will be doing everyone a favour by hastening its demise, clearing the way for something better to be built. I imagine they will start by building a statue of me at the new front entrance.

My act will be remembered for all eternity. Bonfire night will take on a different complexion when people have someone to celebrate who was able to get the job done, unlike Guy Fawkes and his crew. Models of me will be made every year, not to be burned, but to be saluted and applauded before the festivities get underway.

I think of that Round Table fool having to lug my deity into place. It makes me laugh out loud. If only he had taken the opportunity to learn how to light a good bonfire while he still had the chance. His friends, if he has any, will doubtless mock the notion that a buffoon like him could ever have met someone as famous as the great Tennessee Greenbecker.

Every serving chess official in the country will be overthrown when Parliament burns, of that I have no doubt. A new State will rise from the ashes. One in which a man of my talent can be properly appreciated. Perhaps I will survive to take the plaudits. I don't know. I am more tempted to go up in flames. To leave my failing body behind and seek immortality in the ash.

Perhaps I will live longer than I think. It is feasible that I will endure forever, not just through my chess, but literally and physically. The case for the inevitably of my death has not yet been proven. Who can say anything with certainty? I cannot really imagine a universe without me. Am I not the stars and the sun and the sweet mountain air? It is more than possible that I *am* the universe. That everything I think and feel and see all around me is nothing other than the product of my imagination.

Perhaps, before I embark on my final heroic act, there will be time for one last game. I will sit on the steps of Parliament and get out my pocket set. I will play through one of Bobby's *60 Memorable Games*. 'Sheer Pyrotechnics' perhaps. Possibly one of my own equally famous offerings.

I imagine feeling the weight of the miniature chess men in my hands. The ease with which they will slot into their anointed squares. Stroking the surface of my board, a piece of wood worn smooth by millions of games. That feeling which comes from playing chess that even fire cannot wholly replicate. Yes of course I can still lose myself within these sixty-four black and white squares one final time.

Perhaps Guy Fawkes did something similar that fateful night. It would not surprise me if he became so engrossed in a game of chess that he let his guard down, even if no historian has been astute enough to discern this obvious possibility. I will not make the same mistake.

Chess will burn in me, long after people think I am no more. My firelighters will make the place go up like a treat. A man of my skill has no need for gunpowder, my mother's first editions or the assistance of others. I no longer have need for anything at all.

I have written all that needs to be said in my folder. I stand by my story. Once Parliament has burned, my words will surely be turned into the best-selling book of all time, leaving my mother, Magnus Carlsen and all my enemies in the shade. I will forever be mentioned in the same breath as Bobby Fischer and Guy Fawkes. Finally, I will be seen for who I was.

A note on the writing of *The Greenbecker Gambit*

For years, a simple idea had nagged at me. What would happen if someone attempted to storm a world chess championship match? Why might they do this? Could such an act appear perfectly rational to the protagonist?

More fundamentally, I was interested in exploring to what extent any of us can determine our own story. Is there always going to be a gap between our sense of self and objective reality? To what extent does this even matter? Is it possible that such a gap is necessary to survive?

As I was finishing work on *Find Another Place*, I found myself thinking about these questions more acutely. It had taken me until I was the wrong side of forty to write my first book. I was determined to write a second. This time a novel.

They say that writers tend to write the sort of books they would most like to read, and I think this is probably true. I wanted to write about chess but also about London, the city where I spend half my working life. I am always as happy to leave as I am to arrive, but nowhere else is as deep within me, just as little else absorbs me as much as a game of chess or a blank page.

Ultimately though, *The Greenbecker Gambit* is not a novel about chess or London. Nor fire, alcohol or what it is to write, even if it is partly about all these things. Rather, *The Greenbecker Gambit* encapsulates one person's struggle to make sense of the life they find themselves living.

Tennessee Greenbecker is by no means an easy character. His mental and physical health are both fragile, his choices are often catastrophic. It does not strike me he would make an ideal house guest. Yet, while much of what he attempts ends in failure, this is not quite the whole story either. He always stays true to a sense of who he thinks he should be. Like all the best chess players, after defeat he is always ready to set the pieces back up. To try again. Perhaps Tennessee knows better than anyone, that every new game brings fresh possibilities.

A note on sources

My 60 Memorable Games – Bobby Fischer (Faber and Faber 1969) is the book that Tennessee Greenbecker carries with him throughout his somewhat turbulent weekend. A source of friendship and comfort to Tennessee, just as it has been to so many other chess players, Fischer's book stands as the most important collection of games ever published. Unlike many other anthologies, Fischer included three of his losses and nine draws and chose not to include his so-called 'Game of the Century' against Donald Bryne. *My 60 Memorable Games* is a work that is both brilliant and all too human. Tennessee was very fortunate to have a copy.

The Complete Chess Addict – Mike Fox and Richard James (Faber and Faber 1987) contains a treasure trove of chess stories and it is no wonder that Tennessee Greenbecker quotes from it. As Tennessee acknowledges, a version of the fable concerning Capablanca, Alekhine and the peasant appeared here (Fox and James also highlighted that this was a story they were unable to source.) Tennessee as ever had ideas of his own to add. In addition, several of Tennessee's recollections on the game's 'sinners' are drawn from this wonderful book.

Searching for Bobby Fischer – Fred Waitzkin (Random House 1993) is a memoir that has always moved me, and it is unsurprising that Tennessee also refers to it, along with *Chess for*

Tigers – Simon Webb (Batsford 1978). *My Great Predecessors* – Garry Kasparov (Everyman Chess – five volume series published between 2003 and 2006) is the definitive assessment of the geniuses who proceeded him, written by in my view, the greatest player of all time. Tennessee's personal reasons for disliking Garry's efforts certainly should not deter anyone from this magnificent work.

I Was Tortured in the Pasadena Jail House! – Bobby Fischer (self-published) is referenced by Tennessee and would certainly have given him pause for thought. There are numerous excellent books that could further have contributed to Tennessee's fear of the State and were equally invaluable in my researching Bobby Fischer. These include: *Russians Versus Fischer* – Dmitrij Germanovic Pliseckij and Sergey Voronkov (Everyman Chess 2005), *White King and Red Queen – How the Cold War Was Fought On The ChessBoard* – Daniel Johnson (Atlantic Books 2007) and *Bobby Fischer Goes to War – The True Story of How the Soviets Lost the Most Extraordinary Chess Match of All Time* – David Edmonds and John Eidinow (Faber and Faber 2004.) *Endgame – The Spectacular Rise And Fall of Bobby Fischer* – Frank Brady (Random House 2011.) *Play Better Chess* – Leonard Barden (Octopus Books 1980) was another invaluable research tool, as was *Child of Change* – Garry Kasparov and Donald Trelford (Hutchinson 1987).

There are many other chess books that if not direct sources, have nevertheless influenced how I see the game. I would wholeheartedly recommend: *The Chess Artist: Genius, Obsession, and the World's Oldest Game* – J.C. Hallman (St Martin's Press

2003), *Kings Gambit: A Son, a Father, and the World's Most Dangerous Game* – Paul Hoffman (Hyperion 2007) and *The Rookie* – Stephen Moss (Bloomsbury 2016), *Chess Behind Bars* – Carl Portman (Quality Chess 2017). Then of course, there is the most famous chess novel of them all – *The Luzhin Defense* – Vladimir Nabokov (1930 Sovremennye zapiski, translated into English 1960 G.P. Putnam's Sons.)

Acknowledgements

The Greenbecker Gambit would not have been possible without the help and support of many others.

The role of the first reader is always crucial. As with *Find Another Place*, Gary Dalkin's perceptiveness, care and attention to detail all enabled me to better navigate this story than I could have done alone. I am grateful for his friendship and his talent.

I am very grateful to James Essinger and The Conrad Press team. James is a brilliant author and publisher. I have hugely valued his counsel, insights and good humour. I also wanted to thank Francesca Garratt and Charlotte Mouncey for their work on the proofs and Tom Darling and Mark Ozanne for their really helpful reviews of the typeset text. Any remaining errors are mine alone. Many thanks also to Charlotte Mouncey for her excellent cover design.

I want to thank the editor of *Chess*, Richard Palliser IM and editor of *Authors Publish*, Caitlin Jans, for the continuing opportunities to write.

To the family on the Isle of Wight and elsewhere and everyone at Kenilworth Chess Club. Thanks also to Jonathan Maughan, Adrian Walker, John and Kate Coughlan for their support, friendship and encouragement. Love you all and the many others I haven't named – you know who you are!

Finally, I wanted to thank my wife Katharine and my children, Annabelle, Madeleine, Francesca and Gabriella. Without their love and support there would be no book. All my stories start and end with them.

Find Another Place, by Ben Graff – Matador 2018

'Families are their stories,' said my grandfather Martin that late autumn day in 2001, as he placed a clear plastic folder containing his journal into my hands.'

An autobiographical meditation on family, focusing on childhood, parenting, the passage of time, loss, love, faith and memory. Anyone who has ever lost a parent; had a child or reflected on the fragility and beauty inherent in everyday life will enjoy this book.

> 'Heart-warming and thought-provoking, a truly amazing read! I adored this book! I laughed, I cried, I nodded in agreement, as someone who has not only lost a parent, has a parent with MS and is a parent myself, I could relate to this book on so many different level and it will stay with me for years to come.'
> Cherrie Walker – Booktuber

> '… a natural flair for words… an enduring piece of work.'
> Kate Jones – Bookbag

> 'This is the brave and honest account of a man who lives his life as he plays his beloved chess. Always curious and intelligent, simple yet complex. Graff drew me into his world of discovery from the first page and taught me that without hope you cannot start the day… A quite remarkable story.'
> Carl Portman – *Chess Behind Bars*